In the
Face
of
Death

Peter Noll

In the Face of Death

Translated by

HANS NOLL

VIKING

VIKING
Published by the Penguin Group
Viking Penguin, a division of Penguin Books USA Inc.,
40 West 23rd Street, New York, New York 10010, U.S.A.
Penguin Books Ltd, 27 Wrights Lane,
London W8 5TZ, England
Penguin Books Australia Ltd, Ringwood,
Victoria, Australia
Penguin Books Canada Ltd, 2801 John Street,
Markham, Ontario, Canada L3R 1B4
Penguin Books (N.Z.) Ltd, 182–190 Wairau Road,
Auckland 10, New Zealand

Penguin Books Ltd, Registered Offices:
Harmondsworth, Middlesex, England

First published in 1989 by Viking Penguin,
a division of Penguin Books USA Inc.

1   3   5   7   9   10   8   6   4   2

Translation copyright © Hans Noll, 1989
All rights reserved

Originally published in Switzerland as
Diktate über Sterben & Tod by Pendo Verlag
Copyright © Pendo Verlag, Zurich, 1984.

LIBRARY OF CONGRESS CATALOGING IN PUBLICATION DATA
Noll, Peter.
[Diktate über Sterben & Tod. English]
In the face of death / Peter Noll ; translated by Hans Noll.
p.   cm.
Translation of: Diktate über Sterben & Tod.
ISBN 0-670-80703-6
1. Noll, Peter—Health.   2. Cancer—Patients—Switzerland—
Diaries.   3. Death.   I. Title.
RC265.6.N65A313   1989
362.1'96994'0092—dc20   86-40268
[B]

Printed in the United States of America
Set in Granjon

Contents

In the
Face
of
Death

Chronicle

DECEMBER 28, 1981, TO

Today is December 28, 1981. I am sitting in the living room of my apartment in Laax, viewing the snowed-in pond and the woods behind it, snow falling from the fir trees. It is rather warm, sultry, a sign of föhn, the sun only a bright spot burning through the cloud cover.

My perceptions concerning the event to be recorded here began on December 17. The slight pain in my left kidney had increased somewhat in the previous days. My younger brother Christoph, who practices internal medicine in Basel, advised me to have an X-ray with a pyelogram, since we both suspected the problem was a kidney stone that had been lodged painlessly in my right kidney for a long time. Only later did I pay any attention to the additional symptom of more frequent urination, which by itself I would not have taken seriously.

The X-ray clinic of Dr. X is very much a standard establishment. In one of what appear to be several X-ray rooms, I am laid on a table and photographed at intervals of ten to twenty minutes over a period of about two hours, during the second half of which I am injected with a contrast medium. The director came in to give me the injection (somewhat late, because he had been busy at a hospital with a biblical name which I since have forgotten). When he returned briefly at the end to say good-bye, he said something about a stone they couldn't really quite see which appeared to be blocking the drain of urine from the left kidney. An X-ray clinic is a purely technical operation: the director is merely concerned with the interpretation of the pictures, not with the treatment of the patients. I found it odd that my X-ray room served also as a changing room for the female technicians, some of whose work shifts started surprisingly late.

On the nineteenth (Saturday) came the call from Christoph: a tumor.

According to the X-ray, my bladder is no longer nice and round but has the form of a strongly waning moon. Christoph is quite alarmed; he has scheduled everything with his Zurich colleagues, and so I turn up at ten o'clock on Tuesday, December 22, in the urologist's dignified offices. On the wall in the hallway are etchings of famous race horses: they all look the same; I'm unable to discern characteristic differences among the various animals.

Cystoscopy is a repulsive procedure in spite of the local anesthesia—not particularly painful, but the pain has a bad quality, with stabbing, itching, burning, and a false sensation of having to urinate. A little later, in his office, the urologist becomes very serious, with an air of routine composure; he is obviously familiar with such cases. In the bladder, he explains, a small growth of coarse tissue, indicating malignancy, can be seen; it is practically covering the ureter, thereby forcing the left kidney to function only slowly and partially. More precise tests are essential; a biopsy to determine how malignant the growth is, and then a computertomogram. Surgery will be necessary in any case; of the two procedures in question, one would be easier, the other more difficult. If the growth is attached only superficially to the wall of the bladder, I can have part of it cut away and afterward live on as before but with a somewhat smaller bladder. If the tumor has grown through the bladder wall, however, the whole bladder must be removed and the urine drained through an artificial opening into a plastic bag, which one carries outside the body and empties from time to time. Then both kidneys would work again. The urologist informs me that the survival chances in bladder cancer are relatively good, especially if the surgery is combined with radiation treatment. How favorable the odds were was a matter of statistics—about 50 percent. In response to my questions, he says that sexual intercourse would no longer be possible, since there could be no erection; but there was no other essential limitation—hiking, sports in moderate measure, even skiing. Patients who survived the critical first five years all grew accustomed to the curtailed life. When I explained that I would never consent to such an operation under any conditions, he said that he had great respect for such a decision but that I should really get as much information as possible from other doctors as well. Did I want to take the X-rays with me? I said no; the case seemed quite clear to me.

Here, I hit on one of my peculiarities with which I ought to have been long familiar: although by nature given to doubts and hesitation, I'm inclined to make brusque, quick, and radical decisions in crisis situations involving myself.

The expression of respect seems, to a certain extent, to be a standard response, for I heard it several times afterward. Naturally it is appropriate to show a patient who chooses metastasis instead of the technological prolongation of death a certain ad-

3

miration, even though, strictly speaking, he hardly deserves it, for he really has only a choice between two evils, and it is almost purely a question of taste as to which he prefers.

Conversation between someone who knows his time will soon run out and someone who still has an indefinite amount of time left is very difficult. The talk is cut off not at the point of death but way before. A basic element of communality, usually taken for granted, is lacking.

According to the usual ritual of death, both the dying and the survivor must adhere to certain rules; but the rules, unlike those for soccer, are completely different between the two parties; "good sportsmanship" becomes quite impossible. It takes a lot of dissembling on both sides. This is why bedside conversations in hospitals are so queasy, and the survivor is relieved when he is outside while the dying person tries to get some sleep.

I must be careful not to overinterpret this business or to give it too profound a meaning. Yet I already find it annoying that acquaintances whom I have told of my situation act as if nothing were the matter, and, for example, make plans without any consideration as to my ability to participate in their realization or not.

Whom have I told? Whom not? At the beginning I explained it rather casually to all the friends I ran into. Part of my reason for doing this was, as I felt from the first and see clearly now, that I wanted to make my decision stick by making it public, just as someone who stops smoking tells his friends so that he will be embarrassed if he relapses. Later I grew more selective and cautious about whom I told.

After the revealing X-ray, I telephoned Martin Gschwind.* At first he reacted according to the medical stereotype, albeit with

* Martin Gschwind was a friend and colleague who held degrees in both medicine and law and lectured at the University of Göttingen on topics related to the psychology of criminals.

his inimitable drama: "You're crazy!" S. has been running around for fifteen years with a bladder that's attached to his belly, and he's happy. "What are you talking about? As long as your brain is intact, you're a whole person." Apparently, though, my arguments convinced him: I don't want to get caught in the surgical-urological-radiological machine because then I'll lose my freedom piecemeal, my will will be broken as hope diminishes, and I'll wind up one way or the other in the well-known death room that everyone skirts. Anteroom to the cemetery.

Meanwhile, I've discovered that I'm beginning to like sleep more and more.

Nor could Gschwind ban all hope from his (second round of) arguments: "It is very possible that the tumor will stop growing or will grow only very slowly; then you'll have another ten or twenty years. I've seen such cases myself, and I think under these conditions the chances are better if you don't have surgery than if you do." (I recalled the mother with seven children who came to Gschwind when he still had his rural practice. The woman had a tumor the size of a nut—"a little brussels sprout," Gschwind called it—and he wanted to sign her into the hospital for immediate surgery. The woman said no: her youngest children were six to ten years old, and they needed a mother at home with them, not in the hospital. When the youngest had finished his apprenticeship and none of them needed her any longer, the mother died of a massive metastasis within a matter of days. She had lived with the tumor for ten extra years to fulfill all her duties.)

December 29

A light snow has been falling interminably, and now again it is snowing very hard; the first line of the forest is still visible,

5

but not the second, and the mountainside toward Falera is dissolving into the mist. I got up shortly before nine (having taken a few sleeping pills too many), went to the swimming pool, and actually intended to go skiing at midday, but it's no fun when it's snowing like this. Or else the weather is serving as an excuse for my increasing passivity. But why, actually? The pain thus far has not been so bad, and a Spasmo-Cibalgin every four hours holds it at bay. Perhaps many activities take on meaning only from their (unknown) future dimension.

I'm trying to figure out what exactly I was thinking when the urologist told me the results of the examination. He sat across from me at his desk, his hands together, palm to palm, not as in prayer but resting sideways on the desk. My main thought probably was, it's not worth it. At any rate, it was not a shock, neither then nor later. Rather, a feeling of bad luck. No rebellion, no despair. Nevertheless, the tumor seems to absorb not only the body but also my thoughts. It is always there, even if unconsciously, though my ability to concentrate has not diminished.

Very soon after the results came back, the liberating and exhilarating thought occurred to me like a flash that my death ought to be celebrated, perhaps even the last stretch of the way from tumor to death, but certainly my death itself. I am a member of the congregation at Grossmünster, a church that takes its name merely from the fact that it is the largest in the city. My funeral will take place there. The congregation will be told what I think about dying and death and how I experience this dying. That should challenge the public to confront what, aside from birth, is life's most important event. Nothing shall be whitewashed or glossed over; I intend to block off the escape route of repression, as well as airs of false piety and the solace of last-minute faith hastily extracted from the bin of old clothes, the vaguest hope for most, to be saved for the last moment. A perversion of the Christian faith, which is meant for the living, not the dead. We no longer come to church except for funerals. The pastor knows precisely what the public expects of him. He talks about the dear deceased, the dear departed, those who passed on. He consoles, and trivializes death, and he quotes the passages from the Bible that speak of resurrection and eternal life. He doesn't talk about the cruelty of death, its dark incomprehensibility. No burial ceremony can change this. Life cannot know death, and neither does it wish to: life aspires only to live. Without this mysterious compulsion of nature for survival, life would long since have ceased. The impulse to live grows stronger the greater the distress and danger. That is why there are so few suicides in concentration camps. Apparently it is easier to do oneself in when external conditions are normal, because there is no compulsion to save one's life from an urgent threat.

Max Frisch doesn't think it tasteless that I want to celebrate my death publicly. We went to the Zimmerleuten* on Sunday, December 27, for a late supper, after a walk through the almost empty city. The Zimmerleuten has become one of my favorite restaurants over the last few years; it shows the friendly side of small-town, middle-class, conservative Zurich. Frisch talks about death-by-choice as opposed to suicide. This has long been a central theme with him, as I recall again now. The suicide acts from emotion—after his girlfriend has left him, the suicide shoots himself, for example, or plunges out of the window. Someone who chooses death deliberately acts (or in my case fails to act) after weighing all the circumstances. This contrast immediately makes me think of the distinction made in the penal

* The carpenter's guild house (Zunfthaus zur Zimmerleuten), a historical building, now a restaurant.

code between murder (premeditated) and manslaughter (out of emotion). He who acts only out of emotion is less guilty. Can this concept be carried over to killing oneself? Certainly it can, according to old religious precepts. Perhaps my decision to refuse surgery is motivated by too much pride and arrogance—very likely, even by contempt of life. Maybe I'll reverse my decision. The dark woods beyond the snowed-in pond and the white mountainside toward Falera are so beautiful that I'd like to see them for a long time to come, even with my abdomen mutilated, the bladder removed, the sexual potency gone. At least, after radical surgery, I'd have from two to five years, and at best perhaps even more than the critical first five. Christoph is trying to persuade me to assemble all the pieces of information I need to make a decision and, above all, to have a computertomogram made. I'll do it, too. But neither of us believes that the result will permit the lesser solution, the partial resection of the bladder. Still, we won't convince each other. He remains convinced that life with a plastic bag on your belly would be of acceptable quality.

Strange coincidence: while celebrating Christmas at Mother's, Markus, my youngest brother, a professor of molecular biology, remarked in passing that American molecular biologists had deciphered the alteration in the gene responsible for bladder cancer and were in the process of developing antibodies. In a year or two, it will be a matter of swallowing antibodies or having them injected, and the cancer will miraculously disappear, just like that.

Christmas with Mother, with the family, with nephews and nieces and my daughters, was noisy, full of fun and excitement, as it always has been, mainly on account of the children. I didn't mention the tumor so as not to ruin the fun. My ex-wife, Almuth, and daughters Rebekka and Sibylle are in the know. Luckily, no shock here either. Sibylle said she simply couldn't conceive of the idea of my not being here anymore. "Imagine that I'd like to see Daddy, and then I won't be able to—I just won't be able to."

Lots of telephone conversations with Christoph since the diagnosis. He's fighting for my life—that is his profession—and against me, which is probably more difficult. I've noticed that I get obstinate, even though I really don't feel any spite or anger, at most a very melancholy calm, not real sadness.

The word that fell most frequently when I told my friends about the findings was *Scheiss,* the high German word for "shit"; among others Christoph and Frisch used it. No coincidence here, because it is appropriate; it describes exactly and without pathos the feeling of sympathy suddenly aroused.

Marrakech, January 3, 1982

For the first days of the year, I flew to the south with Christoph and his wife, Eva, as we had long planned. For years now this "interlude in the sun" has become a virtual habit. The problem of a travel companion has been paramount since my divorce. Traveling alone is becoming harder with time in two senses; the older I get and the longer the trip takes. Since many, perhaps most, trips are beautiful only in retrospect, I have gathered them for a memoir.

Death Valley, March 1980

I was sitting on the side of the highway that runs the entire length of Death Valley. The rental car in which I had left the main road to follow a side road got stuck in the sand. After futile efforts to get it back onto firm ground (in the end the back wheels were buried up to the fenders), I walked for half an hour back to the highway to wait for cars. It was a very quiet, lovely evening: now and then a small bird flew by; a shrub already had a few white blossoms. It was Sunday. Every ten minutes a car went by, always in the wrong direction, all headed toward Los Angeles, and I had to go to the Furnace Creek Hotel, sixty miles in the other direction. All of the drivers stopped, though I was not hitchhiking (or possibly that itself was the reason), and asked what was the matter. People found it very startling and remarkable to see a well-dressed man sitting by the side of the road, a European yet, a Swiss or a Swede or whatever, and they expressed their deep regrets before driving on. Slowly, the twilight came on, and I thought to myself, At worst I'll have to go back to the car and spend the night—annoying but not fatal, for nearby is a little creek; which is why I got stuck, because the sand was wet. I thought to myself, This story is very unpleasant, but as a memory it will assume significance: the beautiful quiet evening, the many colors changing on the earth and in the sky . . . the slow darkening . . . the feelings of fear and tenseness. And that is the way it has remained. At the time I would have wished to avoid the experience; today I wouldn't want to be without it.

No more cars are coming. The sun has just set; it is infinitely quiet. I get up from my rock to return to my car, and here comes the only car going in the direction of Furnace Creek! Slowing down from a long distance, it finally stops in front of me: "Are you the Swiss with the car that got stuck in the sand?" A married couple. They take me along to the hotel, where I am told, "This is why we have Jerry." Already this fellow has jumped into his truck, and together we race off in the dark to the scene of the breakdown, where he finally pulls my car out after several unsuccessful attempts. I drive through the creek to the highway, the windshield practically covered with mud from the dirty water. Unable to find the wipers, and turning on the emergency flash instead (which I can't turn off), I cling to the taillights of Jerry's truck, forced to maintain his insane speed or to lose my way altogether. In front of the hotel, I ask him how much. "It's up to you." I give him one hundred dollars: never before had I felt such enthusiasm for America.

It is obviously impossible to live in the present. The brain-computer has no program for it. That we live only in the past and in the future, in memories and hopes, in past accomplishments and plans for the future, is based on one of those odd laws of the human psyche. If the future dimension is suddenly and decisively curtailed and one knows this, still nothing affects this condition in a fundamental way. Some say they experience the present all the more intensely. That isn't true in my case, and perhaps it isn't true for the others either. For me, dwelling in the past remains the same, but the future accelerates like in a time-lapse movie. I want now to do quickly everything I've put off. Now I'll try to sketch out the books *I still want to write,* which seem actually more important than what I've written up till now:

The Final Days and Self-Destruction as a Law of Inhabited Planets

The Little Machiavelli: *A Handbook of Power for Everyday Use* (and a Weapon for the Critics of Power)*

The Philosophy of Power and of Law

The Birth of German Music from the Spirit of the Reformation

The Book of the Wisdom of Life and Death

---

* A satire on business, published in collaboration with H. R. Bachmann, in March 1987, and an immediate best-seller (Pendo Publishers, Zurich, Switzerland).

Meanwhile, I've come to realize that the writing of books is substitute behavior, no different from the acts of politicians. Erich Fromm, doubtless a wise man, describes exactly what would have to change in order to avoid the catastrophe into which mankind is falling. But his variables are not variable: i.e., what he says must be changed—namely, human consciousness—can't be changed, at any rate not through books, no matter how many copies are sold. So he, like the politician, is fooling us; he, too, responds symbolically and not realistically. Perhaps he is more concerned with fame and the large numbers of printings and so forth. Would he write if he weren't read? I have regard for the many who remain silent because they know it is too late to change anything through talk and writing. Instead, they ought to force our rulers to destroy all weapons of extermination and stop the destruction of the environment. Yet if such movements arose, they would, in order to acquire the necessary power, have to be organized according to the laws of power (as the Church was in the time of the early Christian communities), and the structural necessities of organization would lead to exactly the same manifestations that we now observe with those already in power. And the organizers of the movements, too, will be more interested in retaining their position or in pushing ahead within the power structure than in realizing the goals of the movement. Unfortunately, these are two incompatible aims. To gain and preserve power requires completely different qualities of character and ways of behaving than those needed to achieve peace and ecological balance on a planet with limited resources.

The march of the lemmings: by the hundreds of thousands, they set out toward the Arctic Ocean, plunge into the water, swim on for a while, and drown. Everyone says what we are doing is insane—stop the rush, for heaven's sake; let's redistribute ourselves, find other solutions; we can't go on like this. The leaders, too, declare: we are doing everything to change direction; why would we want to march into death?; we shall find a negotiable solution; but for now we have to continue in this direction—no other way exists. And the hoi polloi say, if the leaders, who after all must know what they are doing, make this decision, we must follow for now; they surely will find a solution in the end. Meanwhile, everyone keeps rushing toward the Arctic Ocean. Mighty debates occur on the way, considerations of alternatives; some even urge turning back, but no one pays them any heed, and so they go along, too; everyone is against what all are doing. Yet, after all, you can't just suddenly turn around such a big trek: those in the front would be crushed by those in the rear. First we'll have to find out where other pastures can be found. We are studying this problem closely, say the leaders. But on they rush toward the Arctic Ocean.

When ideas are turned into action, the ideas are lost and vice versa: often a good deed can be accomplished only by appealing to an evil idea that is reinterpreted into a good one (because the evil idea is not recognized as such but generally accepted). This paradox is what I have tried to show in *Jericho*.* But let's turn back to simpler things—for example, a dark thought attributed to Jesus but not considered to be genuine: that those who sin against the Holy Ghost will never find grace. I must reinterpret this thought by saying that grace—particularly the grace Jesus preached—must be complete and can have no hole. A redemption with exceptions is no redemption at all.

Writing books is an evasion. We writers know we have no effect, but at least we have unburdened our conscience by saying what had to be said. Still, we should admit that it's a useless occupation.

---

* A play written in 1968 and broadcast over the Swiss radio. Later it was published in the original German edition of this chronicle following the text.

It would be better to found and lead an organization that will bring about the necessary changes; but until now, no one has succeeded in suspending the internal laws of organization that always are the driving force of evil.

Christoph is good at discovering the worst possible scenarios (exactly in the Dürrenmatt sense). The latest is that there is also a possibility that the tumor will obstruct the outflow from the bladder. Instead of the lovely death from uremia (with two dead kidneys), the kidney's urine production would fill the bladder to the bursting point, provoking unspeakable pain. A pointless operation would be necessary, or one would simply have to put an end to it all very quickly.

It is good to know all the possibilities. The record of these days will seem harmless compared with that of the final days. Probably, in the end, there will be an incredible acceleration that I'll no longer be able to control. The more dramatic the course of the disease, the worse the description. Vanity and pride will be replaced by helplessness and the muteness of perishing.

Even if only a convention, part of retrospective memory is an effort to be sincere. Such an attempt does not necessarily have to be a particularly subtle form of hypocrisy. Oddly enough, I recall most clearly incidents where I was offended and, next, occasions when I received recognition—both, of course, only by or from people for whom I care. Fortunately, I've long since conditioned myself to regard with indifference praise and insults from people who to me are equally indifferent. That C., for example, cancelled several dates at the last minute, though our relationship has for years now been without mutual demands, has hurt and troubled me deeply. Certainly, to cite such trivialities is petty; but what would be the point of a magnanimity that withheld or repressed them?

14

The usual notion expected in situations like mine of "settling my accounts of life" makes no sense to me. For what I still have to say, it is completely irrelevant what sort of education, training, etc., I had. That I couldn't bear school, didn't take my university studies very seriously—all this has nothing to do with the situation I want to describe. Still, I have known for a long time that I can't endure people who enjoy being in power, and that this intolerance is probably the reason that I chose to study law. That I then became a very introspective, skeptical legal scholar has again to do with my intense dislike of people who push their way to power. Even though power is unavoidable. Still more repulsive to me are people who exercise power under the cloak of the law. Law, if it is to preserve itself, must be the thorn in the flesh and fat of power. Uncritical legal scholars are one of the worst things the current system, including the social system, the schools and universities, has dished out to us. And, to top it off, the practice of law! The absolute worst are the upper-echelon functionaries, for in addition to their positivist legalistic bigotry, they display the arrogance of superior rank.

Point of departure of a philosophy of law and power: the object of law is not the law but power; law is the critique of power.

We are in need of a reformation of dying and death. Funerals, including religious ones, are the most vacuous rituals that exist. What we get are clichés like, "As we live and as we die, thus we are the Lord's." Such clichés are, of course, meaningless without the context of faith. Its enormous historical remoteness has rendered this phrase, which once meant something essential, completely lifeless. A reformation of the funerary ritual: the pastors ought no longer to function as funeral directors who suppress the reality of dying and death. They ought, rather, to present death clearly and to nurture the thought of death. They ought also to be critical of the medical-technical death-ritual. Since we live with death, we ought also think of it while living. To settle accounts, to draw a balance, is important and useful. The pastors should make it clear that it can be anyone's turn next; that everyone's turn comes at some point; that to prepare oneself is good; and that everything might then become quite easy.

Man has always praised himself as an extremely rational being. He ought to stop that.

What, really, is the meaning of solace? I was unable to grasp it even as a child. I got a bump and Mother consoled me, but the bump remained. The tumor and death resist any consolation— i.e., they remain even if I compensate for them with images of an afterlife. If I nevertheless regard death with a certain composure, I probably do so only because (and as long as) I calmly weigh it against life. But the calm this weighing brings, and the additional freedom that comes from no longer having to care about the future, have nothing to do with consolation. The bump remains, the tumor too, and death.

The subjects I planned to write about in my retirement included the faculty at the University of Zurich, this collection of people who are so cautious that to judge from their behavior, the threat of imminent dangers would seem to be lurking from every corner. In such a group, one man's fear creates another man's strength. M., for example, a rather weak, certainly neurotic, though in no way timid man, for years was able to control the whole faculty. My first confrontation with him appeared to be an act of courage, whereas in fact it was merely the result of my complete naiveté and lack of information. I had dared to present the issue of the students' right to have a say in their own affairs as a completely normal aspect of the relations between teachers and students. Then came the issue of faculty meetings, which M., against the will of all the other faculty members, insisted on scheduling for Saturday afternoons, as had been the custom in the past. His argument—that there were no other afternoons free of scheduled lectures—was so tenuous that I contradicted him, still not realizing that this amounted to a sensation. The faculty decided to appoint a committee, and this committee kept meeting until M. finally retired. Thereafter, it was quickly announced that faculty meetings were to be held on Wednesdays, even though this had previously been impossible. A few months earlier, F. had taken me aside and, in his unctuous way, had told me he was saddened that I had brought discord to the faculty, that it simply wasn't for a faculty member to take a stand on controversial questions during his first year. (As if I hadn't been a full professor in Mainz for eight years!)

Another aspect of this experience is reflected in the fixed seating plan that dominates the faculty room. The plan corresponds roughly to a hierarchy—no matter how difficult it is to perceive this at first. Here too I succeeded in making a big mistake. At the first faculty meeting I attended, I simply sat down in a chair by the wall, until someone politely notified me that this was F.'s chair. I moved quickly to the lower end of the table and stayed there undisturbed until, at some point later, I returned to the wall when a chair there became vacant, for I hate talking to people who are in back of me.

Among faculty, the rule of mutual consideration is strictly maintained. This has mainly two advantages. It could, for example, happen to any teacher, especially in view of our present flood of doctoral theses, that he might unwittingly accept a plagiarism. The doctoral candidate would be very strictly dealt with in such an instance, but the faculty would pass over the supervisor's mistake rather generously. Second, unnecessary arguments and aggressions are wisely avoided when the necessary emotional release is sought not by expressing one's disapproval directly to the party concerned but, rather, by doing so in his absence to a third party: in this way, the culprit can't disturb the spirit of consensus with useless efforts to defend himself.

At the Mainz faculty meetings there were fixed seats as well, but they were interspersed with many changing ones, and the fixed seats did not correspond to any hierarchy. Some inhabitants of fixed seats may have liked to believe that there was one, but this view found few takers. These two cities are indeed far apart. In Mainz, seniority was determined by appointment to a professorship, irrespective of university; in Zurich, what counted was the appointment to the University of Zurich. Thus I succeeded in never having to be chairman of the faculty; in Mainz, when it would have been my turn, the call to Zurich came, and here I had to start at the very bottom again. The faculty in Zurich was enormously relieved when I told the chairman I should decline the honor when finally it was my turn. They always saw me as a loner, an outsider—and then, of course, also as a leftist. Probably true on all counts.

Writing and publishing books as the only form of intellectual action must yield to something else. Action and power have long since emancipated themselves from thought—they rule in giant organizations and multinational corporations. To criticize these organizations' expressed or unexpressed ideology either in writing or in some other verbal form is completely absurd. Rather, we should examine how these corporations establish their all-pervading activity and manage to function freely with a minimum of "philosophy." Perhaps the roles should be reversed: the executives of the multinationals ought to be appointed professors of philosophy and, thereby, be forced to reflect on what they are doing. The sheer mass of writings is choking on itself: for every expert testimony, there is a countertestimony; the intellectuals' greatest error is their belief that they can, with their formulations and publications, influence any event according to their own wishes.

Zurich, January 7

This afternoon, I visited B., the biologist. I had called him up, since I knew from H. that B. had had surgery for bladder cancer. I thought that B. was still in the hospital, but he was already at home, having had the operation on December 23. He had tried to reach me on the phone, but I was still in the south.

B. only had portions of the inner skin of the bladder peeled off; the ureters were untouched. We talked for a long time about his case, and I'm of the opinion that I would have done the same in his position. His chances are relatively good. Naturally, the cancer may start up all over again; but in his case, postponement still made sense. As a biologist, he is so well informed about these problems that the imponderables stretch to infinity.

I succeeded in convincing him that my case was very different. To each his own cancer, and to each his own solution, so to speak. To begin with, in my case, the entire bladder would have to be removed with all the consequences that I do not accept: a plastic urine pouch on my abdomen (B. did not consider this so bad at all), permanent impotence, and a 60 percent risk of recurrence. Then I explained my positive theory to him: I have a relatively short, finite amount of time in which I can begin a new, freer life. After the sabbatical during the spring semester, I'm going to retire and do everything that I've always put off. It is a real opportunity to look death squarely in the face. First, I no longer have to be afraid of antagonizing certain people; I can't lose more than my life. Second, I can get everything ready and bring it all to a close. Death neither appears as a sharp

19

break in the middle of living nor comes slinking up on silent, sinister feet to take your life piece by piece, finally tossing you into nothingness after there's nothing left of you. In all of this, death is helped by medical technology and equipment, as each of one's body's orifices is hooked up to a tube. The urge to survive must never be allowed to become so absolutely over-powering that one submits to all of these indignities. The will to live must oppose it.

In the end, we concurred that our cases were quite different. After all, B. is sixty-two years old, and at that age the stuff no longer grows so fast. When, after an hour, we changed the subject, things got really interesting. I developed my theory of programmed death of the planets and was amazed that he—as a biologist—was surprised by it. Apparently, I manage in the end to convince everyone of any proposition. But this theory is so simple that it can't possibly be accepted right away. A natural law states that intelligence originates and develops through con-flict and aggression—exactly according to Darwin. Hence, in-telligence is to be defined as the ability to destroy other living beings or to dominate them. Considering this origin, and in-asmuch as war is truly the father of all things, intelligence is also evil. It ranges and searches incessantly to achieve more power, more pleasure, and finally it must discover how to release the force of matter (the atom bomb). Once these laws are known, they are also applied. Another important factor is the nature of human systems. An Albert Einstein or a Niels Bohr would never have built an atom bomb, much less have dropped it. But their ideas were taken from them and exploited by those who in all systems have the power. And these people are completely devoid of imagination. Their behavior is determined by the system. This situation has assumed totally grotesque dimensions. The apparatchiks in America and Russia are accelerating the arms race because the system demands it. Reagan and Brezhnev would be dethroned immediately if they decided to sit down at a table and do away with all atomic weapons, actually an obvious idea. Immediately, their advisers, who are part of the system, would foil such an attempt, simply by making the questions so complicated that no solutions could be found.* Ergo, all must end with a bang, whether by intention or through negligence.

In our discussion, which naturally took a quite different course than I'm describing here, the biologist immediately tended to agree. I was reminded of Adolf Portmann** when I took up the defense of rationalism, the evil kind in particular, as the only alternative available to present-day civilized man; he would have to postbreed a moral rationality, but in terms of biology it is too late for that.

B. referred to the many peaceful tribes in history and ethnology. I showed that they all died out or were conquered. Love of peace doesn't pay, and aggression leads to a general holocaust. Of course, one cannot overlook that in the power game reproduction also plays an important role. Countries like South Africa and Israel, who suppress majorities or minorities, will be able to do this for only a very short time: the increase in number of the subjugated populations eventually must lead to a reversal of the power equations.

According to B., Christianity is responsible for all the great plagues, conquests, genocides, and for ceaseless warfare. I said, first, don't confuse Christianity and Christ, since Jesus was after all the first to preach love of one's enemy; while love of one's

* The reader should be reminded that this startlingly accurate description of the Reykjavík meeting between Reagan and Gorbachev was written some five years before it took place.
** (1897–1982), professor of zoology at the University of Basel, noted for his studies on evolution and brain structure, especially in regard to traits characteristic of man.

fellow man is simply normal: you take care of your wife and your children, you fight for your community, for the country, and so on. Second, it should be remembered that the Church first took shape in the early councils, as it defined itself in regard to the heretics; and while it is true that it did give its blessings to the murder of Indians and the conquest of new continents, it did not initiate the devastating process we observe today. What provoked the release of matter, the pleasure mania with all its destructive consequences? It was science and technology—and human greed, of course. Yet the Church wanted at first to stop this process for the sake of its own power and thus preserve conditions as they were, let us say, among the Indians: hence the trial against Galileo, and so forth. So the Church isn't guilty, either. What, then? The emancipation of scientific research together with its commercial and military exploitation. The real driving force is the Faustian spirit, that ceaselessly roving, insatiable spirit, forever curious and not afraid to experiment with anything—that amoral spirit which is neither moral nor immoral, like knowledge itself. This spirit originated neither in the great cultures of Egypt or Babylon nor in Greece or Rome, much less among the aborigines of America or Australia. The Faustian spirit probably originated in the Renaissance and among the critical humanists against whom the Church fought. But it broke its ecclesiastical shackles, first in the Reformation and definitively in the Age of Enlightenment and the subsequent French Revolution. It is clearly a product of Western Europe. The scientific age began in England and then spread to the other Protestant Western European countries. The Catholic countries followed somewhat later (an exception being secular France), because the Catholic Church was able to slow down the process a little. Then the competitive pressure of the advanced industrialized nations (most of them simultaneously colonial powers) became so great that the other nations had to reach some form

22

of accommodation: Japan, Russia, China. It was clearly the Western Europeans—and the Jews, who in part followed them—who initiated the process. The peoples who didn't want to comply or who couldn't compete were destroyed, like the American Indians, or subjugated. Peoples such as those of Africa or India, who were set free because of their unmanageable populations, live under the rule of hunger, because the Western Euorpeans and North Americans grab and devour all the goods the earth produces.

Faust, Galileo, and Einstein are all innocent, as I said, though they remain the greatest representatives of that ceaselessly questioning spirit that seeks to discover everything. Yet the present catastrophe would not have come about through them alone. It became possible only through the unholy alliance of the Faustian spirit with the power and economic system of the modern industrial states. Dürrenmatt ingeniously exposed this union in *The Physicists*. But reality is even more macabre. The play should end where it now begins. Physicists don't go to the insane asylum, and it is even less typical of our system that the deranged madhouse doctor, Fräulein Von Zahnd, seizes hold of the research results and thereby gains control over the world or blows it up. The rule of political madmen, like Hitler, is possible only during great upheavals. Yet these great upheavals no longer can occur, if only because the power machines of the state are too strong to let any countermovement arise. Reagan and Brezhnev are products of their systems and just as normal as Federal Councillor Honegger. No one doubts that Brezhnev and all the others in the Kremlin are pure apparatchiks who came to power by conforming; exactly the same is true of American presidents. Admittedly, presidents are elected by the people, and it could happen—theoretically—that the American people might elect a madman. But in America the large corporations, which are structured exactly like the Kremlin or the Curia, see to it that

23

a madman doesn't get elected. Even while in office, the president is controlled by the political and economic apparatus and deposed if necessary—e.g., Nixon when he cracked up after Watergate.

Most people feel reassured that apparatchiks have power everywhere, for these, one assumes, won't make any stupid mistakes. The opposite is the case. The stupidity or madness, while not individual, is, far worse, a collective and colossal madness irrevocably built into the system. No one is responsible for it. The systems act with complete logic and consistency, and they will logically and consistently lead to total destruction. Inevitably, the Soviet Union feels encircled and at least is holding Europe hostage with its new rockets. The same logic compels America and NATO Europe to respond with an arms escalation. Apparatchiks act according to law even if it is the law of mutual destruction. They have neither original ideas nor the imagination of vision; and to that extent, they don't know what they are doing. No apparatchik will be the first to press the button, but he'll do it automatically if he thinks that the other side has already done so or is about to do so.

Power structures, like the computers they use, are incapable of performing very simple tasks of reflection—for example, those dictated by concrete visions of horror. They immediately get bogged down in complexities and lose sight of the whole. It would really be quite easy and realistic and would harm no one if the superpowers agreed to destroy all atomic weapons. But the idea is too simple. The following question also is too simple: What would the United States do with the Soviet Union if it could conquer the U.S.S.R.? And vice versa: What would the Soviet Union do with Western Europe and the United States if a victory over them were possible? Madmen are not necessary when the systems themselves are the sources of stupidity and absurdity.

The high degree of mutual aggressiveness of all systems seems to correspond to an anthropological law. In all systems, power is exercised by the apparatchiks, the average, the mediocre, the conformist, the uncreative. Because of them the world will perish, not because of madmen or outsiders. Of course, the establishment does not produce people who would break with the establishment. Yet only this miracle could still save us.*

I'm wondering if the time has come to start on my will. According to the law, it has to be drawn up in your own handwriting, and by no means must you forget the date and time and place. The most unpleasant thing is that I don't know how much time I have left. Gschwind thinks it could take years. I don't believe that. But about two years would be nice. I am scheduled for a computertomogram on the fourteenth. Possibly I'll know more then. I'd like to know precisely in which direction the tumor is growing. If it blocks the right kidney as well, it will cause a death that is easy but too soon. If it moves toward the urethra I'll probably notice it eventually. At the moment, the left kidney is behaving idiotically, probably because of the tremendous amount of coffee I drank to flush out the effect of the sleeping pills. The body is so austere that it demands a moral and sober life to the very end. Coffee simply has the effect of making you more tense. As for nicotine and alcohol, the pain lord has so far benignly closed the eyes. In the end, only nonpunishable acts are being chastised.

Frisch has already agreed [to give a talk at the funeral]. I still have to speak with Pastor G. and then with the head of the law faculty.

Sometimes I'm pursued by the curious notion that I'll go on living for another five or ten years, as some kind of medical miracle. But the meaning of my project should certainly not be

* A pity that Peter didn't live to see the Gorbachev miracle.—H.N.

contingent on the period of time left to me. Actually, the thought of death ought to be a lifelong occupation for every man. But this would be too great a stress for the human psyche. We have to live as if we were immortal. Life has neither the will nor the capacity to know death. Constant preoccupation with death, long before it becomes a reality, leads only to empty rituals: memento mori.

And yet this sentence rings with truth: "Lord, teach us to number our days that we may apply our heart unto wisdom" (Psalm 90:12). Instead of the German *weise* ("wise") Luther translates with *klug* ("prudent"), which is wrong, for the sentence illustrates exactly the difference between prudence and wisdom. Prudence is purpose-oriented; wisdom is purpose-free, intent on direct fulfillment, if necessary by renunciation and equanimity. Modesty of needs makes us freer than the fulfillment of all needs. According to our usage, the word "prudence" is the same as "intelligence," which is even quantifiable these days by means of IQ tests. Wisdom does not mean something superior to intelligence but, rather, something completely different. Therefore, the Zurich translation hits the exact meaning with *". . . dass Wir ein weises Herz gewinnen"* ("that we may gain a wise heart"). Were old men often called wise because they were so close to death? To associate old age and proximity of death with wisdom is by no means compelling. Still, for me the awareness of being near (but not too close) to death opens the opportunity of becoming wise. Wisdom seems above all to be a process of detachment and also a concentration on the essential. At the same time, I've spent enough time in the school of critical rationalism to know that the above remarks have no scientific basis. But critical rationalism merely poses questions that are answerable and propositions that are falsifiable, and these questions are precisely those that interest us least. Finally, we arrive at the stupid proposition that whatever is not measurable cannot be investigated; and that means all the things that are essential in the existential sense—love, joy, sorrow, contentment, rebellion, and so on. Modern science has developed an enormous capacity of evading these questions. Such questions then sneak in through the back door in the form of pseudosciences like astrology and dream interpretation.

Zurich, January 10

I'm sitting in my small apartment, alone for the last two days. At most a telephone call now and then. The new wisdom: only he is free who can be alone. Today is Sunday. Why are people least able to be alone on Sundays? Why do most suicides occur on Sundays and, in addition, reach a particularly high point at Christmas? The social norms make it a moral responsibility to be with others at these times, and those who cannot fulfill this obligation feel unhappy. Some kill themselves.

Yesterday and today it was impossible to leave the house. Snowfall, then freezing rain. All technical means of locomotion are paralyzed by the weather. Even walking—one would have to crawl on all fours. Tomorrow I'll have to travel to St. Gall for my series of guest lectures on legislation. I hope the train will get through this new Ice Age. On Friday evening, we had dinner here, Ruth, Ursula, and I. It snowed and snowed, and then suddenly freezing rain. After the food and drink, I had the urge to go out in the nude on the terrace, which was covered with ten inches of snow and a thin crust of ice. Like after a sauna. I made an image of myself in the snow because the ice crust broke exactly where the weight of the body came to rest. Ruth and Ursula did likewise, and we finally got so cold that we had to get into bed to warm each other up. I had never experienced anything like that, but had long somehow expected it, and that it all happened so spontaneously was good.

27

Today I read in the *Tages-Anzeiger Magazin* that George Kennan has long believed that the old guard in the Kremlin doesn't want war. Their one anxious concern is to conserve their possessions and their system. Their alternatives are poor. They are in the same situation (and here I am expressing my own opinion) as the Curia during the Renaissance: either they allow their whole system to be destroyed or broken up, starting with the bordering states, Poland first, or they remain the fear-inspiring masters. Evidently, they have opted for the latter. What Kennan does not sufficiently realize is that the political systems have become totally frozen in the rigidity of their inner logic. This applies to the American system as well. Reagan, too, must fuel the arms race so that he and his country are able to maintain their fear-inspiring stance. This inner logic cannot be broken down by saying "Don't be afraid of each other!," for the system has so many heads that it is impossible to rid them all of fear or even to chop them off.

The increased pace of my writing during the last two years is perhaps related to my unconscious realization that I have only a little time left. The writing of many books seems to be a bad sign.

According to the weather report, the temperature in Zurich will fall to a freezing eighteen degrees tonight; in Bern and the rest of western Switzerland, it will be forty-eight. This appears to me like a symbol of the past two years. Zurich is without a doubt the coldest city in Switzerland.

It is always the experts who are most surprised by new knowledge.

Disagreement between Frisch and myself concerning suicide. Frisch is afraid of becoming an imbecile and thinks you should call it quits when you are no longer at the height of your powers, before you become a burden to others, and so on. Being a burden wouldn't bother me in the least. What bothers me is the loss of freedom; having others in charge of you, to be drawn into a medical machine which controls a person and which one cannot fight. Naturally, intolerable pain will disturb me too. In order to escape it, one enters the machine that takes away pain and at the same time freedom. And it's precisely this enslavement that I don't want.

It strikes me how little Jesus said about death and dying. Death and redemption seemed so natural to Him that He committed himself entirely to life. I've described His intense affirmation of life and freedom in my book *Jesus and the Law* and again in *Jesus and Disobedience*. How little death meant to Him as a secular concern can be deduced from His powerful declaration "Let the dead bury their dead." For Him, the coming of the kingdom of God was the real event, not death: "There be some standing here which shall not taste of death till they see the Son of Man coming in his kingdom" (Matthew 16:28). Jesus did accept His own death willingly as full reality and fought it through to the end—i.e., His vision of the kingdom of God and paradise in no way diminishes death's terror. Thus, nowhere in the Bible are dying and death trivialized. Jesus wanted at first that the cup pass from Him; at the end He thought that God had forsaken Him.

Later, many martyrs went to their deaths with outright joy, visions of paradise before their eyes. With Jesus, death was a wholly different matter. Why couldn't He, of all people, die with the serenity of so many of His followers, who were executed no less cruelly? For me, the explanation is that He wanted to accept dying and death in all its seriousness, without a glance to the "compensations" of paradise. The idea that the soul leaps out of the body and escapes into beautiful fields of eternity was absolutely foreign to Him. And hence, the kingdom of God must be something totally different than a reward for believers, certainly different than paradise, something of no use as a consolation. The kingdom of God can clearly come about even without us.

Zurich, January 11

Called up Zach in St. Gall and told him that I can no longer fulfill my contractual obligation to hold the guest lectures on legislative law every Monday. I also told him about my condition and asked that he treat the matter confidentially. He was quite understanding, very sympathetic, and naturally somewhat shocked; but his response was so honest and his reaction so decent that I couldn't have wished it any better. I'm increasingly curious about people's reactions when I explain my situation to them, and I observe them more and more closely.

The city is coated with an armor of ice.

I still hope that I'll manage to finish the semester in Zurich. Sometimes I'm incredibly tired, and I don't know why. Maybe I should write my will right now, but I don't have any desire to busy myself with all the unfinished matters still lying around or to think about what remains to be done for me afterward. What makes me feel good, however, are the ideas that I've dictated and continue to dictate. Lou* just picked up the first three cassettes. I have to impose on her to transcribe all this, and I'm sorry about it.

* Lou Näf, Peter Noll's secretary at the University of Zurich.

Zurich, January 13

If only people didn't ask the thoughtless question "How are you?" Just answering "Not especially well" provokes further questions. Today, on the way home from the university, I fell into this trap twice when I met first one, then another, colleague. The half-truth is not believable, which I should have figured out beforehand. The only choices I have are to say "I'm fine" or to say "I have cancer." The first is a lie, and the second is an unnecessary truth. Probably to lie is better.

All went well with the lectures, just as usual. No one notices anything.

Spent yesterday evening with Rebekka and Sibylle. My case is so obvious that it has become a normal conversation piece. Rebekka said that death couldn't possibly be any worse than life; for even if there were something like a hell, which she doesn't believe, of course, one would get so inured to it that he wouldn't feel the pain any longer. This is, to be sure, the way we think from everyday experience. Yet it could be imagined that an evil spirit would constantly renew not only the pain but also the sensitivity to pain—at least in theory. But pain is something utterly biological. It seeks to conserve life and to warn and protect it from mortal danger. In the rare cases where people are born insensitive to pain, they have only a short life. Some forms of pain seem to go far beyond their physiological purpose. A terminal cancer patient's unbearable pain is pointless; it's as if one were to drive the dead to the cemetery in an ambulance with flashing lights and screaming sirens. Pain makes sense only as long as recovery is possible. Pain made sense especially for primeval man, who had to know when he had suffered injuries, had broken a bone, and so on. Similarly, pain was the body's way of signaling when to draw back from combat or when to be ready for the next fight. The function of pain in natural selection should not be overlooked. Besides this, and since that time, pain has gained an entirely new dimension in the spiritual realm, which is of much greater importance than the purely biological function. To bear pain, to endure it, proves the superiority of the spirit over life. Jesus as the man of suffering. But what should the terminal cancer patient suffer all his pain for? Here all attempts to see any deeper meaning must stop, and the only thing left is morphine.

Jesus and the martyrs were suffering *for something*. Suffering for nothing makes no sense. Hence, one would have to learn how to extract sense from our suffering. But how? Perhaps the reason that war has remained so popular is that sacrificial death provides meaning to suffering in subjective terms. Even this hope will be denied the victims of nuclear war.

Read Montaigne again. His thought was so free (1580!) that wisdom seems to have come to him without effort. Picture this man: he installs himself in a tower, a hundred yards away from his family home, and thinks and writes for half a lifetime. It is hard to imagine a better life, free of obligations and duties, merely following the delightful self-discipline of thought. Constantly preoccupied with death, his wisdom proves that those who say death is not a subject are stupid. I am translating a few passages:

How is it possible to dismiss the thought of death and not think that he might seize us by the scruff at any moment? . . . Let us remove death's strangeness, let us practice it, let us accustom ourselves to it; let us have nothing more often in our heads than death; at every moment of our imagination and in all its faces. . . . It is uncertain where death awaits; let us await it everywhere. Premeditation of death is premeditation of liberty. He who has learned to die has unlearned servitude. There is no longer any evil in life for those who have well understood that the loss of life is no evil; to know that we have to die makes us free of all subjection and constraints.

Antiquity's heroism, however, produced the following bad example: Paulus Aemilius answered his prisoner the king of Macedonia, who requested not to be displayed in the triumphal procession, "Let him address the plea to himself!"——meaning, he should kill himself.

Montaigne was fascinated by death. In book 2, chapter 3 of his *Essays* he writes:

Death is the remedy for all ills. It is a very certain haven, which is never to be feared and often to be sought. It all comes to the same thing, whether a man bring his end upon himself, or whether he suffer it. . . . The most willing death is the noblest. Life depends on the will of another; death, on our own. . . . Life means servitude; to die means to be free. The common course of cure is carried on at the expense of life: they cut us, they cauterize us, they lop off our limbs, they deprive us of nourishment and blood; one step further and behold, we are cured altogether.

According to the notes in my edition, Montaigne follows Seneca here.

Since antiquity, heroism has contributed most to facilitate death and, especially, to promote the cause of war as well. The victim assumes the pose of the victor. The victor uses it as justification for his cruelty—like Paulus Aemilius. After all, he is sitting on a soft chair. At most, he might think in the very abstract that he might share a similar fate and that it would then be his turn to assume the heroic posture. Since the examples of Jesus and Socrates (who normally should not be mentioned in the same breath, but who do join here), heroism no longer has any business with dying and death. It is cheaper to be brave and more costly to accept fate and cope with whatever it brings.

The dying animal—the old elephant, for example—draws back into the jungle. He wants to be alone, and the others want to leave him alone. Possibly this is the case with us as well. I sense that I'm drawing back more and more, not avoiding contacts but not seeking them either. Right now, I'd like to be alone in Laax; maybe I'll go there the day after tomorrow.

Again, I find myself looking forward to sleep.

The right kidney is hurting now, but this could be my imagination. I didn't take any painkillers all day. It's only when others are about to cry that I get all choked up.

Zurich, January 15

To Basel yesterday and again today by train, first class yesterday, second class today. The difference in price is grotesque. First class is mostly overcrowded, but there are always businessmen around who incessantly talk so loudly that you can't even read. Why hasn't it occurred to any of the railway companies to set aside silence compartments or reading compartments?

The fields are covered with ice and gleam in the sun. Near Augst some children were actually skating on a meadow.

Yesterday, the computertomogram, today the isotope scan. The diagnostic possibilities are fantastic. They can tell you exactly what the tumor looks like, how large it is, where it is located, and they can measure precisely the remaining capacity of the left kidney: 31 percent. So it isn't dead yet, and possibly it will recover. Yesterday, the doctors congratulated me for having such a small tumor, a partial resection of the bladder would be quite feasible, and that is just the option that I've always accepted. They said that I absolutely ought not to give up and that I ought to have this possibility precisely clarified. So I'll have to go at least through the purgatory of the diagnostic tests: removal of tissue samples from the whole bladder under full anesthesia. One can certainly live all right with half a bladder; it would only be necessary to stop more often on long car trips.

The precision of the diagnosis compared to the uncertainty of the therapeutic success has an absurd quality, like a slow-motion film of an auto accident or an airplane crash. One is able to see it all very precisely but is powerless to do anything about it.

Alas, those doctors! If I still have time, perhaps I'll set up a typology of medical behavior and personality. But this isn't even necessary, because they resemble each other in the essential aspects. Not any different from the lawyers, they act to cover themselves. They protect themselves, not the patient, exactly as the lawyers protect themselves and not the accused, by adhering strictly to the rules of procedure. This makes it virtually impossible to take an interest in the client or patient or to try to understand him as an individual. Probably I'm being very unfair. How could anyone conduct a real conversation with forty patients a day? And, to be honest, I have been rather privileged; the doctors all had rather long talks with me, in part because of my academic title, in part out of curiosity as they found it odd that someone would refuse the usual therapeutic treatment as brusquely. Exceptions to this stereotype are people like Christoph and Gschwind, each for very different reasons: Christoph because of his conscientiousness, and Gschwind because of his vigorous skepticism in regard to anything that is routinely prescribed or carried out.

Since there was no train back to Zurich for an hour after the examinations, I went back to the Café Spillmann (it has another name now), enjoyed the view over the Rhine, called up Gschwind, and made a date to have lunch with him at noon. Before that, I walked up to the middle of the Middle Rhine Bridge with its little chapel, the Käppelijoch. When you look upstream from this place, the city is at its most beautiful. They've ruined all the outlying old quarters, so that you would hardly recognize the place. The Rhine glistens like . . . (I thought about a comparison for a long time) . . . like silver foil in motion, the sun just barely over the Palatine Hill,* all somewhat hazy, unreal yet very bright. No clear contours, despite the silhouettes of buildings looming starkly in the shadows of the riverbank of greater Basel.

Gschwind is a thoroughly verbal person, much more so than I. In conversations, he spins the yarn of his ideas: sometimes he's rigid, more often flexible; moving in leaps, yet never afraid that someone will steal it from him. On the contrary: he writes practically nothing; he gives it all away orally—not exactly a way to carve out a great scientific career. Since he lives in Göttingen, Basel, he states, appears to him like a foreign city that he happens to know well. I feel exactly the same. Nor has Göttingen become home for him, not any more than Zurich has for me. To be homeless is probably pretty normal for people who don't live from birth to death in the same place. There are memories of childhood and youth, and so on. The emotional

* A landmark: the hill with the red sandstone cathedral overlooking the Rhine.

homeland, as Frisch called it in his famous speech, is spread out over many memories of a great variety of places and, more pointedly, of people who become friends and then are lost from sight. New friends come, but at greater intervals. In a more rational vein, we talk about "citizenship." In Switzerland, your citizenship is that of a community, not your place of birth but the place of origin of your ancestors. The community issues you a certificate of citizenship which you have to turn in for safe-keeping when you move from your home community. Your citizenship in the home community constitutes an absolute legal guarantee, and this creates a bond that may be abstract but nevertheless is very serious. God knows, one should not glorify Switzerland; but admittedly, Switzerland always has succeeded in keeping its citizens emotionally attached, if only by mere legal and abstract devices. That everyone is first a citizen of a community, then of a canton (state), and finally of the Confederation, is at first a mere legal construct, but behind it lies an enormous ability to make the state a living reality for its people. Add to this the concept of heritability of citizenship. In earlier times, before the recent reform of the citizenship laws, citizenship in a Swiss community, and with it that in the canton and in the Confederation, passed unconditionally from the father to the children, even though they might for many generations have been residing outside Switzerland and have assumed other cit-izenships. This is why, after the last war, many Swiss, above all those from Eastern Bloc nations, remembered their Swiss citi-zenship and moved back to Switzerland, and Switzerland took them in. Such heritability ought not to be possible in the future, was the opinion of a revised law. Out-of-state citizens ought to register from time to time, or at least from generation to gen-eration, to retain Swiss citizenship. In revising this law, Swit-zerland has abandoned one of its greatest (perhaps unconscious) ideas. In earlier times, Switzerland acted in a legal sense like

God the Father in the parable of the Prodigal Son. Switzerland was a limitless fatherland, at least in time. One could turn away from it "unto the fourth and fifth generation," and still it would continue to accept the grandchildren and the grandchildren's grandchildren. Swiss citizenship followed them wherever they went. This smacks of patriarchy and ancestor worship, to be sure; but such a comment seems petty in the face of the greatness of such a stance by the state.

A call from Christoph: according to the tomogram, I'm at stage C. In bladder cancer, the urologist and oncologist differentiate among stages A, B1, B2, C, D1, D2. In A and B1, the tumor adheres only to the inner mucous membrane, and a partial resection is feasible. In B2 and C, the tumor has already grown into the bladder wall, and only a total resection with prior radiation seems "appropriate"—a procedure that has a five-year survival rate of 30 to 40 percent. In stages D1 and D2, metastases are already present, and there is nothing that can be done. Which is, after all, what I knew from the beginning.

January 16

How modern scholarship works to make itself obsolete: A takes an idea from B, and in his first publication quotes B, as good scholarship requires. Later, A returns to his subject and in his second publication quotes only himself—namely, his previous publication. B is out of the picture. The same could be done to A by C, and so on. One could write an extended analysis and satire about the art of how to cite and not to cite. Frequently, an author does not cite the secondary reference but only a primary source that he has never read. He simply takes over the quotation from the secondary source. Once I got a dissertation from a doctoral candidate who quoted Luther several times in his historical introduction. I said to him: "You couldn't have read all of Luther to write this introduction. Where did you get these quotations?" He admitted to having taken them from another dissertation, and the author of this other dissertation in turn had found them in a general history of law. Don't believe for a moment that only doctoral candidates act in this fashion.

References to my *Legislative Doctrine** have already disappeared completely from many legal treatises on legislation, though the authors treat the same issues and problems and present the same solutions I proposed. Apparently, after nine years, it is being considered out of date. The legal literature that has appeared in the meantime is predominantly quoted now, and there at least I'm still being cited. So quickly does scholarly fame fade away, scattered and gone with the wind.

What is practiced today in many psychotherapy groups, accompanied by an enormous amount of psychological literature, is love of one's fellow man—not love of one's enemy. If the group members get along well, it doesn't mean that aggression between groups is on the wane. Quite the contrary. This, I'm convinced, Jesus had already seen quite clearly. Today, people are needed who rebel and resist *within* the group, outsiders capable of eliminating the immanent, system-associated hostility between groups. Otherwise, growing affection *within* the group will have to be viewed as a compensation for the fact that the aggression between the groups has grown to infinity and to the point of total destruction.

What do we love most in a woman, and why do we fall in love with her? Fetishes certainly play a major role (for me it has

---

* *Gesetzgebungslehre*, the first textbook on legislation as a legal discipline, was published by Rowohlt, Hamburg, in 1973.

always been above all scent—I'm like a dog in this regard), and, of course, the looks; the way of moving; and then the voice. According to certain accounts, the last sense to go before death is hearing. Before total unconsciousness we can still hear the doctors and nurses say to each other, "Now he's dead; exitus; let's turn everything off."

This afternoon I've bought Fritz Zorn's book *Mars* and read through it quickly. I was interested mainly in his descriptions of how cancer progresses. I did not learn much except that in the metastatic stage people writhe in pain, pound the walls, roar, scream, and cry. The book is full of hate: with hatred Zorn fights for his life, with hatred against his neurotic past; with raging hatred he pursues his parents and the bourgeois society he comes from. He would like to punch God in the teeth and nail Jesus to the cross over and over again. To all of this, his fatal disease and his age (he died at thirty-two) entitles him.

In my case, death, too, lost its youthful freshness. I am a completely different case, and these dictated notes will never become a best-seller. I can understand how one can hate God, but it takes a real neurotic to hate Jesus. Of course, I'm not doing justice to Zorn's story. I am not attempting to, either, because I can't.

I fully realize that a certain aspect of the Zurich youth movement* would have been inconceivable without Zorn's book: the hateful, nihilistic protest without alternative. The police and the law, to be sure, reacted even more nihilistically: conservation for the sake of conservation, beatings and arrests against spon-

* Throughout the period in which Noll dictated these notes, unemployed, alienated students and their radical sympathizers were challenging the unyielding authorities with demonstrations, graffiti, and demands for changes. Some of these demonstrations resulted in law cases that particularly attracted Peter's interest. (See entries of March 11 and May 5.)

taneity. The official representatives of the state and society, the apparatchiks, who are only after votes, overlooked completely and refused to comprehend the fact that within this movement entirely new and better approaches to the solution of social and personal problems were about to take shape. The great majority of the people wants everything to remain as it is. But nothing will.

If there were a God, say the atheists, then He would never permit that hundreds of thousands of people die of starvation every year. Hence, there is no God. Or: God is evil. This sort of reasoning and accusation assumes that God ought to have created and maintained a paradise. For what matters is not how much is wrong in the world, whether millions of people starve or only two or three; rather, from this standpoint, God is justified only if the world is absolutely good, painless, filled with pleasure, a paradise.

Only music is abstract enough to express the transcendental.

Laax, January 22

Up here again in a luminous world. The contrast with Zurich with its constant blanket of fog is almost unbearable. The sun burns and gleams; above the shadow of the forest, one great ocean of light. I've let the blinds down a bit, and the sun is heating my chest but not blinding my eyes.

Between one and two o'clock, shortly after I arrived, I went skiing, a few times down the upper runs of Crap Sogn Gion. The snow was so hard that I quickly got fed up. As I came down into the valley, the surface was bare ice for the most part. I ski poorly under such conditions, and that annoys me. In good snow, I still ski very well and fast. Everything is intact; only the future has been cut off.

The pond no longer thaws even on the near shore, itself out of reach of the shadow of the woods. Only the upper right end has water, from the many springs and brooks that come down from Falera. For several days now, my old Citroën hasn't started; yesterday I had to have it towed across the city to the Citroën garage. Even while towed, the car wouldn't start, either. But everything is all right now, with the exception of the doors, which can't be locked anymore, or opened in some cases. I have to open the door to the driver's seat from the outside by lowering the window. The whole electrical system was haywire—nothing actually broken but everything out of kilter. Everyone thought I should buy a new car or at least a good used one, and that there was no point in troubling myself with an old car. But now I'm quite content with it again, waiting for the next breakdown.

The sun is now going down behind the promontory, from which there is such a wonderful view down into the Vorder-rheintal. The sun is setting almost at the same spot as two months ago. I was keeping track then of the sunsets, how they would come seven minutes earlier each day. Accordingly, it is now almost half past four again. Just as then, the sun is no longer able to manage the slope that inclines a little toward the right, because its path arches more steeply downward.

Yesterday, I went to see the pastor of the Grossmünster. He offered me Calvados, and it was obvious that he's no puritan. He has accepted my requests for the funeral as perfectly normal, which pleased me very much. So: sermon by the minister, reading of the curriculum vitae to be written by myself as well as some of my reflections on dying and death, allocutions by Max Frisch and by a fellow faculty member. In the intervals the three most beautiful choruses from the Credo of the B-minor Mass.

How well Bach succeeded in translating this Catholic litany into the language of Protestantism! Music is really the only artistic medium of Protestantism; but more about this later. We talked about Luther, Zwingli, Karl Barth. The differences are clearly in the political realm; Luther and Zwingli were the first to exemplify the difference in spirit between Germans and Swiss (Luther to Zwingli: You Swiss have a different Spirit). Karl Barth, who never had any use for Zwingli and was much more in tune with Luther and in part with Calvin, nevertheless in spirit acted as the Swiss he was—and not as a Lutheran—in his resistance to Hitler. But not without hitting on a neat spiritual trick: the oath of allegiance to Hitler, he argued, violated the First Commandment, "Thou shalt have no other gods before me." With this, he could win to his side those apolitical Lutherans whose first concern was always the purity of doctrine, like Martin Niemöller, for example. Evidently, at this point, no return to political innocence is now possible, as is shown by the Evangelical Church in Germany, now so actively engaged in politics.

Report of my urologist in Basel to his radiologist colleague (translation of medical-technical terms supplied by me):

Diagnosis: *Solid, urinary bladder tumor situated on the left, with hydronephrosis [blocked left kidney].*

The patient has had several previous episodes of urolithiasis [kidney stones]. A recent intravenous urography [kidney X-ray with contrast dye] revealed a caliceal calculus [kidney stone located in one of the cups that collect the urine into the renal pelvis] on the right. In December 1981, on feeling a slight recurrent pain on his left side, the patient went to a urologist in Zurich under the impression that another kidney stone was beginning to pass. The findings of the urography, enclosed here, were quite unex-

pected. Shortly thereafter, in a cystoscopic examination [optical viewing of the bladder interior], a solid left-sided bladder tumor was discovered. Histologically [by microscopic examination of tissue sample removed by minor surgery to determine the extent of the malignancy and spread of the tumor] nothing is yet known, and as a first step a transurethral biopsy [removal of tissue specimens from the interior of the bladder] was considered in Zurich. Professor Noll was very skeptical, however, of all other diagnostic measures, after learning the probable diagnosis. Basically, he did not want to have anything done at all, since the overall prognosis for such tumors would in any case not be good. We have now succeeded in persuading him at least to give his consent for some studies as to the tumor stage, since these will not prejudice any further decisions.

An infiltration of the bladder wall by the existing tumor, the histology of which is not yet known, is probable in view of the hydronephrosis [kidney blockage]. We are expecting information from the computed tomography [CT scan] as to whether an extravesical growth [reaching beyond the bladder] can be diagnosed, and as to what extent indications exist for lymph-node metastasis in the area of the fossa obturatoria [a certain area of the lower pelvis] and the iliac vessels [vessels supplying the entire pelvic area and lower extremities]. . . .

Radiologist's report:

CT scan of bladder: *With patient's bladder filled, X-rays of sections were taken at one-centimeter intervals from the top of the bladder to the bottom, yielding the following results:*

The cranial [upper] portions of the bladder are free. In the middle segment of the bladder, the left side wall is thickened. This pathological alteration continues toward the orifice of the left ureter in the form of a relatively circumscribed, lumpy swelling of the bladder wall; in the area of the ureteral orifice an exophytic [growing out] tumor is observed protruding into the bladder lumen [inside of bladder] (section 4–6 + C). The bladder wall has been completely infiltrated, but the perivesical fat pad [fatty tissue

surrounding the bladder] has not been invaded. Beginning at the
tumor center, one can nicely follow proximally [toward the center]
the distended left ureter on the cranial sections.

Conclusions:
Bladder tumor in the area of the left ureteral orifice with hy-
droureter [blocked ureter]. The tumor has completely grown
through the bladder wall but has not infiltrated the perivesical
tissue. It spreads intramurally [within the bladder walls] toward
the bottom of the bladder, where its boundaries are not well
defined. The growth continues cranially toward the middle of the
bladder. No abnormal lymph nodes are recognizable.

I actually had five years of Greek, yet it didn't help at all; the
medical terms had to be translated for me by Christoph.

Whoever wishes to translate it or have it translated for him
will see quickly how things stand. The tumor has grown completely through the bladder wall and, as is the nature of a tumor,
will go on growing. The only remedy is to cut and cut and cut.
They now have copied the Hydra technique from Hercules,
cutting off all the heads at once. But I'm too squeamish for that.

The radiologists who own the CT scanner, a rare and very
expensive machine, hand out information sheets to calm down
and bait the patients. Obviously, all of this is neither painful nor
dangerous, and any rational person will immediately grasp this
without the need for an explanatory leaflet. Clearly, this leaflet
is nothing but a form of advertising.

What Ruth, an intelligent woman, had to say: "You see, you're
upsetting people with your decision. If someone has cancer, he
goes to the hospital and has surgery—that's what's normal. But
if someone has cancer and goes around cheerfully like you, it
gives people the creeps. They are all of a sudden challenged to
confront dying and death as a part of life, and that they don't

want. Nor are they able to do it as long as they are not in your situation. That's why it is irritating and confusing that you sit here and say 'I have cancer' while refusing to go to the hospital. If you went to the hospital everything would be all right. Then everything would be fine again; people could visit you, bring flowers, and after a certain time say 'Thank God, he's been released,' and again after a certain time, 'Now he's back in,' and they'll come again with flowers, but always for shorter periods. But at least they would know where to find you. They would know you hadn't been run over by a car but have cancer and that you were going to the hospital to have things cut out, all as it is supposed to be. You scandalize them [this isn't the way she expressed it]—you are showing them that death is in our midst and you are acting it out before their very eyes; they suddenly are forced to think of what they have always suppressed. And of course they think only of themselves. Which makes it all the worse. They cannot help imagining what their own fate will be at some future time. They are confronted with something living that ought to be dead already, or at least in the hospital."

The pastor told me that I still would have to endure many trials, and I said yes. I'm not the first dead man who came to him before his death. Some old people do the same and make arrangements with the minister in advance, coming to him in good health and with clear minds to talk about their funerals. At least I'm no exception in this regard, only insofar as the minister has never been confronted with such a young and otherwise healthy person with cancer outside of the hospital. The other cancer victims are all in the hospital, and the family then asks the minister to come and arrange everything—which he later does, dutifully.

Laax, January 23

The sky is misty but very bright, with subdued sunshine on the snow-covered fields on the slopes toward Falera. Föhn weather: the air is sultry, no wind. I should be outside in the snow; then the brightness would dominate the dull gloom.

This may well be the temptation to which most people succumb, even though surgery doesn't have a chance of success: hand yourself over to the hospital, and then others take care of you and decide for you, arrange various things, and one is content to know that everything possible has been done. What sort of reassurance is that? To become a child again? Only without a mother's warmth—and here, I believe, lies the fallacy: a dying person who relinquishes himself to the medical machine is truly helpless, because the help he receives is cold.

The physicians, by the way, were indeed not completely honest, in spite of their candor, which in the face of my skepticism simply could not be avoided. What, I wonder, would they have told a less skeptical patient? Only Christoph made it absolutely clear that even a total resection, which I didn't want anyway, offered only a 30 percent chance of survival. Now I see it from the medical reports myself: the tumor has grown through the bladder wall and is even much larger within the wall than in the bladder itself. The case could not be clearer. "Hope" to the medical profession seems to mean any possibility of prolonging life. My conception of hope is different. I have been settling accounts with death for so long now that I view death as something quite natural, which it is anyhow, and at the same time something almost familiar. . . . Is it really true what I am dictating here? At any rate, I believe it, and that should do. At the same time, I am aware that the final days will be very different, probably hard, and this uncertainty, as to the point in time as well, makes me worry. Will I recant and regret everything and think I was a fool back then, five, six, or however many months ago?

The triumphal victory over death expressed in the "Et resurrexit" of the B-minor Mass corresponds exactly to the Christian confession of creed. But I cannot subscribe to this belief, nor do I believe in a resurrection in that sense—that is, I am not convinced of it. This may lead to misunderstandings when the choruses are played in the Grossmünster, but I have to accept that. Since I cannot explain it to myself, how can I explain it to others? It sounds shallow when I say, "This music itself is a triumph over death, and as long as it resounds, death is vanquished, not the least for him who hears it as he dies and for him who dies in the expectation that others will hear it at his funeral." For me, very personally, this music, and this work in particular, are very closely linked to the reason that I no longer—or, perhaps, do not yet—fear my death. If something new begins after death, this novelty will be all the more a welcome surprise. And I shall always admit that the idea of an eternal kingdom of God, whether I experience it or not, is one that continues to overwhelm me: *cuius regni non erit finis.* I can do nothing against it.

Zurich, January 24

Returning from Laax late in the afternoon yesterday, I stopped on my way to see Hansruedi Bachmann. Klärli came by, and so did Gredinger. Paul Gredinger is a rich man who enjoys doing good provided it can be done with some originality, which, as everybody knows, is the opposite of most rich men: they dislike doing good, and if it is unavoidable, they want to do something as conventional as possible. I exploited this aspect of

Gredi's strength and asked him if he would help in having my reflections published after my death, along with *Jericho* and the funeral speech by Frisch. He agreed immediately and asked if I wouldn't like to include one of my short stories as well. Definitely not!

The rediscovery of a good friend! Of course, we have always been fond of each other, without interruptions and incidents, while at the same time neglecting each other. Now I know better than before that one must nurture friendships; otherwise they wither. Not all friendships are equally sensitive, though: some endure years of total estrangement, while others begin to suffer after the relationship has been discontinued for only a few months.

I've long since come to terms with the large pictures of ducks which decorate one of Bachmann's walls. Evidently, with colored etchings of flowers, birds, and so on, several of the same sort must always hang next to each other. Good taste requires it! A flower next to a bird and an old cityscape would be incompatible. But five ducks always go well together. And yet, I must admit, I did the same thing with the folios of colored birds out of my original edition of Buffon* that are hanging in the hall.

The evening was so entertaining that I never gave a thought to my disease, which is not normally the case. I ate and drank a lot and then drove home early. People don't seem to mind anymore. We talked mainly about *Machiavelli,* and we kept coming up with new examples that have occurred since we finished the manuscript and that followed exactly the pattern we described: victims of the scapegoat principle at the Volksbank, the piece on the Exxon management in *Der Spiegel*, and so on.

---

* Eighteenth-century French naturalist, famous for his beautifully illustrated books on animal life.

It is harder to describe people one knows than people one doesn't because, I think, it doesn't matter if one gives a false picture of somebody unknown. You've merely described someone else, perhaps someone who doesn't exist, but still it is a good description. I would be unable to describe any of my acquaintances well enough that everybody would recognize him. It would be easy for me to describe an old farmer, a stuffy professor, or a drug addict. These are mere types; practically all of literature consists of types. Drama has no need of individuality whatsoever; all it needs are the roles.

The setting sun is reflected in the windows of the Bodmer House; it looks like glaring searchlights. A sign that the days are growing longer again.

I have asked quite a few people to take care of certain tasks after my death. I have written them the appropriate letters, with copies to the executor of my will. Then I'll write an "immediate testament," which I'll carry with me constantly in the final days and which indicates who should be notified promptly upon my death—namely, those to whom I've dictated today's letters. Almuth will have to engage an undertaker, send out the death notices, and contact the pastor at the Grossmünster. Lou will transcribe my last dictations and pass them on to Gredinger. The pastor of the Grossmünster will organize the funeral service: sermon; curriculum vitae and reflections on dying and death, both written by myself; funeral oration by Max Frisch; choruses from the B-minor Mass; a big feast afterward, with lots to eat and drink for the mourners. Gredinger is to publish the writings from my unpublished works mentioned earlier, together with Frisch's speech. Professor R., the executor, will be in charge of probate and estate and will deal with the legal problems that might arise. For legal reasons the "immediate will" will have to be safeguarded in the actual will, a long-drawn affair, all written by hand, in accordance with the old-fashioned rules of article 505 of the Civil Code.

Zurich, January 25

On Christoph's advice, I telephoned Professor Zingg this afternoon to find out what to expect without surgery. His prognosis: the tumor will fill out the bladder, which means I'll be urinating ever more frequently, urine mixed with blood, at the end every ten minutes, and I'll die in convulsions. The gentler possibilities of uremia and metastases are less likely at my age. "Couldn't I go to the hospital at the end to let them alleviate the pain?" Zingg: "At your age, you'll still have nine months to live. It is unlikely that the metastases will overtake the primary tumor, and it is highly uncertain whether the tumor will close off the right kidney [uremia] before filling out the whole bladder." I should think it over very carefully and not hesitate to call him back, as it is his job to help. Surgery would probably still be the best alternative. (But unless I decided now, it would be too late.)

Then Gredinger came, and we discussed all the possibilities. Then we dined and drank in cheerful spirits at the Zimmerleuten. Gredinger would submit to all surgery; but he admits that he's a very different kind of person and, in addition, not confronted with the same situation.

It is late tonight. The day after tomorrow I'll try to do some hard thinking so as not to miss anything I owe to life.

Morphine isn't easy, either.

Zingg: "Subjectively you are now in a good and normal condition, but this will change in a few months, and you ought to think about this now." The "subjective-objective" distinction, which is used in other disciplines to mean anything and nothing, still has a very central reality in medicine, since we are dealing with man and his inborn contradictions. Subjectively, he may still feel absolutely fine, but the objective diagnosis will sooner or later catch up with him also in his subjectivity. On the other hand, pain—perhaps the most subjective feeling known to man—may or may not be present, regardless of the objective diagnosis.

I'll have to practice the art of dying all over again, because my present subjectivity will founder in the end on the objective diagnosis.

Why are animals, but not people, allowed to be put to sleep?

If I have the major surgery, it will just be a delayed form of suicide under foreign direction. The decision will still be mine, except that I don't have to carry it out myself. Fear of suicide is the fear of doing it yourself. I would be more than happy if I could make my exit during surgery under anesthesia. But doing it myself, being alone—that still scares me.

I took the "Death of Basel"* with me to Zurich. Nowhere in the world are there supposed to be so many depressives as in Basel; and I recall a conversation at the university cafeteria with Karl Barth many years ago, when I was still a student, in which he told me there are two spiritual powers in Basel, the Carnival Spirit and the Hörnli Spirit ("Hörnli" is the name of the big municipal cemetery between Basel and Riehen). The fact that the most famous *Danse Macabre* was painted in Basel is certainly a mark of the depressive, sterile, analytical, ironical, self-ironical Basel spirit. The streetcar stop near the church in whose cloister (later torn down, like so many other beautiful historical buildings) Konrad Witz's *Danse Macabre* frescoes were located used to be called Totentanz—Dance of Death—until the new State

* The "Death of Basel" is a recurring theme in this old city on the Rhine.

Hospital was built directly behind the church. That is when the Baselers lost their sense of irony and even their historical fidelity. The streetcar stop is now called Kantonsspital, and, logically, the Dance of Death today takes place in the hospitals, in enormous rounds with all the dancers gathered in the same ballroom.

January 28

The most highly developed thinking machine we know is the human brain, at least from the view of the brain thinking about itself. This brain, in contrast to all the computers developed by it, which despite much greater speed will forever remain dependent on it, has produced two concepts, the second of which is as compelling as the first: Death and God.

Death is empirically verifiable. The dead man can be seen, the cold body felt. I've always been against the notion of man as the philosophical animal, which is used to emphasize man's unique capabilities: "In contrast to the animal, man can do this and that and . . ." This argument ignores that the gap between a chimpanzee and a human is much smaller than the gap between a chimpanzee and a worm. The gap between an extremely talented chimpanzee and a feeble-minded person would probably be hard to determine. Despite this, I now state that, in contrast to the animal, man has imprinted into his brain the two ideas of Death and God. Only it would seem that mankind is regressing in regard to the two greatest ideas that its brain ever generated. Today, people behave like the chimpanzees, who might glance briefly at their dead relative, perhaps touch him, then turn away and quickly forget everything. The thought of death is even more repressed than the concept of God, which so far as we know is unknown even among chimpanzees and dolphins yet is implanted in the human brain. Why? Because we know that we know nothing, as Socrates said so well. Wisely, he did not *write* it. Plato took care of that, unfortunately. Or perhaps fortunately, for otherwise we would know too little about Socrates. With Socrates I would be most eager to talk, should I ever meet him over there. He had all the qualities I admire: he was courageous, intelligent, wise, tolerant—pitiless only in regard to stupidity when associated with power. The brain thinks God—which doesn't mean that He necessarily exists; but it does mean, compellingly, that the question regarding His existence is irrefutable and that logical positivism is a dead duck. Already Pascal saw that the infinitely small and the infinitely large, the microcosm and the macrocosm, call for the question of God. Also, as a sign or symbol, God can stand only for Himself. The mind cannot imagine anything without origin; and the brain, after all, is a creation out of this origin. And this brain is capable of thinking that the unthinkable exists.

Nor are these thoughts of mine about God purely a product of a Protestant education. Still, an actual grace of God appears to exist, extending over several generations: unto the fourth and fifth generations. The astonishment of those friends to whom I have told my story and my decision may have something to do with it. God's blessing bestowed on my great-grandparents, grandparents, and parents reaches just down to me. I do not really like this God, but I wish to know Him.

M. said that all Fromm did was to translate the Christian teachings into the realm of the psychological—nothing new to M., who, like me, grew up in a Protestant home. One might add that Fromm proceeds very selectively, transposing Jesus' basic views into the modern way of thinking but without the additions of Paul, and even less those of the later Church Fathers.

Several days of laughing less frequently is enough to change the facial expression. "Somehow, your face is more serious," Ruth said. When a person terminally ill with cancer has all his teeth polished or quits smoking, it is just as pointless or profound as Luther's declaration, "Even if I knew the world would end tomorrow, I would still plant my little apple tree today." Such a pronouncement can come only from someone who knows that the world is *not* going to end tomorrow, or who doesn't know that it is ending.

January 29

Some come purely out of curiosity. A few are horrified, really disgusted, and turn away never to be heard from again; they already have my unaesthetic end in view.

But many come out of true friendship, compassion, and perhaps a touch of shame.

Evidently, my situation divides the minds of those around me.

And now still another meeting of the university senate! Attendance is a duty, and you get a written warning if you are absent without an excuse, as I was last time. To have to sit through the one-and-a-half-hour meeting is not much different from the punitive extra hours after school, for the decisions are all made beforehand anyway; discussion is pointless and mostly unwelcome. Besides, the decisions concern only irrelevant stuff. I arrive at the last minute so as not to get involved in conversations with my colleagues. But attendance is an official duty.

January 30

The larger context makes for a more casual attitude toward little annoyances, which, oddly enough, are turning up with increasing frequency. I was hardly on my way to an invitation in Höngg, and no farther than the Seilergraben, when someone slammed into the rear of my car. Now my host will have to come to get me, and next week I'll have to spend a lot of time trying to have the car repaired.

If one wanted to drag God into all of this, one would have to see Him as getting lost in the business of sending out the most subtle cues. That's the way most people see Him, anyway: "a blessing in disguise!"; "by the skin of our teeth!"; "thank God!"; and so on.

January 31

Without telephone or without television, people would live much closer to each other, and there wouldn't be so much sprawl, either. The automobile, too, causes sprawl. Knights in olden times, in their castles, practically died of boredom, and if there was a village in the area, they certainly went to the pub as often as possible. Today, every man lives in his castle, or what he considers his castle, whether a mansion or a little house, scattered everywhere, devouring the landscape like a cancer. All this was realized much too late, confusing means with ends. Without cars, television, and telephones, people would be forced to move closer together, and regulations for the protection of green zones would be superfluous.

What makes me think of all this? After I started to read, and then put aside, a laboriously written dissertation with hardly an idea to its credit, I switched to making phone calls. Claire told me about her sister's death from cancer: first cancer of the breast, then, after seven years, metastases. All at home to the very end; her husband gave her the morphine shots she needed. The woman wanted to live as long as possible for the sake of their adopted nine-year-old. The last two years she lay in the bed, a little bundle of misery, hardly recognizable any longer, very thin, completely shrunken. Claire had entirely repressed this experience; otherwise, she would have told me about it when she first learned about my condition. I told Claire I would leave her my fiery red bird painting by Strubel, because although she doesn't like him, she really likes his paintings.

Dying is primarily an aesthetic problem—that is, for those who have to go on living. The dying person looks ugly, so totally different from the way you knew him. But this doesn't bother the dying man. He no longer turns and stretches in front of the mirror. His appearance frightens the others. If only he were dead, things would be all right again, the matter quickly settled. But the dying person is a portrayal of death; the cancer victim enacts death over a prolonged period, in the end as a living corpse, which, for most of the captive audience, is aesthetically difficult to take. The spectators experience a very different dying and a very different death than the actor does. I must remember this. Toward the end, for the onlookers, it is merely an act of inspection, revoltingly forced on them by friendship and feelings of piety. Is the moribund obliged to respect these feelings? Ought he to clear away his own remains, fastidiously, like garbage?

How long is one still visitable? The doctors and nurses have an unfailing aesthetic instinct for that.

"It was a beautiful corpse," they say in Switzerland after a burial.

A dismal Sunday and a bad dissertation add up to a minor disaster. Good dissertations are read quickly and with pleasure and with the satisfaction of having participated in the creative process. Bad dissertations are like having to walk in the rain for a long time without a raincoat until, finally, one is completely soaked while at the same time being unable to throw off the wet clothes.

February 1

If one excludes borderline cases, which are rare and will be discussed later, justice is a very straightforward matter. But we cannot come close to making it a reality, because power is stronger than its critique. The principle of justice is equality, all old hat. If I will one of my daughters what is due her by law and no more, and give all the rest to my other daughter, that would be unjust, even if I loved the latter more than the first. Exceptions to the rule of equal treatment must be justified; equal treatment itself needs no justification, because it embodies the principle of justice. Whenever somebody is favored over somebody else, this is compatible with the principle of justice only if the privileged party either has accomplished more or has greater needs. Only these two exceptions pass the test of the fundamental principle of equal treatment: the principle of performance and the principle of need. If one worker earns two thousand francs a month and the other gets three thousand, the difference can be justified only on the principle that the second is more productive by fulfilling a harder task, or is more needy—for example, by having more children. That is all.

Of course it is obvious that the world is fraught with injustice. The corporation president earns twenty times more than ordinary employees, and he is not more productive: on the contrary, ever since he achieved this high position there has been nothing left for him to do; even the job of thinking has been taken over by advisers. Certainly the performance principle is used to justify the twentyfold salary, but quite unjustly so. Until he was made a vice-president, his accomplishments were real; after that, he's only gained positions of power. Neither does the principle of need apply any longer; it doesn't matter if the company president has ten children or two.

The principle of need is always argued from below—for

example, for addicts, for offenders, etc. On the other hand, the principle of achievement is always argued from above, for the rich and the powerful.

Socialism, the least intolerable of all political ideologies, has always turned against the formal legal underpinnings of power, chiefly against property. In so doing, it misses its greatest opportunity, since everyone is a property owner, wants to remain one, and wants to acquire still more property. First error: treating property as property without regard to size. Result: the small farmer will stand up to protect the big landholder, because the small farmer too has property he might lose. Second, more important error: formalizing the productivity principle without background analysis. Practically speaking, this means the following: the injustices exist not primarily in that someone has inherited property, a name, and nationality (still my position in the lecture in Dijon)—although this is, of course, true as well—but rather in the fact that the struggle for power is much more rewarding than any productive effort. There is a point beyond which the effort brings no further advantages to the performer. This is evident from all the infighting in the upper echelons. Merit brings an assistant professorship or corporate vice-presidency, but not a full professorship or chief executive office in a corporation. What is the explanation? Very simple. Everybody wishes one day to live in leisure, to rest on his laurels. Therefore, one of the most important driving forces for achievement is the desire not to be under pressure to perform, while still being able to live without financial worries. This motivation is a spur to achievement, and hence a good thing from the point of view of justice. However, its concrete application invalidates all those ideas that appear correct in the abstract. The productivity principle continues to be invoked even though there is no longer any productivity, a problem related to a further set of principles. The higher somebody's position in the power structure of any organization, the better his opportunity to exploit and claim as his own the productivity of others, who likewise wish to advance. On this principle more than on anything else rests all illegitimate power—in the business world, in science, in academe, and in politics. Our inquiry should begin here, not with the more abstract legal concepts like property, inheritance, and so on but with the exploitation of the careerists by the powerful. Only one out of a hundred in middle management will become company president, yet all will work like crazy for him, increasing his power in return for the tiniest glimmer of hope of becoming powerful themselves one day and thus no longer having to be productive. It's no different, for example, in the Kremlin: a modest measure of accomplishment, a great talent to conform, and an uncanny sense for making the right moves in the power struggles propels people to the top. And because people know this, they shun the effort of hard work, cultivate conformity, and prepare themselves for the power struggles. In the free-market economy, and in the free sciences of the West, all this is mitigated by the competition among various systems (for how long, I wonder?) against each other, with the effect that those in power have a vital interest to extract from the lower levels real performance, the results of which they can claim as their own in order to impress others. Up to the point where they become vice-presidents, senators, tenured professors, people work hard and produce results. Whether the achievements are meaningful and benefit mankind is another question.

The philosophies of law that have failed to recognize this problem may be safely ignored. Only the analysis of power is going to move us ahead, not the reflection about what, in the abstract sense, would be legally just.

This general craving to be rewarded (the necessity principle) should be explored in depth: everyone wants to be overpaid for his accomplishments in order to have security and peace in the future. Everyone needs twenty years of nonproductivity. No one can live under a constant pressure to achieve. Hence, a system ought to be invented in which, say, a twenty-year period of productivity is required, followed by rewards that would be equal for everyone. But this system will never come about, because it doesn't conform to the nature of systems. Changing systems is too costly in terms of blood shed pointlessly as long as the desired change isn't accepted by the system itself.

The necessity principle is seldom abused; the achievement principle, all the time. Why? Because the powerful make use in their arguments of the achievement principle; it would be ludicrous if they did so with the necessity principle.

Legal scholars who philosophize about the just law seem to me like anatomists working on a dead object. The living object would be power, to which, however, they themselves are subject.

February 2

I had to fish the copy of that anonymous letter directed against my colleague S. out of the wastepaper basket, where I had thrown it in disgust, because my faculty colleagues, who had also received copies, feel it important to keep it as proof. Really awful hexameters, all humorless, merely insulting. Important only as evidence.

The intervals between trips to the bathroom are becoming noticeably shorter. Today, it took a real effort to get to the end of my two-hour lecture.

Laax, February 4

The question is how closely, if at all, thought can approach death. We definitely cannot grasp, whether through thought or through other efforts such as meditation, what will be after death. Nor can we conceive of nothingness. All we can imagine is a kind of sleep or unconsciousness. Or total senselessness, without any oases of meaning, the whole world as a black hole; but even then physicists and astronomers say that on the other side of the black hole a negative world or antiworld would emerge. None of this can be grasped in thought or speech. At most there remains the *totaliter aliter*—the totally different, all equally meaningless.

Attempts to glimpse beyond the boundary may be stimulating, but it must be admitted that in reality one sees nothing. Nor is this the kind of activity that death requires of us. Rather, my concern is exclusively with life, life in the face of death, life viewed from the perspective of death. Then everything becomes much simpler and clearer. The limitation in time, the clock ticking away: this I can experience. Death stays the same, but life becomes different. I am seeking out the oases of meaning with much greater care than in the past. Many things that I passed by without a thought are becoming oases of meaning. I take shortcuts through the desert; the routine of daily work, the daily calendar of activities assigned to me by others, I postpone.

I'm going to give up the university chair and the judgeship at the State Supreme Court because fulfilling these responsibilities, which has always been a source of great joy to me, no longer makes sense. I can't pretend that nothing has happened. Nevertheless, I'll still complete *Criminal Law, Volume III,** in order to earn my free semester in the summer. Otherwise I might be cheating the state. I have to accept this odd notion. How long can a dying person still accept his salary as an employee of the state? An absolutely grotesque question, but it

---

* A textbook on Swiss criminal law that Peter wrote for his students.

certainly will be raised by the bureaucrats, even if only after my death.

Yesterday evening, Peter G., my oldest friend from elementary school, came to see me. Peter, who is inclined to dramatize somewhat, told me that his mother and my father had been in love with each other a good forty years ago yet would never have dared to touch each other, even in their thoughts. For my part, I can only remember that they liked each other. Peter probably didn't see more than that, either. Those kinds of parental "sins" are hard for the child to imagine, even as an adult.

Yvette called. I'm getting much more love than before—much too much. I used to find solace in a sentence from one of Plato's dialogues: "God is in the lover, not in the beloved." Now I really ought to be comforting others with this bit of wisdom.

Intelligence is diabolical, because it generates not only destruction but also new technologies, such as, most recently, microelectronics, and in so doing creates a world that even man himself, by his very nature, cannot cope with biologically and psychically.

Dürrenmatt is rather like the king in one of his comedies.

Lou told me that she would quit her job after I retire. She does not want to work for another professor (formally, she is employed by the law faculty). This attitude, this gesture, which certainly makes me feel good—not simply flattered—what have I done to deserve it? Then it occurred to me that I had better take into consideration most people's pettiness and defend myself against the suspicion that Lou had transcribed my tapes on the job, at government expense. Here I may be allowed to allude to my puritanism, even if it isn't worth much; never have I, if only for one minute, used for my personal profit work paid for by the state. On the contrary, I have always paid for it with the most scrupulous honesty out of my own pocket. I have to state this here, though it sounds absurd; for one is always suspected of acts that others commit. Suspicion obviously must come from a mind that is busy doing what it suspects others of doing.

I recall a conversation among colleagues accidentally overheard in the faculty room: "And if you act as a consultant for a bank or insurance company, don't try to forget your fee on your tax return." Ergo, they had been discussing which honoraria could and which could not be ignored on the tax returns.

Laax, February 5

The sun now goes down at exactly 4:44 in the middle of the incline that slopes to the right and at the far right rises steeply to Falera. A minute earlier, the sun was behind the big fir tree that stands on the promontory above the Vorderrheintal, and it looked like a bush aflame that refused to burn out. Moses may have seen God like this, which reminds me of that silly slogan "The Bible is always right." Mental crutches for the feeble-minded.

The sun is a warm mother in these colder regions; the notion of the sun as feminine only ceases farther south, among the Latins: *il sole*. You can feel the heat withdraw quite suddenly on the shady side of the slopes, where it is dusky and icy. In the snow, light and shadow are more sharply divided than usual, and the transition puts a strain on the eyes as well.

I went skiing as always in the past. The body is still in full command, completely alert. If it weren't for the slight symptoms, I'd think I was healthy to the core. I wasn't sad for a moment, though my awareness of the context remained the same. You have to concentrate so hard on the rhythm of turning that it is difficult to brood about death.

I wanted to be back by two o'clock to read and to dictate, but I missed the trail to the valley floor, kept skiing into side valleys, took the ski lift or chair lift up again, and finally gave up at three o'clock at the mountain station, where I took the cable car down into the valley, something I used to think shameful. I got back here again at half past three.

Laax, February 6

Intelligent people who do not have to professionally represent religious institutions generally agree that nothing exists beyond life. Death is meaningless; knowledge about it, an unnecessary burden. Nevertheless, three questions remain: the question of meaning, the question of death, the question of God. Some say that these are no questions at all; but they are fooling themselves, are illogical, since a question that is not answerable still remains a question. And it is quite obvious that everybody is asking these questions.

The agnostic and psychological answers are, to be sure, somewhat more honest. The agnostic answer: We know nothing and will never know anything. The psychological answer: The religious, the mystic, and the transcendental are parts of the human psyche; one must overcome them (Freud), master them (Jung), or make the best of them (Fromm).

God the almighty lawmaker, commander, and judge, Whose every gesture is interpreted down to the smallest detail by His earthly representatives, has certainly abdicated and never existed as such: so much for the Second Commandment. We do not know God's wishes and intentions. The Church served for a long time as proof of God; today it proves the opposite, which does not mean that in the Church apparatus—especially in our time of general unbelief—people couldn't be found whose activities are well pleasing to God. Name one other structure that does so much for the oppressed and downtrodden as those genuinely devout ministers and laity in the Christian churches in, for example, Latin America and South Africa, to whom the Church lends at least a certain protection. This doesn't speak for the Church as an organizational structure but rather for the idea that this structure can never completely lose its conscience.

This leads to the idea of God as the final authority for appeal that can make the individual strong and free, even when all the rest of society is against him. This—most important—psychological function of God is not recognized by the psychologists, not even by Fromm, despite his fairly religious orientation and tireless invocation of the examples of the prophets, of Socrates and Jesus. How can a person stand alone against all others and still hold his own? Such a person is always in need of an authority superior to all others. This power can and must always be God, even if other symbols are employed—for example, Socrates' *daimon,* or the individual's conscience, or a universal consciousness. But in this instance, God must be reasonably well defined and conceptually structured, a God in solidarity with human concerns, a God who distinguishes between good and evil. A vague inclination toward the religious or the numinous or the mystical can never produce such an attitude (of nonconformity in the face of evil), which, rather than being self-serving, seeks to reduce universal injustice.

Second, God is made manifest in that things exist in the first place, including the universe. Thus, a pine cone poses the question of God no less than all the spiral nebulae in the universe. According to the way of our thinking, everything must have a reason. Since behind every reason there has to be another, and since there is no end to the questioning, science will be able to catch up with only very simple gods. The only witty passage that I have found in Fromm reads like this: "Man took refuge in the gods for the fulfillment of those practical needs that he couldn't satisfy alone; those for which he did not pray, he was already able to satisfy on his own." One could say it the other way around: As soon as man has solved a problem, he stops praying. Meanwhile, we have learned that the solution to every problem creates at least two new problems. Because man of our scientific civilization pushes his problems along in front of him, still believing he might be able to solve them in the near future, yet unable to see that the unsolved problems are growing ever more numerous than the solved ones, he no longer prays, having correctly recognized that prayer does not solve any scientific-technical problems. If prayer were generally and everywhere understood as purpose-free, intense reflection, it would certainly improve the world.

The second and third cardinal questions: the question of the meaning of life and the question of death. I am discussing them together because at this point they belong together for me. Besides, I have already talked about life's oases of meaning. What interests me here is the contrast between those who say that they are not concerned about death, that it is not essential and so forth (Elias Canetti, for example, as quoted in Frisch's diaries), and those who maintain that only the thought of death gives true meaning to life (Montaigne and Psalm 90:12). The psalmist says that our heart grows wiser from thinking about death.

What wisdom does thinking about death impart? Neither Montaigne, who thinks as the psalmist does, nor the psalmist himself tells us. Somehow, we know they are right, but we can't define the sentiment and its object. I will try to do so with the following reflections:

1. Time becomes more valuable, much more valuable than

money, to allude to that stupid cliché "Time is money." Time is everything; money is nothing. Money is everything for those who have nothing—the unemployed, for example. For those who have enough money, money is only a symbol and a fetish. Instead, time becomes all the more important the clearer we know its boundary. How often we loathe certain hours—waiting at the airport, for instance—and think, "If only this time had passed already!" What we really mean is, I'd rather be dead for this span of time, for this is time taken off my life. If we kept an exact count, we would probably realize that there are long spans in life during which we would rather be dead.

You grow more selective toward the countless possibilities of life and no longer simply accept those that conventionally lead to an escalating career, for instance; or if you are already near the top, you don't heap position upon position merely in order to have a finger in all the pies. This is wasted, lost time, unlike time spent with a woman or in conversation with friends. On the other hand, you'll postpone fewer tasks; you won't conform to the establishment or fulfill what is expected of you by those who keep the system functioning. At the same time you'll ask: What have I neglected? What should I cultivate more? What would be more meaningful? Which time was wasted and which could be used better?

If this sounds all very abstract, there are concrete examples. Why did I go home early that evening just because I had to attend a meeting next morning? Why not go to the meeting with a fuzzy head? Alas, those meetings! All good deeds, if they are to have any social impact, must be organized, and organizations inevitably mean conferences and meetings. Often real decisions result, but more often everyone is looking for help from the other, and the whole point of the consultation is to cover up the general confusion. Crisis management centers are set up to bring a situation under control that everyone knows to be uncontrollable. This use of crisis management staffs has proved useful: nothing produces a better impression of a government's energy and ability to act. Merely by forming a crisis management team, it has proven itself master of the situation. A meeting is held, and the general helplessness is covered up by a tough-sounding communiqué.

By comparison, most meetings—continuing our discussions of the uses of time—are purely routine, rubber-stamp sessions. My idea of hell: from meeting to meeting, endlessly. One devil is in charge who sees to it that nothing is decided that hasn't already been decided earlier, and another devil drags the meeting out by making hopeless motions, requesting discussions whose outcome the first devil, together with a few minor devils, has long since determined.

You watch less television and read more—fewer newspapers and more books. You are wary about the books, and quickly skip the flat passages where the author has run out of ideas but written on anyway. With the help of the table of contents, you can determine what you're interested in. Why don't novels—why doesn't literature in general—have tables of contents and indexes?

2. Viewing life from the perspective of death, we are made freer; much becomes easier, some things grow more intense. Seeing something for the last time is nearly as good as seeing it the first time. The first time I saw the ocean, it was on the Atlantic coast in Brittany—I said to Nicole, "I want you to tell me now, tell me twice, that this is the sea, the ocean." She found that funny, since she, a rich Parisian, had been at the ocean many times ever since she was a kid.

If I were to go to the ocean now, I'd experience it with the same intensity. Take a good look; it's the last time. By now, I've come to know the sea rather well from the coast; mainly from spits, where you can see the curvature of the earth, the separation of water and sky as a slightly bent line.

3. The relationship to others assumes a different quality,

something you can't change much in the short time before you die but can manage earlier.

Love those more who love you; devote yourself less to those who don't love you.

Become more patient where you were impatient, calmer where you were restless, more open and firmer where you gave in too much and just went along.

Unfortunately I can only come up with trite phrases: you stop chasing things; you become more moderate, at the same time more obstructive; you stop letting yourself be coaxed into chores, commercialized, booked up until the appointment calendar is full. This behavior will make you more isolated, because those who have full calendars can see you in two weeks at the earliest, while you, by contrast, have no desire to commit yourself, at least not that much in advance, because you might not be in the mood at that time. No one seems able to make a date for tonight or tomorrow night.

Laax, February 7

Again the light is dazzling. The blue titmice and the crested titmice are starting to trill, a sign that spring is coming. It's supposed to be raining in the country, here apparently a clearing-up by föhn.

Strange that not a single contemporary writer considers the quest for God a subject of interest. Dürrenmatt once wrote a piece about faith, "The Blind Man"; later he moved more and more toward skeptical detachment. It is more embarrassing to talk of the faith of one's youth than of one's youthful sins.

Dürrenmatt and Frisch: why are they both always mentioned in the same breath? Actually, they have nothing in common.

Why aren't Bichsel and Muschg mentioned together, why not Frisch and Grass, or Dürrenmatt and Hochhuth? That Dürrenmatt and Frisch are Switzerland's two most important writers is really not a serious reason to keep comparing the incomparable and of asking the question which of the two is the more important. What's the point? To play them off against each other until they themselves begin to participate in the game?

Dürrenmatt is a storyteller even when he is dramatizing and philosophizing. The main thing for him is a good story. He is forever inventing stories. Frisch observes and analyzes. You can recognize the characters he describes in real life. Dürrenmatt pulls everything out of his head; if he were blind or deaf, he would hardly write differently. Frisch uses his eyes and ears; he looks and listens very closely. Hence the many "aha!" experiences when reading Frisch—for example, his description of a boccie game played by two married couples, who behave very differently depending on whether or not they are playing with their own spouses. Everyone has had similar experiences but missed the hidden dynamics of these situations because of their familiarity. You discover how the rain falls in Ticino only—again—when you read Frisch's "Man in the Holocene."

I met Dürrenmatt in 1943 (probably; I can't remember exactly), in Bern, when his parents still lived in the old part of town. Our mothers were friends. I was still a high-school student in Basel; Dürrenmatt was at the university, studying philosophy, so he said. Every time I had a little money, I visited him in Bern; I was totally fascinated by him. He sketched, painted, and wrote, but he thought of himself mainly as a painter. About himself, he told me the most incredible stories, and I believed them all, which spurred him on to dish out still more incredible stuff. Only much later did it occur to me that it was all invented. For example, once, when he was drunk, he supposedly went to the Bärengraben.* Thinking himself an Angel of Peace, he stripped down to his shirt, picked up a branch, and talked to the bears until the police came. Later, when his father was retired, the Dürrenmatts lived on the other side of the Aare—inasmuch as such a statement is applicable to Bern.** Fritz occupied the attic, the walls of which he covered completely with black-and-white paintings of grotesque faces, devils, moons, exploding stars, all in the same angular and pointed shapes he also used in his later india-ink drawings. When I told him, as it was getting dark, that the weird frescoes were scary and were getting to me, he laughed and looked proud. He was working on a drama called *The Button* in which a man had the formula for blowing up the earth by just pressing a button. This was before they dropped the first atom bomb, mind you. His mother was worried that her son was not serious about his studies, and one couldn't even know if he was going to be an artist or a writer. In response I told her—my prophecy was so presumptuous that I still remember it exactly—that I'd bet anything that in ten years her son would be world-famous. Actually, it took only seven or eight years; in Switzerland and Germany, he was famous after only five. Much later, in Neuchâtel, he showed me a Japanese translation of his thriller *The Judge and His Hangman,* and I asked him if he thought the translation was any good. He immediately joined the game, replying that parts of it were better than the original but that certain Bernese idioms could not be expressed adequately in Japanese.

I was with Dürrenmatt when I got drunk for the first time, not having had any previous experience with alcohol ever. It happened at the Klötzlikeller in Bern. He ordered Fendant, and I drank the wine in huge gulps, just like a beginner. On the

* A pit near the center of town displaying bears, the heraldic animal of the city.
** Bern is both inside and outside a nearly closed loop of the Aare River.

train back to Basel—my family lived in Arlesheim, outside Basel, at the time—I felt elated, blissful, summoned to the greatest ideas. Naturally, I started to write dramas as well, and I gave Dürrenmatt my first finished play to read. It was called *The Partisans,* and it described the final battle of the Polish resistance against the Germans in Warsaw in 1944. After he read it, he said, "At first I became very unsure of my own writings, because yours is more realistic, but then I realized you aren't original at all, in contrast to me." This really was the truth. My play, which I considered very important at the time, was a mixture of Steinbeck's *The Moon Is Down,* an adaptation of which I had just seen in the theater, and Georg Büchner, who along with Dostoyevsky was my principal literary fare of the day.

Later, in 1945, Dürrenmatt wrote his first publicly produced play at a friend's cottage in a remote part of the Jura mountains. Originally, the play was called *The Anabaptists,* and then, in a later version, *It Is Written,* and finally, in a third revision a few years ago, *The Anabaptists* again. Then followed the famous premiere in Zurich with booing and catcalls—what an incredible stroke of luck!

Before that, when I was at the university in Lausanne, during the winter semester of 1945–46, he sometimes came to see me, since his girlfriend, an artist, lived in Lausanne. I had to keep supplying him with paper for his sketches; otherwise, he probably would have painted his visions onto the walls of the room in the pension where I lived. We talked about a Kleist story, and he immediately produced two sketches of the officer who was to be executed and, as his final wish, asked to be shot up the asshole so that his body would have no more holes than necessary. I still have the drawings, and several pastels that he gave me earlier.

Then came the Basel period, which I still feel was Dürrenmatt's most productive: *The Blind Man, Romulus,* the mystery novels. I was studying; we saw each other at least once a week. He found all of my attempts at writing to be pretty weak, and I quit for a long time. He already knew Lotti, his present wife,* which required him to keep house. Since he never had any money and always spent more than he earned, he lived in houses that had been condemned to be torn down, where the rent was as low as the deadline to move was near. Occupation of condemned houses by squatters was unknown at that time. Dürrenmatt lived in a constant state of having to dismantle everything; everything was provisional, everything was about to be demolished. That is how I liked him best. He played the role of a bankrupt con man, not of his own choosing but dictated by the situation. Because he played this role so naturally, he quickly became a neighborhood character. When he left the finished manuscript of *The Blind Man* at the butcher's while he was shopping, the butcher himself brought it back to him.

Those who are familiar with Basel know that the condemned buildings in which Dürrenmatt lived were in the old part of town. In such a large old town, a few new buildings don't matter. Yet his last place was not in a condemned building but merely in a "building in need of renovation." Dürrenmatt had the whole monstrous building to himself. It was empty except for two sparsely furnished rooms. In one of the many rooms, Dürrenmatt had found a small plaster bust of Goethe, which he painted over to look like Hitler and gave to me as a gift. To this day it still makes my guests wonder: What is Noll doing with a bust of Hitler?

In those days, Dürrenmatt enjoyed living within walls that were about to cave in.

In this "building in need of renovation" in the suburb of St. Alban (today a private school for the dumb children of rich

* She died in 1983.

people) he led me one afternoon down to the cellar. He had just discovered, he told me, that it was full of wine: no one knew why the former occupants hadn't taken it with them. And indeed, within the enormous vaults there were racks of unopened wine bottles lining two walls. Cautiously and with a halfway-guilty conscience, I took a bottle out—the label was moldy and no longer legible—and opened it with the corkscrew of my pocket knife. I took a sip and immediately spat it out: vinegar. Dürrenmatt thought we should keep trying, so I took another bottle—vinegar again. Finally we were simply bashing the bottle necks on the wall, sniffing the contents, and throwing it all away. We worked ourselves into a real frenzy, smashing at least a hundred bottles of what once must have been precious wine. To no avail: we had to go back upstairs to Dürrenmatt's already opened bottle of Mountain Red. Only later did it occur to me that he must have inspected the cellar long before and that I had fallen for another one of his "stories."

At that same time (1949/50), I met Frisch through Dürrenmatt, via Antoinette Vischer, a harpsichordist and patron of the arts. Kutter* and I were at Dürrenmatt's when Dürrenmatt told us that he was invited to a Mrs. Vischer's, that Frisch was there, and that it would be okay if we came along. So that was the day I met Frisch, and Kutter got started with Antoinette. Antoinette was lying on her sofa, Kutter sat at the foot and was stroking her feet, and Dürrenmatt admonished, "Where are your hands?"

From the early fifties, when Dürrenmatt lived, or reigned, above Lake Neuchâtel and had become fully aware of his world fame, my relation to him grew more difficult. When I visited him there, I felt like a pilgrim; but despite that, we still spent many fun-filled and enjoyable afternoons together. Later—for

* A school friend with whom Peter edited the student newspaper.

about fifteen years now—this stopped completely. I didn't like it when he said, "Next week I'll be in Vienna and then I'll have to go to America, you may call me again in three months." If a touchiness arises in a relationship, then it is dead, at least in a relationship of this sort. Somewhat earlier was Dürrenmatt's grand lecture in Mainz on law and justice,* yet at that time, I already felt as if I were trying to cling to the coattails of celebrity. What had been a friendship had become important connections in which I was a link. I was appalled when people thought it such a great thing that I was friends with Dürrenmatt, a world-famous writer. And because I was a jurist besides— that is, from a completely alien field of activity—this seemed more remarkable than it would have had I been a colleague from the theater, a director or a critic. The lecture took place in the Liedertafel, which at the time was the largest hall in Mainz. The hall was completely packed, mainly because we had notified the gymnasia, since we were afraid not enough people would show up. We wound up with three-quarters of the audience consisting of high-school students who came to have a look at the great Dürrenmatt, whose work they had read in school.

Being a student at a humanistic gymnasium inevitably fosters the prejudice that the fame of the writer, the laurels of the poet, are the highest prizes on earth and the only ones really worth striving for. But fame is also governed by laws of power, particularly since the invention of the copyright law. Before it, writers had to court the nobility or starve. Later, the copyright was granted to printers as a "privilegium" and most merciful protection from competitive copying. Ever since artists them-

---

* Following a proposal of Peter's, the faculty had invited Dürrenmatt to receive an honorary doctorate. Dürrenmatt's acceptance speech was later published under the title "Monster Lecture" (1969).

selves became entitled to copyright their own work, justice and injustice in this field have reached bizarre proportions. J. D. Salinger can live for decades from a best-seller without continuing to be creative. On the other hand, well-known authors have to maintain their popularity with ceaseless efforts. They need the cooperation of publishers, directors, television people, journalists, and so on. The genuflections are mutual. The writer cannot afford to be "out" because a "comeback" is difficult.

In the relationship between the prince and the court poet everything appeared much simpler, though probably even then numerous courtiers and sycophants forced their way between these two exponents of celebrity.

It begins to be really embarrassing when people start to write memoirs using the celebrity status of their friends to prove that they themselves are celebrities too. It is like someone referring to his aquaintance with Goethe but not his acquaintance with Gretchen, though he first met Goethe through Gretchen.

The reproach could easily be made that I'm doing the same thing right now. The "sympathetic" or "attentive" reader, however, will note that the names I mention are either not really well known and prominent or at least not cited for that reason. They all are people who were a part of my life and whose memory I would like to preserve.

In trying to have our book *The Science Racket* published, Hans has had the bitter experience that in America the point has already been reached where no book is printed that the publisher and his apparatchiks do not assume will be a best-seller.* Frisch confirmed this as well.

This is truly Sodom and Gomorrah: the prostitution of the spirit. Thought and creative ideas are peddled in the brothel.

* What I really said was that factors other than the quality of the book and the importance of the message determine the fate of a manuscript. Potential sales are only one aspect.—H.N.

On the other side of our polarized planet, they lie in the chains of censorship. Rationally, it might be futile to ask which is better: censorship through the "taste" of a public kept childish by the mass media and, of late, those horrors, videos, or censorship by power, which feels it necessary to suppress any stirring of the spirit.

Zurich, February 11

At Max Frisch's yesterday. He has left New York, temporarily, he says, precisely at the point when his loft was furnished and ready. A metaphor? When something is completely finished, then it is ready to be torn down.

Frisch takes everything personally and gives everything personally—his strength and his weakness. He asked me if I did not want to go visit Dürrenmatt. I said, "Why?" I had thought about it, especially after my recent dictation; but I feel that death ought not to be used to beat someone's door down. People are defenseless in the face of my situation, and I don't want to exploit that.

The kitchen was full of smoke and steam, because Frisch had put the spinach in the pan and forgotten it. We had to open all the windows, including those in the living room. Fortunately, the steak and the spätzle had not yet entered the cooking process, and after a glass of champagne, we were more careful.

We confided a great deal in one another. Discretion in regard to my own person is no longer important. Hence, I shall report here only my part of the conversation. Observation dissects, tears down, I told him; the more precise it is, the more effective. Thus, there are no characters in your work who are described in a "positive" fashion, none that elicit the reader's compassion, except the women you were in love with. Here the dissection process metamorphoses into composition: here is your great talent. Marianne and, above all, Lynn*: the transformation of love into literature, thus it is possible for literature even today to be "beautiful, benevolent, compassionate." Which is the reason I don't write literature.

Women: Frisch is complicated and moody and chooses complicated, unstable women and is always astonished to find that in this realm, minus times minus doesn't yield a plus. Since unstable, excitable women in contrast to well-balanced ones also have more to offer on the public scene, they are in this respect certainly more interesting. By means of complicated situations, Frisch keeps alive. If he didn't, the play could not go on. Sometimes, he reminds me of Molière, who died onstage in *Le Malade imaginaire*. It took death to get him off the stage. Perhaps the reverse is true for Frisch: as long as he is involved in complications with women, he can't die. And so he has to live through situations of increasing complexity until he is ninety or one hundred years old and happens by chance to meet a very uncomplicated and loving woman. A Bluebeard with *still* more women would be hard to take.**

An idea of death: I'm falling deeper and deeper down into myself, just the way I am now almost solely occupied with myself. Some do not fall very deep at all, and neither live nor die, in contrast to those who keep falling deeper and ever deeper.

February 12

I'm cleaning up. My father did the same after his first heart attack; he destroyed bags and bags of paper, letters, notes, all

* Marianne was Frisch's last wife. Lynn is the female character in "Montauk"; her real name is Alice, the woman Frisch was living with when these notes were written (see page 219).
** A reference to Frisch's latest book, *Bluebeard*.

the sermons he wrote out every Friday and learned by heart on Saturday.

I've got boxes full of papers, all in scraps and pieces, soon gone with the wind; again and again I have started something, then put it away and forgotten. These notes, pages, notebooks are confronting me with a completely alien past. Why did I save all this? For example, a page from an appointment calendar of August 30, 1949, with the note "Satigny, 1 kg. peaches." I must have invited friends for a bowl of punch from cheap white wine and peaches—but whom?

In 1959 I started a diary because Ursi made me the present of an appointment calendar whose empty paper invited this use. I called it my Day and Night Book. The first sentence was "Now, I shall begin."

I can't bring myself to submit to surgery that leaves me hollowed out, like a dugout canoe that floats along with no one in control.

A that time, I loved Ursi "above all else in the world," but not in these words. The lover, in order to be loved, makes error upon error and as a result is loved less and less, and so his errors grow ever greater. When Nicole broke with me and, in my despair, I couldn't think of anything better to tell her than "I love you above all else in the world," she answered, "I never loved you above all else in the world, not even earlier"—as dryly as that. I, too, found my way back to reality, later on. Then it occurred to me that the phrase "above all else in the world"— "über alles in der Welt"—comes from the German national anthem, and for that reason alone it is not compatible with love.

In 1959, a well-known writer gave a talk about the backward state of the masses. The writer seemed to me, according to my notes, like someone who has slept late in the morning and rushes out to the fields to wake those already awake. Their amazement about his behavior he regards as sleep.

Andi tells me that my handwriting is hieroglyphic and a substitute both for drawing, which I was incapable of doing, and for writing, for which I likewise lacked the talent.

In order to be loved, you need sympathy and admiration in the right proportions: a sympathy grown in the soil of admiration, the touching realization that the grown man, so big and strong and clever, is still to a certain extent like a child who needs his mother.

"It is incorrect that Herr Korbes *had been a very evil man as claimed in that abominable fairy tale of the Grimm brothers. The fact that a millstone fell on his head is no indication of his, but rather of somebody else's, malice. Korbes was a just and well-meaning person who fell victim to a terrible crime. To solve this crime is the task entrusted to me by the authorities. But the inhabitants of the village who probably killed him themselves are trying hard to foil my efforts. Everywhere, they spread the word that Korbes was an evil man. I am up against the wall of hostile public opinion. One group seeks to cover up a crime; the other, the ideologues, won't admit that it is possible for a just man to die in such a manner. I am unable to overcome this opposition, and resign myself to writing my report to the authorities in the form of the fairy tale as recorded by the Brothers Grimm."*

Most people want to swim with the current, but very few of them know in which direction the current is flowing at any given moment.

———

People who have nothing worth reserving are considered reserved.

How can we feel ourselves "struck" by someone's look, when a look is after all not a bullet, the eye being much rather a cavity into which falls the light of the other person's image. Perhaps what is unbearable is the idea of being an image in an alien brain.

Columbus's egg was a completely ordinary egg.

The words are fighting each other on the page. What would happen if these complicated, abstract, highly composite philosophical words, equipped with feelers and tentacles, were to leap the fences of their quotation marks and suddenly attack innocent pedestrians in the street?

From a notebook of 1949: After ability, the greatest virtue is restraint.

The husband shoots his wife's lover and is acquitted. Presumably it was self-defense, because he simply could not believe that his wife had *not* been raped. *Noted in 1946:* Blind action is a form of passivity.

Otherwise my notes from before 1950 are very weak in content. Dürrenmatt was right on that count.

I came out of the nocturnal forest. A village of dogs howling in the föhn.

1950: Throwing artificial pearls before swine is not only permissible but required.

1951: I am almost unable to see anything. Death has already taken hold of my face. It is not heavy, but darkening.

Undated: The verse "Lord, stay with us, because the night falls" has an eerie ambivalence. The disciples thought they were inviting the stranger in order to protect him from the dangers of the night. But the reader knows that in reality they were the ones pleading for protection and that He would give them protection from the darkness of night.

1949: B. talks so loudly that one always feels prevented from saying anything, even when one has nothing to say. He conducts tachistic conversations. Formerly, artists painted their pictures and, besides, were more or less religious, more or less imaginative. Nowadays they first have to found a religion. Otherwise they can't sell their pictures.

Again from 1959: We would gaze into the light and feel torrents of flowers and think deeper thoughts, inhale and exhale air castles, have angels for chauffeurs, God would press us to His heart, whose beat would waken us every millennium from our blissful sleep; we would dream only dreams about dreams, soar upwards weightlessly and fall perhaps, softly, without memory, painlessly.

1959: Story of the man who wants to marry his niece, which is not permissible under the civil code. He succeeds only after falsifying a lot of records, murdering civil servants and witnesses. Finally, they manage, he having reached ninety, she seventy, to step before the altar of a bribed priest. Hardly has the marriage become seemingly valid when the niece kills the uncle, because the only thing she had in mind all along was the inheritance.

1960: The Swiss are proud that none of them invented gunpowder.

1961: The Wolf and the Seven Kids. This story is to be told in many different styles—as a political appeal, as a manifesto, as a historical, theological, or legal treatise. A wolf is a wolf is a wolf. The wolf tells his story, the old goat tells hers, as do each of the kids, as well as the country doctor, who cuts open the wolf's belly. The wolf's defense lawyer pleads his case: nobody would give him anything when he was hungry, the mean old she-goat locked up his natural food. The kids to be witnesses, the old she-goat co-plaintiff. Later the story makes the rounds: Mr. Mundwiler tells it one way; Caesar another; a forgetful man mixes everything up; a little girl, whose mother has just told her the story . . .

A pastor interprets the text: Who is the wolf? We all are! Would the wolf have turned criminal had he been respected instead of being ostracized? If we had met him as a fellow-wolf? And thus the catastrophe was inevitable: we wolves didn't see another wolf going astray and we behaved like goats, pettily and without compassion. Or God: Wolf, where are you? Where are the little goats, to whom I gave my blessings? The wolf: Lord, I have sinned and paid dearly for it; they surgically removed all the little white kids from my stomach and then filled up my belly with stones and drowned me in the well. God: You have atoned and are redeemed; here you can eat kids for all eternity. The wolf: But I can't stand them anymore.

I have made up all of these additions just now, but I used to tell fairy tales to my children similarly, always in a dialectical fashion, and they didn't like that at all. The question that amazed and annoyed them most was "Which is taller, a giant dwarf or a dwarf giant?"

I am sitting in judgment of my past. The most that remains out of fifty pages is one page. Everyone should take note of this.

Striking how many psychiatrists have symbolic names: Freud, Jung, Adler, Fromm [Joy, Young, Eagle, Pious]; presently in Zurich—Ernst, Angst, Kind, Knab [Earnest, Fear, Child, Boy].

January 9, 1948: Dress rehearsal of *The Blind Man* at the Civic Theatre in Basel.

In hindsight, the lifespan of an individual tends to have an absolute quality about it, at least in the case of those who "continue to live in their works." Georg Büchner, still solitary, lived to be only twenty-four years old and revolutionized literature while Goethe was still living, a point on which I won a bet (twelve bottles of whisky) from Jürgen Baumann. Imagine, we say in cases like Büchner's, how much more he would have contributed to culture if he had at least reached fifty. Certainly a great deal; and yet it is precisely because his work was completed early that it is alive. We could invert the example and ask what our culture would actually have lost if Goethe or Schiller had died at thirty: the classical literature, certainly; but it would have been created by others. Then again, Goethe created those incomparable works of old age, while in between he produced much that was standard for his time. They were epoch-making, Goethe and Schiller (who are always referred to as a pair, like Dürrenmatt and Frisch), above all because of their early works. Yet try to imagine Goethe without *Faust II* and the *Conversations with Eckermann*, or Schiller without *The Bride of Messina* and its extremely classical theatricality elevated to the point of abstraction. Every life is complete and forms a whole, and death comes at the right time. This is the trite phrase due at this point. It becomes less trite if we invert the problem: could we conceive of an eighty-year-old Büchner and the kind of works he would have left us? An eighty-year-old Mozart? An eighty-year-old Schubert? We are unable to imagine lives that were never lived, thoughts that were never thought. Schubert's "Unfinished" Symphony is a symbol that such notions are themselves incomplete. There are, of course, also those lives whose spans seem right, as viewed from the inside and outside, as it were. Bach died at sixty-five, but the works of his old age were still better than the works of his youth. Listen to the B-minor Mass. The same for Mozart, who reached only the age of thirty-five. Formally visible, age-related declines of creative power are rare. And then, of course, there are people like Fontane, who started to write only at the age of sixty. In the upper echelons of corporate management, people are fired at fifty-five at the latest if they do not already occupy an incontestable position of power. Blame our hectic age, which would not tolerate an "Unfinished" Symphony, even if written by a thirty-one-year-old. The old man is no longer on top of the current state of knowledge; he makes mistakes; he can't keep up. It's as if one had told the old Goethe: "You finally must realize the only thing that counts now is romanticism and the new German nationalism, and nobody gives a hoot for the reflections of your old age."

Zurich, February 17

We say "naked power," but we never say "naked law" or "naked kindness." The angels never take their clothes off. Or we suspect that evil is veiled, disguised, masked, and we see it only when it lets its cover drop and stands before us naked. Or maybe the word "naked" in and of itself has a pejorative meaning; decent people are dressed—the first thing that the missionaries taught the heathens.

Today in front of the university a student handed me a flyer:

Yesterday evening an "undisturbed" lecture by [Federal Councillor] Georges-André Chevallaz* was enforced by the deployment of squads of civil guards and about thirty police officers. By the application of force the police dispersed several hundred students who were waiting outside of the auditorium. At least one student was arrested; several were beaten up. Apparently, a confrontation strategy was intended from the start. The waiting students could have been seated in the auditorium without problem, and the lecture begun on time. This was deliberately prevented, because the lecture's organizers feared an audience with a majority opposed to the speaker's views.

There never was any real danger. The deployment of the police and almost two hours of waiting sufficed to change the composition of the audience such that Chevallaz's half-hour speech could be reeled off to an audience of uncritical listeners. During the entire waiting period additional people were admitted, though many within had lost their patience. This is the way to do it. . . .

The university rector, Hilty (this was reported in the newspapers as well), had previously had an announcement distributed to those who were "waiting":

You are taking part in an unauthorized demonstration and are thus disturbing the proper functioning of the university.

* The office of chief executive in the Swiss government is divided among seven equal office holders, designated federal councillors, each heading a department comparable to that of a U.S. cabinet member. Chevallaz was in charge of the Department of Defense.

Please leave this building immediately or I will be compelled to have you arrested for trespassing (article 186 of the Swiss Penal Code). If you are subject to university regulations, you can, in addition, expect disciplinary action to be taken against you.

Once more through sheer inattention I have missed out on a tiny aspect of world events that passed by quite closely. Yesterday at six o'clock I was leaving my class just before this controversial event. I noticed nothing except two army generals in uniform with their pretty gold ornaments on their hats, and I thought, How young they look, and a second later, Probably here for a military lecture.

One group says that all they wanted to do was listen and have a proper discussion; the other says of the first that they, in fact, wanted to break up the lecture. Now we will never know the truth, because the experiment was not carried out. Personally, I think there would have been trouble: to invite Federal Councillor Chevallaz together with army generals to, of all places, the university, was rather naive. But we will never find out whether the fear of one group provoked the aggression of the other or the other way around. Meanwhile, we know only that fear and aggression go together and that in Zurich, especially, this duo has developed into a smooth working team. The traditional forms of cultural life are being shattered. An opera or, worse, the B-minor Mass under police protection doesn't work. The protection crushes what it is protecting. The young people want to make the remaining days of their elders miserable because they think that the older generation has ruined the world for them. They are looking for an opponent; and since they do not yet know that no such enemy exists in the anonymity of a system that follows its own laws, they shoot symbols and think,

That'll show 'em. The hatred between the groups increases, and the formal mechanisms that make it possible to interact with the opponent in a civilized way are being destroyed.

The right-hand side of the student flyer contains a huge paragraph sign showing at its center a helmeted policeman's head that looks like a skull—a clumsy drawing. The paragraph sign as a symbol of force and illegitimate power. The law's protective and critical functions in regard to power seem to have been lost in the public mind. So is the Socratic function of questioning. The only thing seen in the paragraph symbol is the fat belly, but no longer the striking truth that it consists of two inverted question marks, one of which covers the nakedness of the other.

My left kidney no longer gives any sign of life.

Yesterday, before the incident that I described but didn't witness, the *NZZ** reported that the so-called movement was different from the movement of 1968 in that the instigators remained in the background, in contrast to 1968, when they were trying to attract public attention. For that reason, said the article, the movement of 1968 had been easier to bring under control than the present movement. Today, the *NZZ* stated, the masterminds are operating completely behind the scene, with little chance of being apprehended by the police and the law. The idea that there might be no masterminds at all, that these demonstrations were spontaneous, without program, the raging participants being constantly replaced by others, is inconceivable for the editors of the *NZZ*. To these editors, where there is trouble, it must have been the work of organizers. An ominous aspect is

---

* *Neue Zürcher Zeitung,* a daily newspaper mostly reflecting the conservative viewpoint of industry and finance.

precisely the fact that there are indeed destructive movements (in most cases unfortunately) that need no organization. The relations within groups are constantly changing; and there are many loners, including those who now and then join some group for a limited time. Their behavior is determined more by fashion and mutual imitation than by ideology, and in a few months might no longer be "in." For a few years now there has been a fad of defacing buildings with spray cans, especially at the university. The administration always has the mess cleaned off as quickly as possible. Nothing tempts the sprayer more to go back into action. A blank piece of paper acts like an invitation to write or to draw; a page full of writings or drawings doesn't.

A conversation with Frisch never gets boring, at least not for me. I never find myself having to wait until I finally may express a thought that's occurred to me about the subject under discussion. Each of us contributes equally to the development of the ideas; the conversation never gets stuck; there are no silences that are felt as such, and there is no pressure to come up with something brilliant. It's conversation as a good meal, cultivated as pure delight, a feast for the brain. Sometimes he lights up his pipe, even if it is almost out of tobacco, and the juice boils and crackles. Sometimes he stands in the middle of the room talking, but never lecturing. He is a good listener, which means he doesn't merely wait for his own point of entry but follows your train of thought. An analytical thinker without a system: hence his many diaries. Literary history will make a great mistake if it does not perceive him as a thinker, the same mistake that historians of philosophy make in vastly overestimating the founders of systems—Descartes and Hegel as against Montaigne and Schopenhauer. Neither do we legal scholars acquire fame through critical analyses of law and power, but rather through the compilation of monumental works, ideally a real book of statutes, a criminal or civil code that systematically summarizes all legal knowledge, or, next best, through a comprehensive commentary, a systematic treatise, or, at the least, a textbook.

Frisch's writings tend to reinforce the mistaken notion that literature deals with the life of the writer in substance and theme; indeed, that in the end, literature is life's description. His topics, it appears, are taken from personal life: identity with oneself, relations with women, difficulties with oneself and others. In reality, he stands at a much greater distance from his writings than his writings suggest. In his best writing, though, the personal factor becomes exemplary; and typically these are the works of his advanced age: the aging man with the young woman in *Montauk,* the old man alone in the rain of Ticino in *Man in the Holocene.*

If the themes are treated in an impersonal, general, and abstract manner, then we are in the realm of the classics. "Eternal" subjects: Iphigenia, Oedipus, Medea (the latter as the "Old Lady" in Dürrenmatt's *The Visit*). As it happens, these classical subjects are far less "eternal" than most people believe. Do away with the revenge killings imposed by the conventions of blood feud, and Orestes is out of a job; get rid of discrimination against unwed mothers and Faust's Gretchen as well as Hebbel's Maria Magdalena are reduced to figures of mere historical interest. But the psychological plane opens up instead; Orestes, Medea, Oedipus (the Oedipus complex) are events in the human soul to be finally declared archetypes in the works of Jung. By means of this intellectual transposition, the reality of an earlier time may live on as an imaginary or fairy-tale world.

Goethe remains exemplary as an author who from start to finish combined the personal (individual-concrete) with the classical (general-abstract), though in varying emphasis, to be sure. He almost always described his own life, and sometimes he succeeded in raising individual episodes to an exemplary level. With him began the deplorable mania (of which I am guilty myself) of regarding oneself as extraordinary and flaunting this image before others. We know nothing about Sophocles' personal problems, still less about Homer's and the other ancients', which is generally considered to be an advantage but in the end is regrettable. The total separation of personal life from the literature created out of this life has an air of antiquity about it. Only objectivity and generality remain, because we know nothing about Sophocles. Yet there are scenes in his plays that make us realize immediately that he must have witnessed them. Or was that already then purely a matter of literary convention?

You shall not describe your case but, rather, raise it to exemplary status. You shall make of your case a case for everyone. For this, death is just good enough.

You shall make a law of your case, and you may do so only if your case is exemplary, which it is only after you have reflected long enough about it. In its thematic selection, literature should, like the legislator, find the rule for many cases and apply it like a good judge, so as to do justice to the unique. Yet who can do this but God?

The inventor of the conditional sentence, or probation, one of the greatest achievements of the penal code, is unknown. It probably was an English judge who simply explained that he would suspend the sentence (probation), let the accused go free, summon him again in three years, and talk about how he had fared in the meantime. Perhaps this English judge thought as Jesus did (John 8) when Christ said to the adulteress: "Go and sin no more." This English judge is unknown to us; we do know, however, the legal scholars who, lacking ideas of their own, had strictly methodical minds and an irrepressible enthusiasm for compilations. Changes for the good in the world are not the work of the great but of many small and unknown people.

Laax, February 19

Yesterday, at two o'clock, I arrived here, fog down below, up here sun. At three o'clock, Yvette came. We sat in the sun, went to the swimming pool, went to bed, ate and drank, went to bed, ate out, went to bed. Today we were in bed all day long with a short break in the swimming pool. Then we drove to Ilanz for lunch, and at two o'clock she had to leave.

There was fog from morning on, then it snowed, and later it cleared up somewhat.

This afternoon, I read Voltaire, fell asleep for a while, and then continued to read. *Le Christianisme.* It did not occur to Voltaire, as he described the historical falsifications that the state church, its councils and legend makers had produced, that he was fighting the same battle as Jesus did. I believe this because it is immediately obvious that Voltaire was not interested in Jesus at all. He was concerned with the fight against the Church whose power was still nearly total, and he failed to see that this was the same battle that Jesus waged against the official church of His time. This is forgivable, since Voltaire did as much in his writings for the sake of truth and justice (Jean Calas) as Isaiah or Amos. He should have seen himself as a prophet but was probably too busy turning himself, Voltaire, into a great man.

The fog drifts in closer, occasionally releasing from its hold a nearby fir tree, sometimes the entire clutch of firs that forms the backdrop behind the pond. Right now, the fog is so thick and close that I am staring into a white wall of nothingness.

————

In addition to one volume of Voltaire—Voltaire, whom I revere because he is a reformer, a prophet; that is, a critical moralist, to whom political action owes more than to any systematic philosophy—I took along a volume of my three-volume edition of Goethe, an early popular edition from the last century, two columns to the page in fine print. I'm reading from *Elective Affinities,* chapter 3:

> The Captain arrived. Previously, he had written a letter which had put Charlotte completely at ease. So much frankness about himself, such a clear insight into his own circumstances as well as into the situation of his friends, promised a good and cheerful outcome.
>
> Conversation during the first few hours, as generally happens with friends who have not seen each other for some time, was animated and very nearly exhaustive. Toward evening Charlotte suggested a walk to the new grounds. The Captain was delighted with the entire setting and noticed every beautiful spot which, thanks to the new paths, had come into better view and could now be enjoyed to the full. He had a trained eye but, at the same time, was easily satisfied. Although he could see that all was not perfect, he did not— as is often the case—dampen the good spirits of friends who showed him their property by asking for more than the circumstances allowed; nor did he remind them of anything more perfect he had seen elsewhere.

There really was a time when this sort of literature did exist. We do not see the Captain, we do not see Charlotte, we do not see the garden. Büchner should have made his appearance sooner.

That could be said of Goethe as well; there were times when he wrote less abstractly.

As I continue reading, always somewhat annoyed, I realize

how I do Goethe injustice. This is not simply bad literature, compared with that of today, but, rather, a different language—a language foreign to us. Every language is conceived anew by everyone who writes in it.

Hence, it makes no sense when guardians of language like Emil Staiger throw up their arms and say, "We don't want any gutter language, we want the beautiful and sublime." Nothing can be turned back. The guardians of language cannot stop the process. Every word uttered stands forever and changes the language. So you should watch each of your words. Nothing is superfluous.

How to handle alcohol: You should not start drinking wine in the morning. You should drink wine in the evening with your meals. Wine is not inspirational. You can drink whisky or vodka from five until eight in the evening, preferably mixed with water or orange juice, and your thinking will not deteriorate provided that the temporal limits between five and eight are strictly observed. The great American authors started drinking in the morning, nonetheless, but just whisky. As a result, these authors wrote only novels. A play—not simple prose transcribed into conversation—would no longer be possible. Great literature is, to a considerable extent, the literature of drunkards. Even Goethe is known to have consumed three quarts of wine a day.

Laax, February 20

Over and over again, the question of what reason can actually accomplish. And again the answer: very little. Most important, it cannot motivate action, but only develop techniques that satisfy existing motives like the survival instinct, the lust for power or pleasure, and so on. Precise, scientific thought can produce cars and airplanes, weapons and drugs, all with the same dedication because the motivation and demand for these objects is already present. These motivations and desires cannot be changed by exact scientific thought. Just look at how completely ineffective the analyses and appeals of the Club of Rome have been. Equally ineffective have been the psychological and sociological analyses whose very subject is research into human motivation and the striving for power. No appropriate technique exists for it that could guide the action; and if there were, it would only be used to consolidate and enhance power.

On the other hand, speculative thought within the philosophical tradition since Plato is more of an aesthetic pastime than an attempt to change things through new ideas. At best there are fashions of thought like existentialism, structuralism, etc., which primarily influence the idiom of the educated. Such fashions, through a process of vulgarization, may then influence the affectations of the hoi polloi. In this respect, the social result of philosophical fashions comes closer to other, lower-class fads, like "rock" and "punk."

Collective reason could be established only through an exact religion. Something of this order came to pass in ancient Judaism with the help of the prophets.

The cult of an empirically defined reality becomes the cult of power. This is the idolatry of our day. On the heels of basic research follows the greed for profit. And the military is always out in front.

I wanted to read Isaiah's angry description of injustice, the best that I know, but I forgot to bring my Bible along.

One remaining hope is that the dominant power structures will perish from their own inner tension, collapse before they have the chance to bring about our total destruction. I am not thinking here of the uprisings of satellite states such as Poland or El

Salvador, or of revolutions from within, since such situations could merely cause the powerful to throw the bomb at the last minute anyway. Rather, I hope for a quiet, gradual, almost imperceptible disintegration; a process beginning with the system breaking down at one point or another, forcing us to go back to a more basic stage, to get by with simpler means, because it takes too much time to repair the robots or possibly because no one is available who knows exactly how to get to the source of the trouble. A situation rather reminiscent of the last days of building the Tower of Babel: it will come to a stop by itself because it has grown too complicated and nobody is capable of grasping the whole. Those in power will stay where they are, but they will become helpless, because the communication on which power depends no longer functions. Chaos would descend, but without destruction; people would simply go home and "organize" what they needed, like the Germans after the war. On further reflection, I have to admit, however, that this fantasy has no real merit except as an appealing vision. The systems will preempt their own decomposition by destroying the other systems and themselves. For the first defect in the overly complex machinery would suffice to trigger the alarm.

Now the fog has returned, at first from above, then from below as well. A milky, blind whiteness, which the blackness of the fir trees, with their normally sharp contours, penetrates only faintly, like a very distant call. Instead, the firs near the house seem all the closer, with their upwardly outstretched arms on which the cones dangle, pointlessly. Rilke: *Soviele Penisse über niemandes Beischlaf.* (So many penises over nobody's intercourse.)*

* The inscription on Rilke's tombstone reads: "O rose pure contradiction, no one's sleep beneath so many eyelids."

———

I should dictate two thousand pages, Frisch telegraphed me after I sent him the first hundred pages of this chronicle. Yet I realize with increasing clarity that I must cut more and more; much of it is too weak, a lot is nobody's business. Perhaps this garrulousness heralds the weakness of approaching death. At the same time, I must admit that Frisch's telegram really did cheer me up.

Christoph says the tickling sensation in the urethra can't result from an infection or I would have a fever. E contrario: the cancer with its feelers, lightly stroking, reconnoiters and inspects the spots it will later attack with its shears. And I am silly enough to portray it so flatteringly. Actually it is a stupid, blind, vicious animal within me, perhaps the stupidest part of me. At least it won't outlive me.

I told the pastor at the Grossmünster that he should read a curriculum vitae written by myself, and some of my thoughts on death and dying. This has been the hardest order I've issued to myself. It would not be good if I were to disobey it now.

I have a number of curricula, several that don't agree with each other, not to this day. There is the achievement C.V.—that's the one that's normally used. There is a love C.V., a sex C.V., a laziness C.V., and a frustration C.V., a C.V. of defeats and Pyrrhic victories. On the whole, my life was slow and tortuous, despite the contrary impression one might get from my legal writings. Only now has it become faster and more linear, except for a few small deviations of which I cannot rid myself anymore. Whatever data I select, the portrait will be misleading.

By contrast, my thoughts about death and dying are much clearer. Thus, I imagine a very short sermon in which I confront the audience—a congregation of mourners doesn't constitute a community—with the only certainty that is inescapable for each: his end.

The sermon could go like this:

Since December 19, 1981, I have known that I have cancer. I declined the surgery that was recommended, not out of heroism but because it did not agree with my conception of life and death. I had an alternative. My bladder would have been removed; I would have been radiated; and even with all of these procedures, I would have had only a 35 percent chance of survival, able to live for a limited time, diminished and mutilated. You will all die, some of you very soon and others much later. My experience is that we live life better when we live it as it is—namely, with a fixed time limit. Then the length of the allotted time hardly matters, since everything is measured in terms of eternity. Though I have a strong Christian heritage in my genes, I speak now as a non-Christian and refer to non-Christians. Not only the Christians but particularly non-Christians from Seneca and Montaigne to, if you wish, Heidegger, were of the opinion that life made more sense if one thought of death rather than shoved the thought of it aside or repressed it. They also said that it was easier to die if one thought about death throughout one's life rather than being surprised by it. I have found all of this to be true. I had time to acquaint myself with death. That is the true benefit of dying from cancer, which everybody fears so much. I know that my time was briefer than I had imagined earlier and that I had thought too little about time and its limits before. I felt a great deal of sadness but also true joyousness and, astonishingly, no despair. We naturally are aware that we must die, yet we still act as if life would continue forever, as if death applied only to others, about whom we hear that they finally died in the hospital and whose funerals we attend, out of piety mixed with a certain revulsion.

What ought to change in our lives if we think of death?

Much, but not everything. We shall gain a wiser heart, as the psalmist says. We shall use time more carefully, be more considerate of others, more loving, more patient—and above all, more free. No one can take more from us than our lives, and this will be taken from us anyway. This thought generates a feeling of freedom, like a breath of fresh air. The tyranny of imagined needs—the career, the status symbols, the social pressures—becomes increasingly irrelevant, and we feel free, for example, to say exactly what we think without regard to the conventions or powers that seek to prohibit it. In Zurich, for example, we can freely engage in efforts to help solve the problems of the polis, sit down with the discontented youth and talk with them, or at least try to, without fear of being censored by the authorities. Whether we are from the right or the left, dialogue with our opponents will force us to think, and to think means to be free. Thus, the necessity to think is part of freedom. What does all this have to do with death? A great deal. If as a socialist or a conservative, I adopt the ideology of the group into which I drifted more or less by chance, then I have handed over my independence as a thinking individual and lost my freedom. I would get stuffed with foreign ideas that replace my own—a comfortable but ultimately degrading and enslaving situation. What is fascinating about death is that it is at the same time the most general and the most individual of all things: a dead president is as dead as a dead immigrant working as a garbage man and, viewed from life, as dead as a dead fly. At the same time, death is a person's most individual event. Everyone dies alone; no one else can be with him, even if he were to die at the same time. The old ritual in India whereby the patriarch's widow was to be burned after his death is a futile, even ludicrous, attempt to break down the total individuality of death.

Because of my experiences over the last several months, I can say to you that the thought of death makes life more precious.

A few words about the Beyond. You have heard from the B-minor Mass choruses that most exactly express the musical thinking of the Protestant Bach: Jesus was buried, Jesus is risen. This triumph over death can only be expressed by music thanks to its abstractness—for death, too, is ultimately something abstract. Other than through music and completely abstract visions, the idea of eternity would be impossible to bear. That it will be better, more luminous than this existence forced upon us, could be deduced from many indications. Let us wait until it is time and then talk with each other again.

End of sermon.

Hans asked on the telephone, "Can you still ski?" Despite their innocence, I still hear the undertones of such questions.*

Zurich, February 22

Counterpresentation:
The university rector reports:

> On February 16, 1982, the Swiss Institute of Foreign Studies invited Federal Councillor Georges-André Chevallaz to present a paper in its lecture series "Security Through Equilibrium?" The title of his talk, which was to have taken place in the university's large auditorium at 6:15 p.m., was "Opportunities and Risks of the Small State in a World of Labile Equilibrium." The appropriate request for auditorium space had been approved. The rector's office was therefore responsible for the orderly implementation of the event.
>
> In the days before the lecture, there were indications that certain circles intended to disturb the presentation. The VSU [the university student union] addressed the public in an ad

---

* The question was motivated by my desire to go skiing with Peter.—H.N.

on the front page of the *ZS* [the student newspaper], nos. 27–28, as well as in two handbills—one of which referred to a "Cervelas action"* in the large auditorium. Also, two anonymous handbills were posted in the university, the second of which contained as its text "Our Recommendation—Assassination." Finally, on the day of the lecture, the *Telephonzütig* announced that an "action" would take place in the university auditorium. In view of these indications, it was clear that the rector's office had to take certain security precautions.

Shortly after 6:00 p.m., all the seats in the auditorium were filled, and some listeners were already standing along the walls. About one hundred fifty people were also standing outside in front of the auditorium. On my direction, they were informed by megaphone that they could listen to a closed-circuit transmission of the lecture in lecture room 101. That a portion of these people were interested not in listening to the lecture but, rather, in disturbing it was borne out by their subsequent behavior. They did not proceed to room 101 but instead were blocking access to the auditorium, making it impossible for the speaker to enter undisturbed and without risk. Thereupon, I had a handbill distributed among them threatening legal action for trespassing if they did not leave the university grounds. When this warning proved equally futile, I decided to request the state police to intervene, in order to secure free access to the auditorium.

The behavior of the people outside the auditorium as well as some of the audience in the hall who were equipped with noisemakers clearly demonstrated that certain groups were not interested in an intellectual debate with the speaker and his message but, rather, in disturbing the event. Such behavior in a university is deplorable. Admittedly, these disruptive actions were caused only in part by students.

I should like to thank all those who helped make it possible for Federal Councillor Chevallaz to deliver, though after a long delay, his lecture in the auditorium of the University of Zurich on February 17, 1982.

* Cervelas is a popular Swiss sausage.

What is the truth? I find the rector's account more convincing than that of the students. Cultural life is highly vulnerable. A single troublemaker is sufficient to disrupt an entire event, because the forced removal of the culprit is by itself a serious disruption. It follows that the police would have to cordon off the access roads further out; and such measures, too, would tend to stifle cultural life—which may, in fact, have been crippled already. No society can live without the minimal consensus needed to guarantee the formal expression of opposing opinions. At the same time, one must realize that the potential trouble-makers acted out of the conviction that the *others* would not let *them* speak, or at least would not listen to them.

Paradoxically, as increasing complexity makes systems more vulnerable to disturbances, ever more massive ways of causing disturbances arise within them.

Yesterday after returning from Laax, I went to see Almuth, my former wife. Hans came specially from Basel; he is once again shuttling between the U.S. and Europe. On Thursday, he is taking the boat to Palermo to continue his work at an institute, where he takes sea-urchin embryos apart into single cells and reconstructs them into new individuals. As a molecular biologist, Hans sees the apocalypse much more clearly than I do. He wants to write a book about the doomsday character of technology, its incessant, implacable acceleration, its destructive potential. Everything is going to happen faster and more radically than we expect today. Molecular biology has discovered that the human life span is genetically programmed because it is not in the interest of the species' survival and evolution to prolong the nonreproductive life of its individuals. Within the foreseeable future, it will be possible to program the genome of the gametes (sperm and egg) so that the resulting offspring will live for a thousand years or more. This will not be possible for those already born, because the program has already become fixed in the somatic cells—which is a comfort. Who would want to have a son who would live for two thousand years? They will be able to restructure the man of the future in a botched-up imitation of creation. And if they can do it, it will be done. And in another dimension, too, development is proceeding much more quickly than we dare to imagine: the descendants of our computers and robots will not only think but will also see, hear, feel, and be like a human. Man will create them in his image. Every conceivable tragedy or grotesque fantasy is innocuous in the face of such visions. For these artificial creatures will develop their own visions. The idea of the homunculus is obsolete; there won't be just little humans who do the lowly labor for us but, rather, huge machines that we no longer will be able to control, machines without souls whose only purpose is to restore the chaos from which God once created the world.

Though Hans feels that Genesis, the creation story in the Bible, foresaw some of these developments, he rejects any conception of God. I told him, "You are an apostate. You were too pious, too devout, and now the counterreaction has set in." I've always been just marginally concerned about God, always skeptical, but never totally disbelieving; His fire never seared me, because I did not get too close. "You say," I told Hans, "that no conception of God is meaningful, because it is either a relapse into the worship of the lost father or an empty cliché." I say, however, that it is part of this diabolical technology to dismiss any metaphysical thought. Yet—I repeat myself here—man's existence is unequivocally drawn between two points: being (that something, rather than nothing, exists, as already recognized in antiquity) and death. On this line lies the question of God. (I am not engaging in self-consolation, as I am not in the least expecting to enter into heaven or into any kind of eternal life.) If only we could rid ourselves of the idiotic image of God as a bearded grandfather. The Jews, who discovered the one and only God, prohibited making images of Him—above all, no grandpa pictures. It is ridiculous to assume that what we perceive with our senses is all there is. Of course, reason, not logic, postulates a spirit who created our world, an infinity of other worlds, and—the decisive point—who implanted in our brain the compulsion to imagine Him. Why talk about faith?

Hans began to agree with me only when I explained "God's function" to him: with God, you can be alone against the entire world, courageous, proud, humble. The godless world, which ours really is, is a world of power structures in which no one rebels, everyone conforms, and everyone increases the anonymous power and mindless activities of an unthinking apparatus or system. Even the notion of God the Father is preferable to that. Whatever conscience He may inspire is still better than an absence of conscience adapting to the forces of circumstance, to power structures and anonymous systems.

Hans admitted I was right. One could have supposed the two pastor's sons were about to have a reconciliation. But that wasn't the case at all; rather, that our views converged on but one of many controversial points. Uncontrolled, unleashed power is diabolical, though no one who accepts or serves it has a diabolical feeling. What should have long been recognized becomes apparent only with technology's unleashing: if man breaks all bonds with what lies beyond his own experience, but which (for lack of better words) transcendentally envelops the whole and incessantly poses the question of meaning, then man will *automatically* (in the true sense of the word), without deliberation and against his will, bring about total destruction. Man is putting himself in the position of the Creator, who took billions of years to produce something that one now and then can sense as being beautiful; and man has botched it—one cannot describe it otherwise—for he hasn't even succeeded in producing a real hell as a counterworld to creation. The only accomplishment has been to put everything out of joint, making a mess in which life is no longer possible.

Zurich, February 24

The semester is over.

It often occurs to me that this chronicle will be read by my colleagues and students and, quite generally, by people who only vaguely know me—as a teacher, as a legal scholar, or as a middle-level prominent figure. Meanwhile, I have doubts whether all of these notes should really be published. Isn't this merely a critical discussion with myself, which concerns only me? No; death is universal, and what is universal ought to be public. This authorizes me to cross my threshold of shame, or shame-lessness, if you prefer. I must demonstrate to others what is happening to me now and in the coming weeks. In the end, they will strip me naked anyway, before they wrap me in the winding sheets.

Zurich, February 25

Is not the worship of God a worship of power—the most absolute worship of power?

Au, February 26

To escape the noisy nights of the Zurich carnival, I drove to the Bachmanns'. I'll spend the night here, tomorrow night at Almuth's.

If I had submitted to surgery, I would have assumed the role of a patient for the rest of my life. This way, I'm not a patient;

though not in the pink of health but, rather, dead sick, yet still not a patient. I can "play" the role of a healthy and normal person right to the end. Yet what is at stake here is not a game but the decision between two forms of existence. I still feel I've made the right choice. People still take me for full; I sense a certain vague feeling of sympathy but not the embarrassing display of consideration accorded to patients, the endless conversations about the last operation, the further course of the disease, what the doctors said, when one has to return to the hospital, etc.

Adolf Muschg [contemporary Swiss novelist] told me yesterday on the phone—we had been talking about the case of the two German lawyers who are to be declared insane—that a certain German doctor treats cancer with a very different and much more successful method than that of establishment urologists; Muschg wouldn't tell, but I suspected psychological treatment. Not one of his patients is supposed to have died. Not even later in the hospital? When I described my case to him, saying that the greatest likelihood was that the cancer would "close off down below," he quickly replied that somebody talking like that, about "closing off down below," would be unsuitable for the doctor in Germany. I was relieved at having to explore one fewer alternative.

Laax, February 28

Under the shadow cast by the clouds the forest appears like a black wall; and far behind it, as contrast, the sky and the mountains lie in bright sunlight. The clouds are creeping slowly from west to east and rarely, even for a short time, leave a gap for the sun.

I still haven't found any theoretical work on the question whether, and in what way, the intellectual process is altered by the mass of published ideas exponentially accelerating at what already is a furious pace. Scholarly thinkers and writers outside the sciences don't seem to give much (published) thought to this phenomenon. They just keep scribbling cheerfully. In the *Festschrift* for Peter Schneider,* I wrote that I need much less time to outline a new idea that seems original to me than to determine if it is truly new. Whoever tried to be scrupulous about this second task would never have any time left for his own thinking or writing.

Here, too, the end is approaching inexorably.

In the arts, which for this purpose include jurisprudence and the social sciences, publishers publish only those manuscripts that have a guaranteed market, like textbooks and other teaching materials, or else are financed from outside sources. Examples of this last type of manuscript are dissertations whose printing costs are borne by the doctoral candidates themselves, and periodicals, reviews, and similar publications financed by institutions (mostly with state funds) such as the National Foundation or by professional organizations and associations.

The situation is quite different in the natural sciences. Here the latest state of knowledge is obvious and generally recognized, and the object of knowledge does not change in the short span of a lifetime. Natural scientists always stand on the topmost turrets of the Tower of Babel and do not have to worry about the lower stories. They find out everything and generate new knowledge all the time without ever asking if past knowledge would not have been better. Unconsciously, the thought process is directed toward practical application. The very selection of the field of study is determined by potential applications. Hence, the most ambitious and talented scientists today rush into molecular biology and atomic physics because in these fields the

---

* Born and raised in Zurich, Schneider was a professor of civil law at the University of Mainz, where he and Peter first became friends.

lure of reward is strongest. The insights of astronomy, on the other hand, are not likely to return such profits to the current powers; in that sense astronomy is the only pure science.

To be sure, so-called basic research, even in the sciences that are closer to earth, often is conducted selflessly, driven only by the pleasure of discovery. Still, two phenomena make me skeptical. If someone discovers an area rich in potential, hordes of less imaginative workers rush in with squads of assistants, like gold diggers to a new gold field, exploiting everything and leaving ghost towns in their wake. Secondly, basic researchers are like animals about to perish: the vultures of profit-oriented technology hover over them, ready to settle on the cadaver of pure thought as soon as something becomes exploitable. The role of the vulture and the cadaver are interchangeable; the basic researcher can himself have the idea of exploiting the cadaver of his thought—as recently happened in the United States and in Switzerland among professors of molecular biology and gene technology, who have founded large, profitable businesses to exploit their own thought and that of others.

Will we have a culture that functions without thought? More so than today's?

In the arts, dangers of the kind described for the sciences are not a problem, as exploitation by industry is less likely. At worst, careers may be obstructed or cut off if scholars stand for ideas that don't suit the establishment—which is no lesser evil. On the contrary. The silenced or ignored scientist who has made a great discovery has his discovery to speak for him (the earth *is* round; time and space *are* relativistic); but no one speaks for the scholar of the arts. Bans on speaking and writing are much more effective against them.

Back to the question of how the proliferation of writing influences thought. Just as in economic life, attention is focused on the most prominent of prolific writers. With the exception of

Viehweg, not one legal scholar in the twentieth century has become famous through a single small book. Most of them do it with quantity. I'm thinking here more about philosophers and sociologists, who, to be sure, don't have a larger subject but who have more to say because they are less hemmed in by systematic thought. Habermas, Luhmann, and before them Adorno, Gehlen, had a lot to say because there is a lot to be said. Almost no one talks anymore about Karl Barth, Heidegger, or Jaspers, but all of these greats have attracted a host of secondary thinkers, some starting as secondary and becoming primary thinkers, others always remaining tertiary or quaternary thinkers. Alongside these figures of greater or lesser fame are the many unknowns who have developed many interesting, maybe even great, ideas but have never managed to receive the attention necessary to attract secondary and tertiary, etc., thinkers. Which means: inflation in writing leads to a concentration that results in an impoverishment. Hardly anyone nowadays dares to imagine a blank surface as a basis of his thinking. All are toiling in libraries. More and more footnotes, less and less text. The number of those who think evidently doesn't improve the quality of thought. What others have said before is constantly—unconsciously—repeated. Since the pressure of their careers keeps them moving along at a pretty fast pace, hardly anyone can afford the time to check the primary sources. At best, they work their way through the scientific arguments of the last decade, occasionally spicing them with quotations from Aristotle or Montesquieu pulled from secondary sources.

Finally, thought will lose its foundations, and, toppled from its high cultural plane, perhaps it will start all over again from below.

There are things, experiences—misdeeds mostly, or at least embarrassing occurrences—that everyone takes with them to the grave and never communicates to anyone in a lifetime, even posthumously.

How does one select what to tell and what not? To demonstrate the principle of my selection, I now would have to tell everything I don't want to tell. A passage from Dostoyevsky: At a little dinner party, a game is suggested in which each person has to tell about a time in his past when he felt he was the vilest, most despicable character ever. Nearly everyone comes out with a story in which he indeed doesn't cut the best figure but which is nevertheless met with general understanding. Only one of the group tells a story from his past in which he truly behaved in a rotten, depraved way, like a swine—whereupon everyone present is outraged and indignant. The game has blown up.

We all have such dark spots in our past, about which we cannot ever speak with anyone.

Laax, March 1

Around four o'clock, the sky grew quickly overcast. The landscape has taken on a frozen quality that I have never seen before. Nothing is moving. Usually at this hour, solitary skiers are still coming down the slope from Falera.

I skied wonderfully well, but I believe I tire more quickly now. At about twenty-three hundred meters, I noticed a sharp transition, below which the snow is soft and heavy. Above, it is lighter but still not very good. Lots of people, mainly Germans. At the ski lift, I talked with several of them—nice young men, not uptight, not pretentious, very appealing. What probably bothers us is only the fact that the Germans outnumber us so drastically at these ski resorts, at least during the holidays. We feel invaded, and, subconsciously, many of us are reminded of the German assaults of 1940–41, even though we were not victims. This must be the explanation for our discomfort, for we don't have the same uneasy feeling when we are in Germany.

Which visions, which thoughts take on more depth by thinking of one's impending death? Taking, for example, an aesthetic-cosmic vision: I see the sun, the clouds, their movement, the change of light and shadow in a larger context. I think more about the fact that these elements are the visible parts of the moving atmosphere: that we are in a great whirl of elemental forces and that the small portions that we see can be very beautiful. I used to think: More rain again, or, What a beautiful sunset! Now I'm looking at the lower clouds beneath the upper cloud blanket, which, still receiving sunlight at a slant from the west, will soon be blown away or fall to the earth as rain. This, at least, man will never be able to destroy.

But let there always be eyes to see it.

A famous photographer, whom I do not know personally, has offered, through a friend, to photograph me right to the end. He had Hodler* in mind, who painted his lady friend again and again when she had cancer, until she lay before him as a corpse, emaciated: a long, narrow painting as one views it slowly from foot end to head. It is an inevitable reminder of Holbein's *Christ in the Tomb,* hanging in the Basel Museum. A drowned man's corpse, greenish-yellowish, stretched, rigid; Holbein had only to add the wounds and stabs of Christ's torture. The drowned man's corpse serving Holbein as model was as dead as only a human corpse can be. Dostoyevsky, after seeing this picture, wrote: Who paints Jesus Christ like this does not believe in the resurrection. Dostoyevsky was right, inasmuch as Holbein,

* Swiss painter and lithographer Ferdinand Hodler (1853–1918).

more than any of his contemporaries, was a painter of the visible and only the visible. In this respect, an ingenious positivist.

Being photographed by Holbein: not a pleasant thought.

The sky is now covered by a thin rose-colored layer of clouds, the foreground frozen and somber; if painted, the picture would be bad. Only reality, the landscape itself, can afford to be so kitschy and tasteless. Thus, criticism should be redirected at our taste, which has seen too many of those department-store pictures painted like this. And hence the aberrations of taste causes the confusion, or more precisely, the disorientation of taste.

Again I have forgotten to take the Bible along, as I wanted to read Isaiah and Amos up here. I went to the only bookstore in Flims and asked if they had a Bible. "No, of course not—what for? . . . Where can you get one? Maybe from the pastor." But they have books on herbs, books on mushrooms, books on cooking, books on all kinds of shit. The point has been reached where one feels ashamed nowadays to ask out loud for a Bible in a bookstore; to ask for a porno magazine would be less conspicuous. This remark should be regarded *only* as a statement of fact. The thresholds of shame are in the wrong places, on *all* sides.

Laax, March 4

At two-thirty, I telephoned Max Frisch to tell him that I'm unable to come to Überlingen tomorrow, as I haven't finished grading the eighty-four test papers I brought here with me.

Until two o'clock, the sun shone brightly; then the clouds gathered around the mountains and a thin haze covered the sky. The sun disappeared and snow began to fall; the whole change took no more than twenty minutes. The flakes are small and falling densely, interminably, muffling all sound. But it took a long time for the fir trees to accept the snow, having already been attuned to spring. Spring was also on the mind of the green finches, the blue titmice, and the chaffinches, who mirrored the light acoustically with their twittering and short songs. Now, all is quiet again. The biologists say that birdsong has the sole function of demarcating and defending the future nesting territory. That it might also express joy is too anthropomorphic an idea. Apparently, the birds are not logical either, because the moment it started to snow, they stopped defending their territory with their singing and twittering!

Antiquity and Christianity were in agreement that death takes on meaning when someone is dying *for* something—for his fatherland, for the faith, for his work, for his conviction. Both were confronted with the normal case as well, where death is not a sacrifice but where someone dies only for himself. Christianity solved this problem with a faith in Paradise, which could be attained by a life pleasing unto God, whether through good deeds, according to the Catholic doctrine, or through solid faith, according to the Protestant. Thus, death deprives life and life deprives death of its importance. The thinkers of antiquity, in contrast, embraced death fully as part of life and regarded it as an important act of a good life. This idea has aspects of a forced heroism; the desire for redemption is lacking—or was it repressed? It seems odd to me that the pre-Christian thinkers of antiquity, despite their sense of cosmic order, did not speculate whether the account would tally in the end. Also, no philosopher took seriously the widespread folk belief in the underworld, Hades, with its shadow figures, a vision of hell.

Today death is no longer an issue. Too much dying is going on, serially; death is becoming more and more frequent and banal. Too much murder is occurring, also serially. Individual death has been abolished as a superfluous luxury. At the same time, unconsciously, the idea takes hold that if everyone is dying, it won't be so bad for a particular individual.

The martyr's death, dying for a cause, is not an individual death either, if we disregard isolated executions like that of Socrates. The cause for which he dies is not all that important. During his stay in the Berlin Gestapo prison before his execution by the Nazis, Bonhöffer was astonished, indeed shaken, that convinced communists went to their deaths as bravely as the convinced Christians.

Giuseppe, who comes from a very Catholic family, told me recently about his uncle, who is dying of cancer after several operations. Since the metastases have attacked his larynx, his uncle can no longer speak, but he can still write and of course understand everything. His wife visits him every day in the hospital to read him the litany of his sins, like a purgatory merchandising catalogue of the Catholic Church. He had led a sinful life—frequently coming home drunk, smashing dishes, ranting at his wife—for which, according to her, he now had to do penance with his disease, later in purgatory as well, and if worse came to worst, in hell. He is now writing several checks every day: a hundred francs to the St. Anthony Fund for the Sick, two hundred francs for the Z. Monastery, so that the monks there will pray for him. When the secretary of the monastery wrote back that the monks were praying for him, he seemed, for a while, nearly content. But his wife didn't relent: he shouldn't be handing out too much for these good works; rather, he ought to be thinking of the family, which he neglected during his whole life; he shouldn't think he could get off the hook that easily by buying his way out of his sins, especially ones so serious and numerous—and again she reminded him of this and that. I couldn't believe it, but Giuseppe assured me that in central

Switzerland the power of the Catholic Church is still absolute. His uncle does penance with his dying; he does penance in purgatory; and maybe it was all in vain and he will go to hell. Why doesn't a priest who really understands something about God intervene here?

Laax, March 5

Alone again the whole day. It snowed until evening. For lunch, I fried some frozen potato cubes, but I didn't touch them. The kitchen is messy. I've read a lot, in several different books, but only brief passages. I couldn't get interested.

A few days before my father died—he didn't know that the next heart attack was to be his last—he wanted to reread world history from the Egyptians to Eisenhower and Khrushchev, properly following the chronological order. He was always more interested in history than in theology.* I have brought along with me a world history (which, interestingly enough, was written by a German nationalist in 1918—the last sentences concern the armistice offer made by the German General Staff to the allies), because I originally wanted to check up on the history of the Reformation. But then the chapter on Louis XIV caught my interest, because this king with his countless wars, alliances, peace treaties, peace breaches, and so on illustrates with particular clarity how little meaning there is in history as such. This history, too, has all fallen into oblivion. When read today, it is exactly the same as those battles between tribes in central Africa

---

* Johannes Ernst Noll (1884–1955) was a minister of the Swiss Protestant Church and author of a scholarly biography of Johannes Buel, a Swiss educator of the eighteenth century.

which we find so comical. Not to mention that the very writing of history, perhaps unfortunately, has eliminated a lot of what its writers deemed unimportant. Yet the remaining principal facts don't make much sense either, nor do they yield a coherent picture. The lust for power, war and more war, conquest of territories and loss of territories—a stock-market gamble with blood and destruction. From a still greater historical distance one could, of course, argue that under Louis XIV the centralized French state took shape. Yet, if this is true, then it was certainly not because of the wars but as a result of internal politics, and most certainly without regard to the question of the worth, if any, of such a centralized state. Still, it made possible the French Revolution; all that was needed was to overthrow the central government in Paris. But this definitely was not the Sun King's intention. Rather, his many wars must be viewed today as an unsuccessful attempt to bring all Europe under his power, perhaps inspired by Charlemagne, later imitated by Napoleon with short-lived success. Since history itself describes little but conquests and wars, it almost invites those, or vice versa: the conquerors, war lords, and big shots have always kept their own historiographers as well.

The air is getting thinner and thinner . . . as is what I am dictating.

Laax, March 6

Reflection, abandoned to itself, runs into emptiness. It needs objects, observations, outside opinions.

Thinking that attempts to think itself, without an empirical object, either remains inarticulate meditation or leads to juggling with words that turn on themselves: Heidegger's "nothingness nothings," "language is the house of being," "being there* is a precursor to death."

The mind, with its compulsion to think, is an insatiable animal, a glutton. It poses its rapacious questions even where no more answer fodder is to be had. It takes hold of metaphysical speculation. Here too, creative thought needs an object, or else it is disembodied, reduced to word play and linguistic acrobatics. We must give it real nourishment, not mere empirical facts, not mere "beings"* whose hidden meanings are to be discovered by reduction to a set of rules—otherwise thinking is not real but merely a technique that makes use of the thought process. Thinking needs material metaphysics for food. Speculation should again be permitted, but measured by the highest standards. It is absurd to speculate about men on Mars when rocket probes can be sent there; it is absurd to speculate about life in the universe when we can show statistically that the planet Earth is not a unique case. The magicians and the dream interpreters, the astrologers and the fortunetellers, these practitioners of the cheapest form of metaphysics really ought to get out of our way.

Only when thought has recognized its limits can it remain precise and credible in the limitless as well. I claim that such a thing as reasonably exact speculation exists; aspects of it used to be known as faith. We cannot escape the exact thought that the empirically perceptible world is not everything. Beyond the perceptible world extends an infinitude of other worlds. To think otherwise would be ridiculous, similar to the worm that believes that the soil it is creeping through is the universe, with the idea, of course, that the universe is all soil, including the worms creeping through it.

* The German *Dasein* has been rendered as "being there" and *Seiendes* as "beings" in a translation authorized by Heidegger (*Philosophy in the 20th Century*, W. Barrett and H. D. Aiken, eds. [New York: Random House, 1962]; vol. 3, p. 206).

I'm stuck.

If so many worlds exist—and they must exist—what business do they have with us? The simplest and most convincing solution still is God, God the Father. All five billion human brains on this earth, when they think, cannot think otherwise. Still, this proves nothing; the concept never is proof of its object.

Over and over I must emphasize to myself as well that the idea of eternal life does not prove the reality of eternal life.

It would be very easy to ask "What is proof?" and then quickly escape into imprecise, but comfortable, speculations.

But not I. Precise speculative thought can occur only for a post-Copernican, post-Einsteinian "age"—better yet, for a corresponding agelessness, in which Einstein's data, too, become relative; our astronomers' cosmology is reduced yet again. Which means not only that this earth is a little grain of dust in the universe but that the universe itself is a little grain of dust in the universe of all universes. We can't return to the idea of the earth as the center of the world, only leap forward into the unknown. Possibly we shall see God then, though it may be that our senses are too dull, as they are made for this world and nothing else.

Nothing is easier than to describe death in similes. A whole tradition of it has not enhanced our understanding. Holbein attempted it; Frisch attempted it through the rupture of communication (in his *Triptych*), each person talking as he always had, a kind of talking noncommunication. This is death for the living—but what is it for the *dead*? Nothing, of course.

Nevertheless, I would like to encounter God. If He is nothing, I would like to see this nothingness. I would like to know why out of nothing everything came into being. Perhaps all is a diabolical whirl from nothing to nothing. Why, then, the human brain, which poses such stupid questions?

Hence, let's return to the oases of meaning: No thinking that goes beyond feelings. The fir tree in front of the house, the mountain behind it, the woman at your side, events you can feel—may they suffice you!

What later flowerings these final days of mankind are bringing forth! New York, for example, is having a new building boom; skinny, shiny skyscrapers are shooting up in Manhattan with luxury apartments affordable only by the richest, who obviously must be plentiful. At the feet of these pencil-thin buildings with their luxury apartments lies poor Lazarus, those thousands of slum dwellers and homeless. Nice to be rich again without having to feel ashamed. The infrastructure of this city of millions is in decay; soon no more soil will be available for the flowers among which the rich are dwelling. They couldn't care less, because they know that everything will be over soon anyway. When Sodom ended, God asked for only seven just men. Perhaps He Himself forgot the many thousands of poor Lazari.

Amos or Isaiah in New York—the street noise would drown out their call "Woe unto you!" The rich are so high up anyway that no call from below would reach them. Hell would seem to be up, and not down below as we had always thought.

Laax, March 7

I'm still at peace—have been at peace all along—with my cancer. I have grown used to the idea of death and dying. It would pull me out of my routine if this development were to take another course.

Yesterday evening I really enjoyed watching television, not because of the show that was on but because of the many ideas about it that came to my mind while watching. Entertainment as a pastime: time has to be passed. Entertainment as a giant industry with millionaire recording stars and so on: all of this as a consequence of the copyright law. Schiller, had he died in 1910 or 1920, would have been a wealthy man: *Wilhelm Tell* playing somewhere every month and Schiller cashing in on his royalties.

Then, during this completely stupid show of schmaltzy German songs—done by a Swiss, of course—came the song, or, rather, aria, "O Mein Papa." The girl plays her dead father, a mediocre clown, better than he would have played himself, not only because everyone can play another person better than himself but because her adoration raises the dead clown into the infinite.

Zurich, March 11

I vomited twice this afternoon—don't know why; only thing I had to drink was tea. Before that, a crew from the Swiss TV was here; they wanted a statement from me about the last Supreme Court decision on one of the riot trials. I told them that the court's extreme interpretation of the riot laws amounts in practice to a curfew, especially for people like myself who live in "endangered" areas like the Old Town. If every peaceful citizen who finds himself in a "riotous assembly" (article 260 of the Swiss Penal Code), no matter how he got there, either as a passerby or as an observer ("gawker" in police jargon), is violating the law, to the extent that he knows the crowd might commit acts of violence, then he must avoid such places at such times and stay at home. Thus, justice bows to the disturbers of the peace by advising the peaceful to relinquish a part of their freedom.

With the approval of a powerful majority of the uninformed public, the Zurich and the Swiss federal judiciary are currently giving their blessing to the actions of local governments, which, with the help of the police, hope to solve or repress the problems of public life, regardless of where the chips may fall. With nostalgia, I recall the times when the judiciary knew its true task, even if it never actually achieved it in practice: the task of protecting minorities, of making unpopular decisions even in the face of inflamed public opinion, of handing down unpopular verdicts; of remaining cool and drawing distinctions when the masses of televiewers, the mindless masses, demand red-hot verdicts and global damnation.

How is it possible that time and again so-called peace is confused with law and order? How has the teaching of law failed over the centuries? Or is its voice simply going unheeded in the practice of law because its practitioners cannot resist the pressures of the political climate of the moment?

Once again it takes great courage to be a good judge.

Yesterday I went with Ursula to see Max Frisch at Überlingen, where he has already taken off nine kilos at the famous health and weight-loss clinic. He is not drinking anymore—except on the afternoon when we arrived and promptly went to a restaurant on the lake. A classy restaurant, which struck us as German, despite our inability to say exactly why. Outside the window, the lake with waves like huge dinner plates, and a boardwalk with older ladies and gentlemen, *comme il faut*—above all, ladies, not merely women.

It struck me how little there is to tell about my cancer. It is not only silent and invisible but currently producing only very few symptoms. All the tension is in waiting for the fifth act.

I was surprised, delighted, and a little disturbed as well, at Frisch's suggestion that I fly with him to Egypt in April. Ten days together with Max Frisch—how would that work? But Egypt is an enormous historical catalyst, with the world's longest continuous history, with too much to see. And Frisch is a good viewer and a precise observer; he loves the visual and the concrete, all the things I'm not good at; in this regard we shall complement each other perfectly.

My attractiveness: the abrupt contrast between my healthy, relatively young and cheerful appearance on the one hand and the deadly but invisible disease on the other requires from the onlooker certain dramatic experiences and talents. He must be able to anticipate already, in the first act, the undecided possibilities of the fifth act and to recall during the fifth act all the earlier acts. In short, he must see order in chaos.

Zurich, March 13

A dark day. It rained, then it snowed, all of it without landscape. Nothing elementary, only disturbing effects of atmospheric fluctuations.

I'm not making much headway with the second volume of my textbook on criminal law, which I promised to the publisher. It is a routine job, with no fun and lots of frustrations because the problems I am particularly interested in are precisely the ones that are unsuitable for discussion in a textbook. What is needed for a textbook, anyone can present as well as, if not better than, I can. Thinking becomes standardized. For example, in dealing with the statutes concerning property crimes, I was enormously tempted to explore the ideological and economic background; but that clearly doesn't belong in a textbook. On the other hand, the task of writing a textbook has the advantage of exacting discipline, especially in comparison to preparing a lecture; one realizes that everything has to be thought through again more systematically. A lecture is less balanced but more imaginative, more captivating. A book can never be like a lecture. Books in lecture format are hybrids written from lecture to lecture and read from the manuscript; they contain neither the spontaneity of the oral presentation nor the concentration of the written expression. Karl Barth was wrong to have his lectures printed as *Church Dogmatics*. The many volumes appear loquacious; he ought to have strictly separated the oral from the written, possibly to have had the oral transcribed by his students, as Hegel did, or Luther in his *Table Talk*. Then we know that the material, even though printed, is a dinner speech or a lecture, something conceived for the listener, not a product made for the reading public. These are two totally different things.

Finally, Isaiah. His raging, insatiable hunger and thirst for justice! He saw too much injustice and he wanted too much justice. How I can empathize!

> Woe unto them that decree unrighteous decrees, and that write grievousness which they have prescribed; to turn aside the needy from judgment, and to take away the right from the poor of my people, that widows may be their prey, and that they may rob the fatherless! And what will ye do in the day of visitation, and in the desolation which shall come from far? to whom will ye flee for help? and where will ye leave your glory? [Isaiah 10:1–3]

And the preceding vision:

> And I will restore thy judges as at the first, and the counsellors as at the beginning: afterward thou shalt be called, The city of righteousness, the faithful city. Zion shall be redeemed with judgment, and her converts with righteousness. . . . And he shall judge among the nations, and shall rebuke many people: and they shall beat their swords into plowshares, and their spears into pruninghooks: nation shall not lift up sword

against nation, neither shall they learn war any more. O house of Jacob, come ye, and let us walk in the light of the Lord. [Isaiah 1:26–27; 2:4–5]

O God.

In the evening I called up Rose, the theologian, and asked him for the citation that he had quoted in his inaugural lecture concerning materialistic atheism in the Old Testament. It was Zephaniah 1:12: "And it shall come to pass at that time, that I will search Jerusalem with candles, and punish the men that are settled on their lees: that say in their heart, The Lord will not do good, neither will he do evil." Which is to say, the Lord no longer intervenes in human events: he remains outside, remains passive. Rose is going to send me a reprint of his inaugural lecture.

Zurich, Friday, March 19

I think I had better hurry. For several days a new symptom has been added: a slightly painful pressure in the lower part of the bladder. I wanted to call Professor Zingg to ask whether this symptom was going to affect my allotted time span, but he was already in a meeting with his assistants, and I'll be able to reach him only on Monday. I simply must know about how much time I still have; virtually all my decisions depend on it.

From Tuesday until yesterday I was in Düsseldorf, at Gredinger's main office. All the streets in that city look the same: I couldn't even remember if I had been there before. The Rhine flows past, but the city has no relation to it; the river here is like a water superhighway—very different from Cologne or Mainz.

All our mutual acquaintances regard Gredinger as inscrutable, which could mean that he evokes a desire to be scrutinized, whatever is meant by "scrutinize." It could mean that he never talks about very personal things without an analysis. For example, he says: "I make as few decisions as possible or I keep delaying them; most problems solve themselves. I can't figure out what to do with my money, which is why I don't sell my advertising agencies and why, instead, I plough nearly all the profits back in and buy or start new agencies in foreign countries; in the long run, only twenty advertising agencies will be left, anyway." But he does not say: "I'd like mine to be one of the twenty survivors." Instead he says: "I can always sell the agency—that's no problem. But I wouldn't know how to kill the time." Or it could mean that he is unconventional in an unconventional way while at the same time making you believe that it is deliberate. A lot is subconscious with Gredi, but nothing subconscious is out of control so as to puncture the surface. He always does the opposite of what you would expect, but consciously so. He deliberately assumes a lifestyle that is the opposite of the lifestyle typical of owners of advertising agencies large and small. This makes him conspicuous, which is important in advertising. Farner, who used to have the largest agency in Switzerland, kept an excessively elegant and lavish house, gave parties, and so on; but he was not clever enough to refrain from printing the speeches he gave every year at the Sechseläuten* before the chamber of commerce—that way, they became available to everyone, not just to fools.

Everything about Gredi** is modest. He might be thought of as Max Weber's puritan: someone who accumulates capital through modest and simple living. Nothing could be farther

---

* A Zurich festival held in the early spring in which a figure of Winter is burned.
** Paul Gredinger, sole owner of the international advertising agency GGK.

from the truth. In contrast to most people, he is simply not interested in investing money in status symbols (which I would not do, either). His apartment in Düsseldorf, which he showed me after I asked to see it, would hardly be acceptable for a Zurich student. To sleep there without earplugs would be impossible, even though the apartment is on the fifth floor. (It even has a view of the Rhine, which looks rather miserable at this point.) A big duct winds itself through the narrow staircase. Although it leaks, it is supposed to carry the exhaust or the fumes from the restaurant below out over the roof. Gleefully, Gredi showed me the dark streaks that the fumes left on the carpeting below the doors to the apartment and to the bathroom because of the draft at these spots. Trails of grease: the last traces of the french fries' soul.

Gredi is not stingy but a puritan without a puritanical ideology. The most accurate analysis would probably be this: he observes himself and his relations to others so scrupulously that he refuses to take on any role one might assign him in his social context. On the contrary, he prefers to compensate by means of deliberately atypical behavior. By this very scheme he maneuvers himself again into a role. More than ever, he is the boss who does not behave like a boss, the conversational partner who does not behave like one—the "not" being important here. Again, a deliberate compensation. Of course, these reflections are merely a matter of speculation—as is the question, for example, of whether his stereotypical cynicism isn't simply a form of sadness.

I am attempting to describe a person who is close to me.

What makes people so crazy about Gredi? His charm in combination with the unusual, the atypical. In addition, his joy at taking risks, his optimistic vitality, both of which he balances with declarations about his passivity, the power that he has but does not use. His joy in other people's ideas whose magnitude and value he recognizes instantly, and to which he either adds or which he streamlines critically. An example: At one of the lavish suppers we had, I told him I was so intrigued by the "bar-B-Q" signs on American eating places that I sent postcards to my friends using the same semantic principle—for example, "XLNt" or "mRvLS." Gredi immediately: the principle can be applied to every written language. A little later, a German example came to my mind: "ND DR RD."*

How come nature enacts on only one planet in each solar system this immensely creative and immensely miserable competitive experiment for the development of the species? Why is there no competition among the planetary systems and spiral nebulae? Why are the galaxies flying away from one another? Do these phenomena have anything to do with the meaning of the universe? Could it mean that the infinity of space provides a limit to competition and offers many possibilities of protection and shelter for creatures not so insane as we are? That no inhabitants of planets of other suns or of other solar systems are able to visit us can only mean that war is to be excluded from the interstellar realm. Possibly God really wants to try the experiment of a peaceful planet. The distances between continents on individual planets are not large enough to let peaceful tribes develop undisturbed; as soon as unpeaceful, "more highly civilized" tribes "discover" the other continents, they destroy or subjugate their inhabitants. The meaning of the expansion of the universe for peaceful creatures might be in their protection from discovery.

Zurich, March 20

Because of the understandable self-interest of the judge in reducing his workload, one of the most important but unarticu-

---

* *Ende der Erde:* end of the earth.

lated principles of the administration of justice is the "disposal principle." Judges are forever searching for reasons for not having to hear either the arguments of the opposing parties or the case as a whole. These reasons are necessarily technical. I see this quite clearly in my job as a judge at the Zurich court of cassation* as I observe the activities of my colleagues as well as my own. What the plaintiff fails to fault will not be examined, which is entirely within the law. Evaluations of evidence and procedures by the lower court will be annulled only if they are found to be arbitrary, something that occurs very rarely. At most, the court of cassation approves 10 percent of all appeals. The judges of the appellate court are upset not so much about having been disavowed by the higher court if the appeal to it was approved as about the fact that according to the law, the court of cassation only confirms or sets aside the appellate court's rulings but does not issue a new judgment, with the result that the judges of the appeal court might have to do their work all over again—not a good system from a psychological point of view. For his verdict, the judge generally looks for that argument which costs him the least amount of work. In this regard as well, justice is an utterly human institution. Order is more important than justice; putting an end to the fighting and the arguing, more important than all other tasks of the law. I don't subscribe to this reasoning, but that's how things work out in reality. The disposal principle contributes to the reduction of disorder. As long as it doesn't result in screaming injustice, as in totalitarian police states, the citizens are content with the system, because they don't thirst for justice but have a need for peaceful order. A West German survey revealed that most citizens think that too many legal remedies are available to the defendants and too many opportunities to drag out litigations.

* The canton's supreme court.

They should end sooner. Citizens relate to the law like church-goers, who always find a short sermon better than a long one. At the "Amen" everyone is relieved.

My increasing shortness of breath, says Christoph, could be due to a metastasis in my lung. Then everything would go much faster.

How about suffocation?

Since I want a natural death (Christoph asked, "Why actually?"), I have to be prepared for its cruelty. Nevertheless, I am inclined to a compromise: a natural death only insofar as it is not extremely cruel. Alcohol from five until eight in the evening is a good companion in life and in death.

Criteria of a good conversation (at least as important as a good meal):

1. Subjects that interest everyone, subjects that change now and then and have sufficient significance to meet certain objective criteria;

2. To force one another to think, for example by means of questions (Socrates), even when they digress;

3. To permit digressing freely, but always to ask for the line of thought;

4. When another person is talking, to ask him what exactly he saw, heard, and felt, what was peculiar, and what general conclusions he drew for himself;

5. A balanced exchange of speaking and listening, which means refraining from expressing sudden ideas if that interrupts your partner's train of thought;

6. Immediate cessation when people are beginning to tell jokes.

Zurich, March 21

I'm sorting things out again. A notebook falls into my hands in which I wrote the following under the date May 11, 1952:

> J. is lying in the hospital. Comments about cancer. Its proliferation. The body against the body. The bad cells against the good. I'm turning against myself, from hope to hopelessness . . . unrolled life from the vantage point of death, like a superior enemy rolls up a shrewdly erected front . . . cancer discovered too late. Its inexorable course. Marked by death from the beginning. Birth in the hospital, death in the hospital. Pain as a fixed idea. Until release from the idea succeeds. The story begins in the hospital. Review of life. Interspersed with the progress of the disease. Sand running through the hourglass.

A paltry idea turned visionary only in retrospect, by mere chance. The cited passage was embedded in a larger story, "The Treasure in the Field." According to the parable in the gospels, someone sells everything he owns in order to buy a field which he believes to harbor a treasure. Then he begins to doubt, and in order to avoid disappointment he procrastinates the search for the treasure until he becomes ill. Now it is too late. He can't tell anyone that a treasure is in the field; besides, he still doubts whether there is really a treasure; has he risked everything for nothing? The disease finally relieves him of these doubts.

Yesterday evening, dinner with Frisch at the Münsterhöfli. After Easter we will go on our journey to Egypt. For me, everything is now subject to St. James's condition: "If the Lord will, we shall live and do this and that." Frisch told me that among the original inhabitants of Mexico, the highest-ranking were the priests; the military stood on the next to lowest step. No wonder the Spanish robbers had it so easy! According to Toynbee, on the other hand, the end of a civilization is signaled by the rule of the military. Toynbee was probably thinking chiefly of Rome; the theory hardly applies to Prussia, Sparta, or even the kingdom of Alexander.*

When the priestly caste is on top, it naturally has the effect of repressing the kind of free-roaming spirit that, if exploited by technology, finally leads to destruction. Hence, under the priests, society remains stable. But not under military rule, which is even more hostile to freedom; for the military is interested in nuclear researchers and biochemists and so on, in order to improve the technology of its weaponry. By contrast, the power of the priests, however cruel, never leads to the total release and manipulation of the natural forces of which man only appears to be in control. What has technology actually brought us? Prosperity, we say. But for whom? Not for the people of the third and fourth worlds. Medicine, while the most humane part of technology, still is responsible for overpopulation and all the intractable problems associated with it. Motorization brings us more quickly from one spot to another (what for?) and destroys the environment. And then there's nuclear energy.

Over the last few days, I've read Hoimar Ditfurth's book *We Are Not Only of This World* [*Wir sind nicht nur von dieser Welt*], first from the end, then from cover to cover. His idea that the evolution of the world is creation still in progress, and leading into the beyond, where the spirit reigns, is majestic and plausible. The natural sciences themselves confirm religion: the beyond and the spirit that, independent of matter, must have decreed these cosmological laws. We cannot understand this spirit; but

---

* Of course none of these latter qualifies as a civilization in Toynbee's sense.—H.N.

at the end of the world, everything will become intelligible. For whom? This question remains open. The book is full of optimism and fills a real need; the natural sciences are finally confirming that the religious, the transcendent, the spiritual do exist—indeed, that we are soaring toward them. The only problem is that the author bashfully conceals that the laws of evolution, at least on this earth, will first lead to the destruction of this planet; or else that the universe might quite possibly end in the cold of thermodynamic death. Only in one little passage does he say, "When we ponder to what extent our behavior is still irrational, that inborn instincts and fears still prevent us from doing what we recognize to be right, aware that our survival is at risk—we need only remind ourselves of the insane arms race—then the contrary is more likely"—by which he means that we do not represent the apex of development.

What Ditfurth overlooks is the palpable fact that at least one law with which evolution operates must finally bring about the destruction of what has been created. It is either an evil law or it is a law enacted by the spirit to punish evilmongers, which amounts to the same thing. How is man to shed his "inborn instincts and fears" if they served him earlier to endure the battle for survival, to win out under natural selection? Ditfurth would have done well to reduce somewhat his sales-inspired optimism, though he moves with utmost caution on the outer limits of his feeding ground. The word "God," for example, is scrupulously avoided.

If the preservation of the species is everything, no meaning is left for the individual. Yet our sensory experience obeys the spiritual, and the spiritual is precisely that power which does not serve the preservation of the species. An entirely generalized God does not yield any meaning either, in contrast to an individual God who has not simply been derived from natural laws

133

but who is compassionate precisely with those whom the law of selection keeps throwing into the void.

Death could be conceived, if anything individual remains, as a thought or at least a memory, an escape from time. But no man can comprehend the meaning of timelessness.

When will the natural sciences discover compassion, or at least justice?

The fact that someone writes is a sure sign that he does not belong to the powerful. The powerful do not write books; they have their writing or speeches composed by others according to their instructions, and sign, if need be, important decrees. The fact that someone no longer has to do his own formulating and writing reflects quite accurately how far up he is in the power hierarchy. A minister or corporation president no longer does his own writing, except, perhaps, as pure hobby or in highly personal matters such as a will, where execution in one's own hand may be stipulated by law. Up to the rank of vice-president or ministry director, one still has to do his own writing. At these lower levels, one continues to rack his brains to formulate precisely and to substantiate an idea that the boss outlined vaguely in the form of a general suggestion. A king or dictator can get away with being utterly illiterate, but not a government clerk. Which means that ultimately power can be neither won nor retained with the written word.

Zurich, March 22

Postscript on the subject of the philosophy of power as a basis for the philosophy of law. Almost all power is illegitimate, justified neither by achievement nor, least of all, by need. Farthest from the law is power that is won through gambling and speculation, especially when the odds are not the same for everyone: they never are after the game has been played for some time. At that point, the most powerful players, who according to Dürrenmatt's parable in his "Monster Lecture" on law and justice have most of the chips, can change the rules in such a way that it results in more and more profit for themselves and ever-increasing losses for the others. If billionaire T. buys tin mines for $1.5 billion, it cannot possibly be a losing speculation, because all the tin coming to market belongs to him. Of course, he does not actually possess anything like all the tin, but he knows (that's his "intelligence"), first, that the demand for tin is increasing and, second, that the other tin owners are not interested in underbidding his prices—except if the demand were to sink drastically. The powerful's third advantage, aided by the law, lies in his easy assumption of any risk of litigation, which is enough to scare off any weaker opponent who would like to take a stand against him.

I read Isaiah, whose terrible solemnity is sometimes hard to take. But his blazing sword of fire is what it took to hold his own against the powers of his day. Also his unwavering conviction to speak in the name of God. Isaiah 5:8–10.

> Woe unto them that join house to house, that lay field to field, till there be no place, that they may be placed alone in the midst of the earth! In mine ears said the Lord of hosts, Of a truth many houses shall be desolate, even great and fair, without inhabitant. Yea, ten acres of vineyard shall yield one bath, and the seed of an homer shall yield an ephah.

Here the prophet has clearly seen that extensive landed property and the expropriation of small landowners render the land infertile, converting it into desert. The generalization of this insight would have far-reaching implications.

Why are nearly all Bibles bound in black? To express gravity and sadness? In much of Europe, the Catholics are labeled "blacks"—quite unfairly so. To convince yourself that the opposite is true, watch the outdoor proceedings of the electoral assembly held annually on election day in the Protestant state of Appenzell Ausser Rhoden and the one held in its Catholic counterpart, Appenzell Inner Rhoden. First you should drive to the Protestant town of Trogen and then very quickly over to the Catholic town of Appenzell. In Trogen, all the men are dressed in black; there is no other color to be seen in the entire village square. The members of the state government are up on the wooden podium in black frocks and top hats; there is no discussion, only the business of conducting the election and voting on the issues brought before the people. In Appenzell—you will have to rush to catch the tail end of the show—everything is colorful, with flags, costumes, old uniforms. By contrast, in Trogen, the black magistrates stand on their podium like judges about to hand down a death sentence.

The idea of evolution as creation has little meaning for the individual; he is only a building block in the development, which rolls over and past him. Of what use is the spirit, which merges with matter in the end? Diametrically opposed and of much greater grandeur, even as a mere metaphor, is the concept of the Christian God: the Almighty Himself takes on the role of the weakest, the most despised, those ending at the gallows, thereby declaring Himself in solidarity with all of those who have not survived evolution, who have come under its wheels, wiped out by the law of selection. Taken to its ultimate conclusion, it would mean that God, through Jesus, refutes this world, which was created by the devil, by gathering unto Himself all the creatures lost in the course of evolution, taking them into a counter-kingdom that will in the end be much larger and stronger than the grand finale of an evolution that runs down like clockwork according to empirically indisputable principles called "creation"—but *whose* creation? Who takes pity on the chick that got out of the nest and was pecked to death by the hen because she takes it for an enemy?

The invention of God the Father, who becomes ever more paternal, ever more benevolent, the more power He possesses, comes from the spirit.

Slowly, my philosophical thought is taking shape: the sense oases (as individual and unique experiences) are vistas of the spiritual light that awaits us at the end of the universe.

Tonight the last drops of urine were quite red, but it was that way already once before, a month ago. The left kidney is finally dead; it hasn't stirred for a long time.

Perhaps the sense oases, which, of necessity, are always the result of the unique and individual, are tiny windows through which we see the spirit or feel its breath—the spirit that gives meaning to everything in the end. Then the lost objects of evolution will be gathered up; its rejected designs will be recognized as great paintings. Incomplete sketches will be seen as just as complete as those finished to perfection.

Zurich, March 23

Zingg is like a good spirit to me: "With your symptoms, you don't have to worry about not being able to take your trip to

Egypt. [I keep thinking: flight to Egypt.] If you still have a bladder capacity of half a liter, it's downright unusual." Afterward, I measured it again and found it to be only three deciliters. The difference is only one of degree. If I die in Egypt, I shall be in high society, amongst the pyramids and tombs of kings. There would be many dead to receive me. The reason for going to Egypt in the first place is interest in the dead.

The oncologist is quite severe. He says it is irresponsible on the basis of incomplete information—i.e., without pathological examination of a tissue sample—to make such a far-reaching decision as I did, and such a negative one to boot. I thought I'd heard all this before, three months ago. The oncologist says that only the histological analysis can tell whether there might still be a possibility that the tumor is benign and can be made to disappear. I got the impression (subjective, subjective, subjective) that he finds it inappropriate that for the past three months I haven't had anything more done—no further examinations, no biopsies, no radiation treatments, no surgery. My obstinacy melts in the face of his determination. More precisely: first we argue, then I feel defiant, then insecure; then I give in—only, as I subsequently realize, on formal grounds. For once I'm outside, I return to my original decision, which in fact, as I see more and more clearly, rests not on some whim but on necessity, the inner logic of my life and death.

In order to set himself apart, the oncologist resides in a cheerful room; the walls behind him are decorated with children's drawings or drawings by adults that look like those of children. One was, if I remember correctly (I had to concentrate on the discussion), a kind of collage: two human footprints embroidered with wool on paper, the toes pointed upward, decorated with colorful pieces of cloth, the whole arranged so as to give the two footprints the shape of a heart—not a medical but a symbolic heart. In front of this beautiful picture sat the austere oncologist, who nevertheless was so friendly to me while, at the same time, not being fooled for a moment. He talked about pessimistic attitudes, and we both knew he meant depression.

In the presence of doctors, one always has the feeling of being ungrateful.

Anyhow, in the waiting room I received a sheet with the following contents:

> As a private patient, you will be billed directly by our office. Besides the honorarium, this billing includes:
> 1. Charges for analytical tests in the oncological laboratory
> 2. Charges for medicines and drugs injected or dispensed here. . . . The statement lists separately charges for any tests carried out at other laboratories, particularly the central chemical laboratory. . . .
> Professor V. regrets not to be able to accept health insurance forms. For administrative reasons, we also cannot enter the insurance-rate figures for individual services. At your request, however, we will itemize our bill for your health insurance but *without reference to so-called treatment units* [emphasis in the original]. Any claims for reimbursement must be settled directly between you and your insurance company.

The legal-financial aspects are certainly clear. But would it still be of any concern to the cancer patients, to the mortally ill—if they know their situation?

The compulsion to preserve life at any price—only in the medical profession do we encounter it palpably and systematically.
To make a science of the goal to preserve life—the unconditional goal—a science bound to develop according to its own inner logic, may have been one of the many mistakes of evo-

lution, at least if viewed from the other side. Not that I wish to leave the helpless without help and the weak without protection; but since death is a reality, one ought to cultivate its company instead of believing that life can get rid of it.

Zurich, March 27

No more about evolution. God is both in the infinite and in the individual. At least that is how we ought to think if we are to take things seriously.

I recall a conversation a good forty years ago between my mother and our family doctor. He was a lovable man with a tendency to have his head in the clouds. He walked like a dog, with his feet parallel but at an angle to the direction of movement, had a penchant for nature worship, and was on the whole a bit dreamy, as we said in those days. Diseases, he said, had their meaning, even fatal diseases; they improve the gene pool by preventing individuals from reproducing—one ought to do less in medicine. My mother: "What, then, is the point of cancer? Cancer patients usually have already given birth to or generated their children." At that, he was totally speechless and grew dreamy again.

Collectively, nations create their sense oases by fostering an enclave mentality. The Americans and the Swiss are all very much in favor of having free, democratic, and legal conditions in their own countries (up to a certain limit). In order to preserve these oases, they are prepared to tolerate and even promote inhuman conditions in other countries, provided that quiet and order reign in these other countries. These unfree countries are in a way regarded and treated as suppliers for our own prosperity. Neither the Americans nor the Swiss would ever tolerate a Somoza as dictator in their own country; but they are ready to support him as long as he confines his injustices within his own borders, which—presumably—somehow benefits us.

If God stands only at the beginning and at the end of evolution, we may forget Him without qualms. True, Judeo-Christian religion at times has understood Him in this way, though never exclusively. If He is not also conceived as being present in our minds (and the minds of animals as well), He loses his entire actual potency. He becomes a God who is waiting it out—in part, perhaps, without paying attention. A God of the Beginning and the End—precisely the God who, according to Zephaniah's sermon against the rich, never intervenes in actual events. Nor is He evidently doing that, as He is clearly not continuously shuttling back and forth between eternity and temporality. He does not strike evil people with lightning. But He might be present in minds that continue to develop and must necessarily think of Him, and that's where He becomes most acute and virulent. Karl Barth could never have spoken out as forcefully against Hitler, could never have mobilized so many people against Hitler—I am not talking about success—if he had spoken only about religious generalities, about the psychological necessity of the transcendental and so forth. God's power substantiates itself over and over again, in individual persons; and then, in the here and now, these persons take their stand by invoking the highest authority and perhaps are able to change social conditions—all of which is possible only with a concrete, temporal-nontemporal God, not with a beginning-and-end God who is forever waiting, and maybe asleep.

What I especially like about theology is its unscientific mix of transcendental speculation, quest for eternity, and temporally concrete moral claims. A God who does nothing for the individual, who leaves everything to the free reign of power, is not

141

God but the devil at best. Nonetheless, the human brain has produced the substance capable of resisting this kind of power.

This evening toward seven o'clock, Christoph and Eva came with her mother, their adopted child, and Hans. Eva had a numerically important birthday, her fortieth, and Christoph had invited us all for dinner at the Zimmerleuten. But it was impossible to get there, since the whole Old Town was fogged in with tear gas. They then wanted to go to another restaurant in a different part of town, but I no longer felt up to it. We said good-bye in front of my building; they were all looking at me with expressions of alarm.

I'm very tired, sweating; maybe I should eat something after all. I hate having my freedom curtailed, even if it is only the freedom to go to the nearest restaurant. At the same time, I don't like to give in. And thus, here I sit; I have no other choice.

The signal for the riots now in progress was apparently the destruction of the AJZ.* The city council is behaving just as childishly as the children it has its police beat up. It is only a matter of symbols, exactly as I have always said, written, and published in print.

Opio/Provence, April 1

Yesterday, I flew to Nice and was met by Honegger and Sybil; at the last moment, Ines, Sybil's daughter, managed to catch the same flight as well. For the first time in a long while, I am again completely immersed in company; with friends, in constant conversations, taking in the sights together.

* Alternatives Jugendzentrum—a youth center for dropouts and adherents of an alternative lifestyle, a building made available and later destroyed by the city.

We went to Vence this afternoon to see the chapel that Henri Matisse decorated with stained-glass windows and painted tiles shortly before he died. The tiny building, wedged in between taller ones, looks like a shack, and even from the inside appears like a garage as far as the architecture goes. Since the last war, it has become fashionable for every great artist in France to build or decorate a church (Le Corbusier, Léger, Chagall, Rouault). In Matisse's work—I always had a special love for his paintings, the cheerful colors, the view from a window—the chapel at Vence is conclusion, repetition, and a new beginning without continuation. Over eighty years old and practically paralyzed, Matisse was hoisted up and down the walls, so he could paint the tiles using the sketches he had done while in bed. The Way of the Cross he numbered according to its individual stations. At the base, only lines dashed off without shape; supposed to represent Saint John and the women who witnessed the crucifixion; all we recognize are rough, broken strokes. In the upper center, the Crucified and to His right the Entombment. I am unable to reconcile all of this stylistically with the entirely perfect representation of Saint Dominic on the wall of the long side. All of it in black and white, including the large opened blossoms which he was in the habit of painting. Nor do the stained-glass windows, composed of large areas of yellow and green plant leaves, fit in, with their cheerful light effects directed toward the Crucifixion.

After our long and serious viewing, of particular interest to Honegger because he is himself now engaged in a church project—a bishop commissioned him while mildly ignoring Honegger's protestations of being an atheist—we settled down in the street noise of a sidewalk café and drank wine. On the way home, we drove past the entrance of the Gorges du Loup, and I remembered suddenly my visit there nearly thirty years ago.

The house Honegger has rented is surrounded by terraced

gardens bursting everywhere with green plants that threaten to cover the house and the terraces alike.

In the Matisse chapel at Vence, the Bible was displayed on a lectern, opened at John 8:51, a rather unconvincing passage in which Jesus extols himself as the Son of God. At the end, the Jews are ready to throw stones after him, but he gets away. The passage cannot be genuine.

Honegger thinks about death as B. does: nothing; finished; life alone matters; death is not worth discussing; anything metaphysical is a part of life; death has nothing to add. I am immediately suspected of constructing a system of consolation, and I'm unable to convince them that the question of meaning in the face of death might be answerable without trying to satisfy the need for solace. Honegger's father was a Jehovah's Witness, a Bible researcher, as they say, and as a youth Honegger was forced to peddle pamphlets from house to house; sometimes people spat on him. Now he has conquered these insults by ridding himself of their cause.

Opio, April 4

The weather is cool except for yesterday, when the sun shone all day.

The house belongs to two artists from Paris. One of them makes frames, small and large, out of dark iron; the other paints or glues narrow strips of almost equal colors on the indulgent canvas. The house is very tastefully furnished, overfurnished, full of beautiful objects: old painted plates hanging everywhere on the wall or displayed in wire holders on stands, no longer to be used, and almost too precious for show. Please do not touch. But why bother? As the value of an object continues to increase, it will end up being removed from sight, locked in subterranean vaults, at best replaced by copies. Thus do the fetishes lay claim to God's invisibility. Yet, in the end, a simpler explanation prevails: The beautiful ought to be preserved and brought out only for the most festive occasions, so as not to become an everyday object.

Opio, April 5

Honegger doesn't give the impression of belonging to the international elite of artists. He doesn't give himself airs, nor does he try to attract attention. Yet in the end he does not feel sufficiently recognized. Everywhere he ranks near the top: every museum of some importance in the world has one of his paintings; he is part of an epoch, seemingly at peace with himself, modest and generous toward others. For a long time he lost track of the paintings he had hanging in galleries and exhibitions. He didn't know whether or not gallery owners made off with pictures of his, a practice that appears to be routine nowadays— the dealer sells the picture and hopes the artist won't remember. After Juan Gris died, the art dealer Kahnweiler came and cleared out the house and the studio because only a girlfriend was around who had no inheritance rights. Honegger's stories confirmed what Alex had been telling me for a long time—that art dealing is one of the most criminal businesses in the world. As I respond with outrage, invoking criminal law, all I encounter is tired or condescending resignation. Nor are the insurance companies any better. Four of Honegger's paintings that had been insured by Lloyd's were left standing in the rain for a week after being exhibited in Brazil. The Lloyd's agent offered a fifth of the insured amount and said, "If you want more, you can litigate until you die. We calculate our risks according to tables. If the artist is quite young, we pay a lot, because he'll probably live to see the end of the suit; the older he is, the less we pay voluntarily. You are over sixty at this point—a clear-cut case."

All creativity has its parasites, in nature as in all of human culture: in politics, in science, in art. An inevitable fate of the creative effort is that its fruits are taken away from the creative people by others, who make their living exclusively from selling, trading, or just plain theft. The creative genius is an easy victim of this form of exploitation, because he takes his satisfaction from the creative process and the joy of accomplishment. Any additional benefits he treats with contempt: perhaps he receives them without further thought, perhaps greedily, but never with a sense of proportion and value.

Honegger says I have a negative attitude to art, otherwise I wouldn't be so eager to jump on the seamy aspects of the art business. I tried to explain that I am primarily interested in understanding the general principle that I can most easily recognize in areas in which I have a certain expertise. And behold, the moral and aesthetic elements are joined; selflessness and an ability to endure great privations are the sources of power infusing the greatest works of art, from van Gogh to Giacometti. He who is full of spirit has no need of money.

My arguments were immediately refuted by Honegger, who cited the example of Raphael riding through Rome on camelback for no other reason than to dazzle the people, or of Leonardo summoning the king of France to his deathbed. Picasso amassed enormous wealth but didn't seem to care much about it and lived as though he were a thousand times poorer than he was, without being stingy. Conversations with Honegger degenerate into arguments whenever the subject matter is sufficiently important. Where I attack, he does not put up a direct defense but tries to find a positive angle. Take, for example, the art collectors, whom I regard as money-conscious speculators. Honegger points out that they donate their paintings to the public in the form of charitable trusts. I argue that the superrich develop three types of supercravings: (1) power—for example, through the building of corporate empires; (2) status in the form of conspicuous consumption—for example, as playboys flaunting women, as owners of airplanes, racing stables, and so on; and (3) status (and immortality) as art collectors by establishing foundations in their own names that consist of works created by others. These three forms of foolishness are a rich man's dilemma that neither the truly creative person nor the average man knows.

The three forms of property:
1. Property as an instrument for freedom
2. Property as a means of production
3. Property as nihilism

Property as personal sphere, the ultimate symbol being your own toothbrush, is generally undisputed. Also, property as security—say, for old age, so as not to become dependent on others. All of this is indisputable.

Property as a means of production makes sense as long as it really serves to produce and innovate and not in fact to impede production and innovation. Ownership of the means of production easily changes into pure power; that much we must concede to Marx. The owner of the means of production must justify himself through productivity. The builder of corporate empires has no part in this justification, in contrast to the entrepreneur, who creates new products, discovers new markets, and so on. Even so, the property owner remains vulnerable to the criticism of senselessness if the new market is not real, the need artificial, the owner's activity altogether useless. What alone matters in this connection, it seems to me, is the tautology that ownership of the means of production must justify itself through production.

A precise definition of nihilistic property may be found in paragraph 903 BGB (West German Federal code):

> The owner of an object may, if not opposed by law or the rights of a third party, do as he pleases in regard to said object and exclude all others from having any influence thereon.

I can do whatever I please with what I own, be it a painting of historical value or a factory that supports an entire town. But that's not the decisive issue. Decisive is that I can exclude everyone else from having any effect on the object. I can own a villa on Lake Zurich, another in Tuscany, still another in California, and so on, in addition to numerous vacant houses in many cities; I'm not using any of the villas or any of the houses, but I can nevertheless exclude everyone else from having any influence on them. This is the supreme pleasure of property. How else would you explain, as you take a boat trip across Lake Zurich, that the most beautiful villas on the choicest land are closed year in, year out? No one lives in them, no one is enjoying them; but somebody wants to keep the others out. And he is allowed to do so, for this is the law, and for the owner, the real meaning of property after all other meaning has ceased: "I don't get any pleasure out of it, but at least I can see to it that nobody else does." The nihilistic aspect of property is becoming increasingly important, as the excuses multiply: investing of capital, protection from inflation, and so on. The big landholder owns everything, produces nothing, and doesn't have to. The police assist him in excluding all others from taking any action that would affect his property. Too bad that Marx failed to analyze this most important nihilistic aspect of property.

Zurich, April 11 (Easter)

Resurrection once a year: a strange thought.

I spent Good Friday with Gschwind at the Steinerhof, his Alsatian farm. It was beautiful but as cold as in February. I don't remember what we talked about. Everything seemed frayed and worn out—even the landscape, usually so wide and warm, seemed barren in the cold wind. Wirz brought the news that Uli had died in the hospital after ten days in the intensive-care unit. Uli, a farmer from the Leimen Valley who frequently came to the Steinerhof, had been living with his third transplanted kidney. Before his first transplant, he needed to be hooked up periodically to a dialysis machine. Since his operation, he had succumbed to drinking, which he did quietly and unnoticed. Still, he didn't die from his kidney condition but from heart failure. Coming home from the pub, he fell and never regained consciousness. About six months ago, he told me he would never submit to dialysis again. His arms and legs were perforated from puncturing with the cannulas. Gschwind is not going to his funeral. He hates funerals. Nor are we present at our own funerals.

The Christian confession of faith violates the freedom of conscience and hence ultimately its own foundation. It shouldn't matter whether or not someone believes in certain events claimed for facts—and this includes the resurrection—and nobody ought to pressure any individual for an answer or a decision on these questions. Assuming that Jesus has not risen, why should that make his death meaningless, and why shouldn't God be able to redeem the world anyway? In this regard, God's freedom is also the individual's freedom of conscience.

I find it rather interesting that with regard to the Old Testament no such fixation on faith exists. It is perfectly acceptable to interpret the message of the prophets in relation to their historical context, as the Jews have always done, without risking a loss of substance—on the contrary. In this act of relativization I scrape away the sediment covering the absolute, and from the absolute I can bring to life the message, though only for the present time, to be sure.

Honegger, son of a Jehovah's Witness, seemed to me an impressive example that the either-or attitude of faith serves no purpose. He noticed me reading Isaiah, took the Bible out of my hands, and told me that the Witnesses regarded Isaiah as the most important book and immediately went on to quote passages that from the fundamentalist viewpoint—that is, without regard to a critical analysis of the historical context—are pure nonsense: the end of the world and the salvation of a very small group of sanctified people. That's why Honegger switched from either to or: only life, its colors and forms, and what you make of it, has meaning; all around it is nothing but nothingness. Of course, it is absurd to believe in that kind of doomsday with the chosen few, especially the latter part. Yet such notions don't invalidate all of Isaiah.

The fundamentalist's inability to interpret, to see truth as something relative, to make it relevant to the modern condition, may be taken as a sign of honesty, as it certainly was in Honegger's case—a horror of distorting the truth. If we stay with the original text, however (Zwingli: "The word they must let stand"), then each interpretation in its turn is subject to relativization, and each interpretation must find a foundation that is more basic than the text; for the text itself, the word itself, is ultimately no more than a reflection of the spirit, of which no image can be made.

We should at least have learned from history that what people believe—whether sold as faith or as knowledge—is to an extreme degree subject to the currents of opinion prevailing at the time and hence a function of collective behavior. Only a hundred years ago, nearly all people in Europe still held the Christian credo to be true. Today almost nobody does. I'm disturbed about both situations, especially about the fact that the great minds, the majority in any case, all swim along with the currents of the times. Faith in God and atheism are simply fashions, conventions.

Convention, imitation, fashion dictate human behavior even in places where we least expect them, such as the most individual sphere. Joy and pleasure, for example: most people's idea of pleasure is what others find pleasurable—skiing, traveling, jogging. The more skiers there are, the more there will be. Every summer I swim a few times down the Limmat River, straight through Zurich, pulling my clothes along in a plastic bag. Nobody except me considers this to be fun.

The recent public discussion about the Federal Supreme Court decision concerning the crime of *Landfriedensbruch* (breach of the peace of the land) taught me primarily one thing: the law as an attempt to restrain power with words (in the statutes) nearly always fails. In the past, the Supreme Court defined this crime more narrowly; now it gives it a broader interpretation. Not even a revision of the statutes would prevent the judges from tailoring their interpretations to what they believe to be the fairest decision in a specific situation. It is all the more urgent, as I must reiterate all the time, to understand the nature of power in order to impose on it the rule of law. Neither would it be possible to learn how to subdue a lion without ever having seen a lion, but only bars, cages, and so on.

So long as this state of insight and practice has not been attained, the rule of power will always dominate the rule of law. Consequently, people will fail to see those characteristics of

power that the law may exploit critically to its own advantage—
for example, rivalry, envy, and so on.

The misconception in regard to the meaning of the word "justice": most people see a fanatic who lets heads roll . . . the rigid,
the narrow-minded, the joyless, the systematic, the ungenerous.
Such a picture already reflects a deformation of justice by the
judiciary inasmuch as it has adapted itself to power. It is not
the justice of which the prophets, Jesus, and the apostles speak.
One cannot thirst for this unyielding justice, and it isn't worth
being persecuted for its sake (Matthew 5:6, 10).

Luxor, April 16

The Nile is about as wide here as the Rhine at Mainz. Five
o'clock in the afternoon: I am sitting on the balcony outside my
hotel room; the sun is glaring at me from above and from the
water, and it is still very hot. On the promenade along the river,
cars are moving, constantly honking, intermingled with horse-
drawn cabs, a few donkey carts. With the shadows cast in the
slanting sunlight, the cars give the appearance of having eight
wheels. Only in the far distance, downstream, do I see today
one of the normally so numerous sailboats with the high pointed
sails.

Frisch, who is staying in the room next door, went to the
swimming pool. Today, in almost unbearable heat, we went to
see the colossal Temple of Karnak and then to the somewhat
lighter Temple of Luxor, right next to the hotel. In terms of
architecture, the Greeks are undoubtedly closer to us. The Po-
seidon Temple in Paestum, though also massive, is more luminous and without any of that brutality that characterizes the
buildings of Ramses II, who incessantly had himself sculptured
into colossal statues as well. The columns seem too fat, too close

together, standing in each other's way, at least at the Temple of Karnak.

Yesterday we went to the Valley of the Kings, climbed down the shafts that go into the depths almost perpendicular to the mountain slope. At the bottom, inevitably, the plundered burial chamber.

In the evening, a long conversation about the Egyptian views of death and afterlife. What could they have meant by it? Did an eternal life, equally luxurious as in this life, exist only for the kings and the nobility? What was the meaning of such a selection, which denied even death a moment of justice? What did the kings have in mind when, still very young, they started building their tombs while at the same time knowing that their ancestral tombs or those of earlier dynasties had all been ransacked? If afterlife depended on the burial artifacts remaining intact along with the mummy, a second death would have to occur after the burial chamber had been cleaned out. Did they imagine something spiritual or something material? The mummy is bandaged so tightly that it certainly cannot take part in physical pleasures. What, then, is the purpose of all the objects and figures that shared the burial chamber with the mummy? Clearly some kind of symbolism to point to something quite different, something spiritual.

Luxor, April 18

Yesterday we hired a guide and chauffeur and drove about sixty miles upstream to Edfu, to the Temple of Hator, which has withstood the ages preserved in its original state except for the slashed limbs of the human figures in the reliefs—destruction allegedly caused by fanatical Copts. They couldn't reach the figures that were too high above ground; and those near the

153

base, the prettiest of all, were buried beneath a dense layer of sand and hence were spared.

After lunch and a short nap, new and serious symptoms appeared. No longer able to urinate, the urine appearing in drops and red. Extreme shortness of breath, especially when lying down and at night. Cold sweats all over the body. A feeling of perishing. To walk or stand upright, I had to lean against the walls. I am probably running a fever as well, but what good would it do me to know?

Max took care of me like a good friend. Called Christoph in the late evening, who naturally was out, yesterday being Saturday. Since I had vomited as late as four hours after lunch, Christoph recommended that I continue taking Motilium to compensate for the undesirable side effects of the Spasmo-Cibalgin.

But why this constant nausea, the feelings of dizziness?

April 19

Today, because of my condition, we had to cancel the trip to Abydos, in itself a charming journey down the river. Slept a lot, with bad awakenings. When sleeping on my back, I keep waking up and have to sit and breathe rapidly. Lying on my side seems somewhat better, as the other organs appear to exert less pressure on my lungs. Who knows all the places where the metastases have already gained a foothold. Most likely in the liver: it is hurting for the first time in my life. The way it looks now, it probably can't go on much longer.

Zurich, Triemli Hospital, April 24

Afterward it all went very quickly. I was able to reconstruct the sequence of events only with the help of Frisch. A call to the

Swiss rescue service got through immediately, the same day, April 19. I had to be supported wherever I walked. After some bureaucratic fuss by Egyptian officials, the ambulance jet was able to depart from Luxor at 4:00 p.m. and arrived in Kloten (the Zurich international airport) toward 10:00 p.m. From there I was taken immediately by ambulance to the Triemli Hospital. I have no recollection of these events, as I was unconscious most of the time. While still on the plane, I was given injections, and the backed-up urine was tapped by catheter. I was lying on a stretcher, and I remember seeing Frisch's face for a while; he was sitting at my feet toward the rear of the airplane.

Christoph and Eva came especially from Basel to see me the same evening.

The diagnosis is now reasonably clear: hepatitis.

Later this diagnosis could not be confirmed. A viral infection probably led to a heart insufficiency resulting in the accumulation of water in the lungs and a congested liver. The shortness of breath was caused by a thickening of the blood, which was clotting in the capillaries and led to a weakening of the heart. I must have been rather close to dying. If such a condition develops with fatigue and without pain, it is easy to bear.

On the other hand, death assumes a higher quality when it is more conscious. The only question is whether in dying this activity of consciousness is still possible, and for how long.

Zurich, Triemli Hospital, April 28

My case, seen from various perspectives, is indeed unusual. I have cancer of the bladder, which will certainly be fatal, but lesser problems are now intervening that are stressing the organism more than the primary disease has until now. The chassis can no longer be repaired, yet it still holds together. Nevertheless, one knows that in two years it will be finished no matter what.

And now the carburator is beginning to sputter, the brakes need fixing, and so on. The whole thing isn't worth bothering with anymore.

On the other hand, the incident in Egypt has changed my outlook. It is no longer a question of death as the ultimate limit but rather a matter of what course the disease will take now. Death in the hospital as death of slow approach: no either-or, only the prospect of infinitesimal convergence which at some point must reach a break. Or, inversely, life appears as a completely quantitative construct having, in addition, diverse characteristics.

April 30

Still in the hospital, with a fever that has lasted for days. Great reluctance to continue dictating. A temperature of 99.5 F is already enough to make me feel weak, passive, unable to concentrate.

Medically my case is confusing. The hepatitis seems to be gone, but they can't figure out what's wrong with my heart and my lungs. Since yesterday even breathing is painful.

Every day I have at least one visitor. Frisch comes frequently and encourages me to take little walks, which also according to medical advice should be good for me, except that they leave me completely exhausted. His *Bluebeard* is the saddest and most despairing book that I have read in a long time. If the protagonist is even remotely autobiographical, then Frisch must be in a totally hopeless situation. When I told him this, he said he was helped by the act of writing. Even so, the situation of Dr. Schaad is really without any hope. Frisch admittedly is living a very lonely life, which I didn't realize until now. Still, he has his fame and, more important, the satisfaction of having written his best works at the age of seventy. Besides, he told me, nobody else is reacting to *Bluebeard* the way I did; the majority simply take it for a suspenseful crime story in the form of a courtroom drama. Such an interpretation might apply to any author except Frisch.

With most visitors I have a feeling that they are absolving a duty. Not with Frisch, of course; our conversations are too interesting for him as well. The same applies to Rebekka, who is totally supportive and, in the process, has matured into an adult, responsible daughter. After a visit from my mother and several brothers and sisters from Basel, she said to me: "Why should you always be the one to comfort and cheer up the others—why is it not the other way around?"

Suffering does not steel us; it fills us with self-pity.

Zurich, Triemli Hospital, May 5

Quite apart from the weakness resulting from the illness— mainly the fever I had until a few days ago—the whole hospital routine is designed to force the patient into as passive a role as possible. He is subjected to constant manipulations, never because of his own decisions but always as a result of diagnostic or therapeutic considerations by the physicians or quite simply as a consequence of hospital routine.

DAILY SCHEDULE

7:00 a.m.   A nurse enters the room and asks if I have slept well. This could be taken, without malice, at face value; at the same time it is also a friendly form of waking the patient. Makes not much sense because breakfast is only at eight, and with respect to taking the temperature, it doesn't matter whether it is done at seven, eight, or nine.

7:45   Blood taken for analysis, if ordered by the doctor.
8:00   Breakfast.
            Between 8:30 and 10:00 the bed is made by two nurses and the room is cleaned by a cleaning woman.
11:30   Lunch.
12:00 noon Doctors' rounds.
            In the afternoon, the physical therapist comes to force the patient to have some physical exercise.
5:30 p.m.   Supper.
            With the meals the prescribed medicines are routinely dispensed.
10:00   One of the nurses enters to say good night and to hand out sleeping tablets and medicines where indicated.

From time to time one is called up to an examination or tests: X-ray, EKG, and so on. One has to be prepared for a nurse to walk in at any time to bring or get something. It is practically impossible to sleep during the day.

In the case of certain patients, the early "Good morning" could well mean "Let's check if he's still alive."

On Monday (the day before yesterday), I attended a session of the court of cassation. The day before, Sunday, I had returned to my apartment with Rebekka. Everything went well, even though I was still running a slight fever. In a spectacular case, the court of cassation rendered what by its own standards was a bold decision, though by the barest majority: two superior court judges were declared to have been prejudiced in a riot case. The superior court hearings showed aspects of a grotesque farce, as evident from the transcript.

TRANSCRIPT
September 17, 1981
Repeat of the appellate hearing (testimony of the witnesses).

[Just as the hearings were to begin, a window pane in the hearing room is smashed. Windows and shutters are being closed. According to the bailiff, none of those outside the court building were willing to come inside after being told that spectators were welcome to the extent that seats were available.

Beginning of the hearing in the absence of the public, except for journalists. In the hearing room are two uniformed policemen; outside the building are additional policemen with dogs.]

The following testimony was given:
ATTORNEY G.: I should like the record to show that the glass from the broken window lies outside the building. Hence it is not possible that the window was smashed from the outside. It must have been broken by pushing outward from the inside, from the hearing room.

[The presiding judge indicates to the defense attorney that the pane broke when the bailiff tried to close the window and somebody pushed against it from the outside. The defendant interrupts, shouting, "Liar, liar, it's not true!"]

I merely wish to enter into the record that the greater part of the shattered glass lies outside of the building, only a few pieces are here in the courtroom.

[The bailiff informs the court that none of the persons standing outside wish to come inside.]

I do not believe that the character of the hearing as a public proceeding can be guaranteed when the police are intimidating the people with dogs, as I observed here. . . .

[Interjection by the speaker of the superior court: "Stop this crap . . . sorry." Laughter on the part of the defendant.]

I wish to enter into the record that . . .

[The speaker of the superior court remarks, "It's your fault that we have to call in the police."]

I must, Sir, take exception to this charge. I am here as an attorney acting in the defense of the defendant. I vigorously refute the charge that I am to blame for the fact that the police had to be called in.

[The speaker: "I didn't say that." (This sentence was later struck in the record and replaced with the following sentence: "I did not say, YOU are to blame for it.")]

Yes, you said it exactly like that, I want the record to show it.

Based on paragraph 96, section 4 GVG, I challenge on behalf of the defendant the presiding judge of the second criminal chamber, Dr. S. and also the speaker Dr. K., possibly the adjunct speaker, Dr. P., as well, for being prejudiced, and I request adjournment of the hearing until a decision has been reached in regard to my demand for exclusion.

. . .

[Banging on the shutters from the outside. The presiding judge directs the police to restore peace and order, so that the hearing may proceed.]

. . .

THE COURT DECIDES:

1. The motion to disqualify the appellate court's presiding judge, Dr. S., as well as the AC judge Dr. P. and possibly AC judge Dr. K., will not be entertained at this time.

2. Oral opening arguments.

. . .

160

[The presiding judge declares that as of yesterday evening—
i.e., September 16, 1981—he was in receipt of a communication
from the state's attorney's office to the Appellate Court, II.
Criminal Chamber (Document 48). The presiding judge reads
the letter aloud. (Amendment to section 3 of the request from
the state's attorney's office: denial of a suspended sentence because of participation in disturbing the court hearing of September 15, 1981.)]

[Sprinkling of applause from individual members of the audience. (This sentence was stricken and replaced by the following: "Applause by the defendant.")]

THE DEFENSE ATTORNEY:

I should like to inquire of the court in what manner the state's
attorney learned of the defendant's attendance at the session two
days ago? This question is directed to the presiding judge.

(The presiding judge points out to the defense attorney that
he would have to ask this question of the state's attorney's office.
He further directs his attention to the fact that during the court
hearing in question some forty people were present.)

I am asking whether the court knows how the state's attorney's office was informed about the defendant's participation in
the hearing in question.

(The presiding judge states: "I do have knowledge as to the
manner by which the state's attorney's office obtained the information. I do not, however, owe you any explanation on this
matter."

In response to a question by the presiding judge, the defense
attorney and the defendant declare themselves unwilling to
withdraw the appeal.)

THE DEFENDANT (IN RESPONSE TO QUESTIONING):

Will you please stand, Mr. T.?
No.
I must admonish you again to rise and warn you at the same

time that a refusal carries a fine of 100 francs for contempt of court.

No, I won't stand up.

You have the opportunity to explain the reasons for this behavior.

I have nothing to add to my testimony at the first appeal hearing. I refer to its record.

I warn you again that you will be fined 100 francs for contempt of court if you refuse.

I won't stand up.

[In regard to the contempt fine, the defense attorney refers to his statements on the occasion of the first appeal hearing of August 25, 1981.

A contempt of court fine in the amount of 100 francs is levied on the defendant.

The defense attorney requests the court to check whether some observers would yet want to be admitted to the hearing and to permit it since seating is available.

All persons who request entry at this moment are admitted. Their number is about twenty. The defense attorney states explicitly for the record that he agrees with the choice of hearing room as well as with the admission of the public allowed by that room.]

Two days before this hearing, another court action against a rioter had taken place, and the defendant, T., who was sentenced two days later by the appellate court, was in the audience. When T. laughed at one point (whether out loud or silently: even this became a matter of controversy), the presiding judge, later to be in charge of his hearing, called out: "Mr. T., if I were you, I would rather not laugh right now!" This remark logically signaled to Mr. T. that the judge was prejudiced. Any disinterested party as well could reach no other conclusion than that the presiding judge intended to make the defendant pay for his laughter two days later.

When I later told Frisch about the scene, he found it had a rather touching familiarity. A judge who, abandoning all judicial decorum, directly speaks or calls out to a spectator in the audience, reminded Frisch of Adam, the rural justice of the peace.*

Triemli Hospital, May 7, 5:45 a.m.

A moment ago an event occurred, already now, exactly as Zingg had predicted. Following a normal urge to urinate, all I was able to produce were a few drops of blood. While the urge to urinate remained, I had no real bladder cramps; to prevent them from developing, I took a Spasmo-Cibalgin.

Yesterday I talked with Haemmerli** and asked him whether, in this case, it would make sense to have the palliative operation. He said that it depends on my overall condition, which is excellent. Heart, lungs, liver—everything is in order. Only my legs are still somewhat weak from lying down. Yesterday I took the streetcar up to the Uetliberg and walked from the end stop up the rather steep footpath to the Hotel Kulm on the top. No problems. On the way the chaffinches and the great titmice, even the pine titmice, followed me from tree to tree, sometimes flying ahead and landing in front of me on the ground. I knew, of course, that they are accustomed to being fed by the strollers. Still, being alone in the cold, dreary weather, I felt like Francis of Assisi. I feel quite well again, inclined to go through with the operation, after all; if I decide against it, I'll have to be put

---

* The central figure in Heinrich von Kleist's comedy *Der zerbrochene Krug* (*The Broken Jug*).
** Head of medicine at the Triemli University Hospital and a friend of Peter's.

on morphine already now. The time is short; I have not completed my dictations yet. In one hour, the nurses will be here—another reason I have to hurry.

Yesterday, Haemmerli, on his daily call, noticed that I was reading *The Prophets* by Klaus Koch, an enormously instructive book; I'm only irritated by the author's habit of reducing all words still spelled with a "ph" to a profane "f" (e.g., *sfäre, Katastrofe*). I was amazed how well versed Haemmerli was in questions of the Old Testament and the Talmud. He, too, wants to read Koch's "Die Profeten" ("The Prophets"). Apparently, he, too, searches for meaning.

The prophets have disappeared. Christianity has sanitized its prophet Jesus, forgotten or ignored the Apocalypse; what remains is at best a commonplace morality—or, at funerals, a feeble consolation with the Beyond. And yet: how much our time is in need of prophets! But just imagine what would happen to Amos today, he who castigates the social inequities, the rich who get richer and the powerful who grow more powerful. Fat cows, he called the women of the rich—a very unbalanced and biased statement. Such trenchant social criticism, today more necessary than ever, is rejected in our time by every segment of the population, because no God exists to empower somebody to make such pronouncements. Yet we are engaged in making the rich richer and the poor poorer. Inhabitable houses stand empty because the owner wants it that way; the economic concentration continues; the anonymous machine is in control. Faced with such a situation, politics is not only powerless but agrees with it. It is futile to rage about outrageous injustices. It seems as if society wants to do away with itself as quickly as possible. The elders pretend that nothing is changing, and youth is resigned or despairing.

———

A few days ago, the Liberals* elected a new president. Of course, he calls himself a liberal—it always sounds good—yet everyone knows that in his position he will represent the interests of the rich and powerful. Well, so what?

Today's prophets would be social critics deriving their authority from history and meta-history, ultimately God. They would immediately be declared insane and committed to a psychiatric institution. Evil is given free rein. Freedom is for the few. Ten percent of the people have more than eighty percent of all the available freedom. They know how to consolidate their power, politics is subservient to them, and the laws are either made for them or not enforced; for they know all the techniques of how to evade the law and can buy themselves all the professional help they want. Cries of woe are needed but would be ridiculous. The dispossession of the dispossessed continues, within nations and between rich and poor nations. Nobody wants to face the fact that in the process societies are destroying themselves. The state fills its coffers by taking the money out of the pockets of the poor. But the rich can evade nearly all taxation through their international connections. This is well known and palpably manifest, but a conscience sensitive to these issues is lacking. The autonomy of the individual is missing; "morality" now lies in conformity, for, inevitably, an autonomous conscience some- how presupposes the existence of God. Only the powerless dem- onstrate against the systems of the powerful and the conformists, but without success. The outrages against which Amos and Isaiah, both absolutely rational critics, lashed out, appear rather harmless in the face of the injustices today. The greatest of the prophets would not accomplish anything today.

* The Liberal party in Switzerland is right of center, roughly corresponding to the Republican party in the United States.

The Church and its theologians have failed to translate anew for every generation history's only spiritual-moral continuity, which the Bible bequeathed to us. As a result, the Bible has become almost completely unreadable. At best, its morality was reduced to a technique for living together with a minimum of conflict; which in turn means that the powerful make the rules, the others have to conform; which they do—though reluctantly, of course, since power, as we all know, is no true authority. If God doesn't exist, everything is permitted. For the powerful, we must hasten to add; the powerless cannot use this atheistic license, because power prevents them from doing so. At best they can riot.

Zurich, May 9

I've been at home since the day before yesterday, trying to wean myself from hospital life. When, the day before, my urine contained for the first time visibly blood, Haemmerli said that it was normal, considering the condition of my bladder. Of course, he was right. I, too, recalled the earlier prognoses: actually, I ought to have had blood in my urine much earlier. But then the urologist came. He wants to perform a second cystoscopy tomorrow under general anesthesia. Why? So that we know at least where the cancer is moving and how much it has advanced. A partial resection may still be conceivable. Foolishly, I agreed. I was weakened, unable to resist. If the circulatory problems hadn't intervened, I would have said no, just as before. Now I regret it, but I don't see any opportunity for a graceful retreat. I wanted to phone Christoph, but he was not at home.

What Honegger says about Isaiah is all wrong, by the way. The fourteen thousand redeemed are not mentioned anywhere: the Jehovah's Witnesses must have sought and found that elsewhere;

Isaiah speaks of the rescue of those survivors of the Assyrian pogroms who will convert to God (Isaiah 10:20).

The constant back-and-forth between social criticism threatening divine punishment and promises of redemption for the converted and faithful I find tiresome. Many pastors used to preach this way or still do—sin, punishment, grace. This is very much the worldly God of the Old Testament. White sheep and black sheep. This view personalizes world events too much and overlooks that the totality of events with all its participants has gone wrong and must be replaced by something new. Hence, with a certain inner logic, prophecy turns apocalyptic. For Jesus, the end of the world was imminent. He erred only by about two thousand years.

I believe that the general reduction of civil liberties occurring in Switzerland and other countries with the participation of legislatures and judiciaries is a process of historical significance: processes of dissolution produce authoritarian reactions with real or symbolic constraints which not only fail to eliminate the manifestations of disintegration but, on the contrary, provoke them that much more. That more and more people regard the power and toughness of the state and its reactions as an ideal is precisely the proof that spiritual-ethical concepts that can be realized only in freedom no longer exist or no longer are considered binding. Power and coercion take the place of conscience. What an absurd process! The law loses its critical function with respect to power. Arrests are facilitated; general surveillance and registration are soon going to be accepted as completely normal. Everyone thinks he can save himself by conforming, but soon we won't know what to conform to; for the powerful are, after all, the superconformists and concerned only with maintaining the system, which in and of itself is nihilistic. It has no convincing norms and duties; it exists for nothing other than itself and the preservation of its power. The cry for law and order is in reality a desire to close eyes, ears, and mouths in the face of the breathtaking developments that originate from ultimately uncontrollable systems and are destroying this earth. Refusing to know what's going on, one believes that nothing is happening and that everything will remain the way it is. What a diabolical error! The large majority of the world population simply refuses to be informed about the true situation, and therefore little can be expected from the minorities that carry the movements for peace and the conservation of the environment.

The prophets would have said of those who closed their eyes and ears, and the mouths of others as well, that they were "impenitent." Unfortunately, this word cannot be translated into the modern idiom.

Rebekka says that the younger generation thinks quite differently and will bring about a fundamental change once the older generation is no longer in power. I, too, cling to such hopes. My only fear is that the objective and uncontrollable conditions, the immanent logic of the systems, are even stronger than a majority of well-intentioned people. Unfortunately, everything seems to be moving inexorably to a predetermined fate.

Sunday, May 9

Just talked on the phone with Christoph and then with Haemmerli. Tomorrow's surgery would make sense only if it were really my wish to go through with the bladder operation. But since I'm sure that this is not the case, I'm going to cancel my appointment with the urologist. This prospect relieves me considerably.

Zurich, May 10

Gredinger was here for two hours. The conversation was tiring because he likes to contradict, but none of the topics were uninteresting. He thinks questions about the meaning of life and the universe, of the beyond to be meaningless. To him all such speculations are only a form of solace. Nothing has any meaning. Then he admitted to experiencing joy at certain moments of his life and not at others. Hence, meaning in spite of all? We don't agree on terminology. That he admits. The problem of how to evaluate the accuracy and verifiability of propositions: according to Gredinger, we are dealing with a graded scale, beginning with the extreme inexact, such as theology, following with the humanities, and reaching the relatively exact natural sciences at the other end. If we limit ourselves solely to the measurable, certain competitive sports are the most exact. In downhill races, hundred-meter sprints, etc., we can determine exactly who is the best. Not so, of course, in artistic ice-skating and gymnastics. Gredi: the word "art" by itself is already an indication of extreme inaccuracy. He wants to extend his scale to include sports.

In his view, thought can never be exact, because language is not exact. Sure, we may have moments of perfect clarity in thought and consciousness but these can't even be communicated to oneself, let alone to others. Language is made by the large majority, who represent mediocrity. At the other extreme are the esoteric and symbolic languages of philosophers and mathematicians. But whence this craving for exactness? Perhaps again a manifestation of the search for meaning?

Discussions about mechanisms of power. For example, if the recipient of a private letter in which he is the target of criticism publishes its contents, he does so only if he can count on public approval. Gredi suggested that it might just as well be done out of laziness. Gilgen* published a letter from Frisch declining the Literature Prize** with the explanation that he couldn't shake Gilgen's hand.*** As Gilgen owed the public an explanation for Frisch's refusal, why not simply publish his letter? Nevertheless, it is clear that Gilgen was confident of having the public on his side. An analogous case: Federal Councillor Furgler invited the members of a commission of experts entrusted with the task of rewriting parts of the Penal Code to a banquet after the first working session. One member of the commission thereupon wrote him a sharp letter pointing out that in view of the present need to save government funds, such lavish affairs were wholly inappropriate. Furgler read this letter before the commission at the session preceding the banquet. He could be certain that his audience, which after all had accepted the invitation to attend the banquet, would approve of his action. On the other hand, had he handed the letter over to the press, the public might have reacted quite differently.

It is difficult to understand all this, perhaps unnecessary as well. We talked about the interesting and dull cantons: Grisons somehow is like a cross-section of the entire country; we were in agreement about the special significance of Glarus, Uri, Appenzell, the superfluous character of the canton of Aargau and the dullness of Zurich, St. Gall, Thurgau. We were unable to classify our prejudices concerning the other cantons.

May 11

Used Zomax again, because of my left kidney. Something must be going on there. Strange feeling: I regard the left kidney as

* Zurich's minister of education.
** Literaturpreis der Stadt Zurich.
*** Frisch was opposed to Gilgen's right-wing philosophy.

a friend fighting for his life. And I don't even know if he isn't already dead.

Since I returned from the hospital, so many visitors are coming to see me that I hardly find any time for myself. It is probably better to see my friends now than later.

May 16

The "little books about cancer" have become a veritable literary genre. Increasing numbers of cancer victims, especially young women, who know that they must die very soon, write about their condition, their feelings, their life ebbing away, the reactions of others, marked mostly by mere helplessness and embarrassment. Dora Hauri (*I Have Seen the Autumn*): "Dying has begun, I notice it from my behavior toward the others and theirs toward me. Brothers and sisters want to see me again, to have me with them once more. Visits are hastily arranged." Here again the severity of the dying, and at the same time the inability to refuse playing the game.

Yesterday with Heidi at Claire's, sitting outside in front of her house high above Lake Zurich. A few days ago it was still winter, now suddenly summer, skipping spring. Time has become forgetful. Heidi, completely involved in environmental issues, eats only health food and tries, even if she is the lonely example, to conduct herself in such a way that the world would be a better place if everybody did the same. Kant's categorical imperative comes to mind: "Act in such a way that the maxim of your will may at all times serve as a principle of universal law." Whenever, somewhere in the open landscape, a tin or bottle has been discarded, it doesn't take long until further garbage is added to the place. The virgin quality of nature has been violated; people's inhibitions are gone when they realize:

the others do it too. Nobody wants to be the first to destroy an intact landscape. But once the destructive process is in full swing, the categorical imperative quasi turns around, inverting itself. The use of cars and the enormous destruction connected with it may serve well as the general maxim of legislation, and in fact our laws have done just that. Then the response to Heidi's rigorous standards is: what's the use if I alone act in the interest of the common good when the world can be changed only if everyone or nearly everyone participates but nobody does? Kant's maxim implies not only the responsible conduct of the individual but also a view of the whole in all its ramifications.

I just had to urinate, but the result was only a trickle of clotted blood. Yet the urge to urinate persists as though the urethra were blocked. Perhaps the stuff can be flushed out when there is more fluid in the bladder.

Talked on the phone with Haemmerli, who calmed me down. In the present hot weather, he said, most of the fluid is sweated out anyhow. According to the X-rays, the cancer was not moving toward the urethra but upward to the left; I should better wait until the bladder was full, then the stuff would be flushed out, as I had no signs of uremia.

Zurich, May 18

My birthday—probably the last. Telephone calls, visits, flowers.

The day before yesterday, in the evening, I had to go twice to the Triemli Hospital emergency room. The bladder exit was blocked; with the aid of a catheter, the urine was allowed to drain together with the blood clots. Back home, I was again unable to pass urine, only two drops of blood. Return to the emergency room by taxi. Rinsing of the bladder, first for nearly three hours by perfusion, during which a solution drips by gravity through a two-way catheter into the bladder and out again, then with a large syringe acting as a pump. The doctors wanted to keep me overnight, but I drove home at my own risk. They were right in concluding that the blood clots had not been eliminated. While still at the emergency room, I began on my own initiative to drink a lot of tea. I returned home quickly by taxi, and there luck was finally on my side: at first, despite the strongest bladder pressure, I was able to produce only two drops of blood, and then, suddenly, like a miscarriage, came a clump of blood the size and shape of a date. Then I felt complete relief as the urine passed, still reddish in the beginning but soon completely clear again.

Spending the night at the emergency room would have been a nightmare. For the patient. A fantastic show of realistic theater for spectators and listeners. All the beds next to each other in one room, separated only by curtains. Sounds of groaning from one bed, cursing from another; from still others, whimpering or snoring. Conversations of the physicians and nurses with their patients or on the phone: You have food poisoning? The best thing is to stick your finger down your throat and vomit. . . . It doesn't work? What did you eat? . . . Meadow saffron leaves?* In this season? . . . You're perfectly welcome to be treated here, but then we're going to pump out your stomach, and that's much more unpleasant than trying with your finger. We're going to introduce a real big tube all the way down into your stomach.

Reception of new arrivals: I suppose you smoke as well—say, two packs a day? (No, no, at most one.) And as for drinking, a glass of beer or so now and then? (Yes, certainly, of course.)

Nurses' stock phrases: And now you're going to feel a little jab. Yes, yes, you can go home again tomorrow. You're not

*An autumnal flower containing the poison colchicine.

allowed to get up under any circumstances; we'll bring you the urinal. (But it's for—) We've got a bedpan for that—it'll work just fine. (Let me get up, dammit!) You're not allowed to, and you're not capable of it, either.

The doctors: Yes, he should be taken to intensive care right away. I'll be there in five minutes—I can't be at three places at once.

All of this is played out as if on the stage of a modern theater. The audience ought to sit high up in order to have an overview of the entire scene. The participant sees only the sector revealed by the opening in the curtain and the doctors and nurses rushing to and fro, yet he can hear everything. He waits and waits. A nurse stopping at his bed for a moment is enough to make him happy.

I must try never to become an emergency again.

Laax, May 27

The joy that I used to feel here somehow won't return—perhaps because I haven't had time to get used to the completely changed view, to this sudden summer. The pond has become large; it's filled with murky brown-green water. The birds are singing at me from all sides, titmice, chaffinches, green finches, black caps, serins, and, in between, the rasping of fieldfares, a bird that used to be very rare but now can be found everywhere—obviously an acculturated bird, like the ouzel. A cuckoo's call, beckoning from afar, enhances the feeling of early summer. I missed out on spring, if it ever came. The sun's still burning with undiminished power at five in the afternoon. I can't follow its course any longer, for now it is setting behind the house.

Increasingly, I am assailed by doubts that these dictations have any meaning. No one considers death a problem, except that it marks the end of life; and I'm not making any headway, either.

Cancer books are already plentiful. The authors describe their disease, their feelings, the compassion of their friends, the routine of the hospital personnel.

One of my neighbors has just started up his power lawn mower. Noise can ruin everything. I could imagine hell as an engine running forever right next to me, with no possibility for relief by adapting or becoming numb. Heaven would then be total silence. But that's not the case in real life. Prisoners in solitary confinement, who are enveloped in total silence, describe the soundless condition as extreme torture.

Tomorrow Christoph and Eva are coming for the Pentecost holiday. I've brought along a bottle of champagne for their welcome. We'll drink it slowly, so that the carbon dioxide doesn't give me a lot of discomfort.

I wonder what size lawn my neighbor is mowing? Now it would be nice sitting outside in the sun; it's not so bright and hot as it was.

During the past weeks I've done nothing but chores: *Criminal Law*, volume 3. Nothing that anyone else couldn't do. The field is characterized by the familiar controversies—e.g., those concerning asset losses from fraud, a topic in which everyone takes part, joining one view or another, occasionally contributing a thought of his own—all activities that are not in the slightest changing the way the law grinds away in its routine march, unimpeded by concerns about justice.

The neighbor's lawn seems to be infinitely large.

Evenings are too long during daylight saving time—when one is depressed, at any rate. What is there to do in bright daylight if one doesn't feel like working, going out, reading, watching television, eating, or drinking? One can't go to bed in bright daylight. Possibly the inhabitants of northern Norway, where the sun never sets during midsummer, can get used to it. I found it very eerie, walking as a tourist through towns bright with daylight but dead quiet, places like Hammerfest or Tromsö. That was exactly thirty-one years ago.

Frisch, Gredinger, and the others probably take it for granted that my reflections are meaningless except for me personally, and they remain silent so as not to hurt my feelings. Yet I still believe that I don't need such consideration.

I'm dictating these thoughts not so much to seek my own solace as to portray dying and death as an event imposed on us all, but one that can truly be overcome. But what is the result? A compilation of banal sickness reports alternating with lengthy reflections that won't convince anybody.

The power mower is still going. In spite of it, I'm going to sit outside in the evening sun.

Laax, May 28

If the sun isn't shining, the meadows on the slope of Falera appear yellow instead of green tinged with yellow, as yesterday. The pond is now dark green, almost black.

The curriculum vitae! I still have to write the version to be read by the pastor in church.

What are the elements of continuity that make up the unity of a person over the course of time? Except biologically, I certainly have nothing in common with the infant baptized fifty-six years ago. Is a biography equivalent to reeling off a genetic program under diverse environmental conditions? Every sleep is a death, and every awakening a resurrection. Everything is bridged by memory, which gathers and stores events and attributes them to the ego. The attributions, interrupted by numerous gaps, the forgotten and the repressed, make up, in regard to time, the curriculum vitae. If you write it down, really juicy lies and omissions are put together with selections dictated by vanity. Even a man as modest, intelligent, honest, and, above all, courageous as Albertz* can't help mentioning again and again in his autobiographical diary the many famous and important men he met, although it is impossible to know whether they played any significant role in his life. It seems to be a general principle of memoirs and autobiographies that people who *must* have mattered most to the author—wife, children, "unimportant" friends—are mentioned most lovingly, but only at the margin.

I was born on May 18, 1926, in the Merian-Iselin Hospital, because my mother happened to be in Basel at the time of birth. My family was then living in Stein am Rhein in the most beautiful church-owned manse in all of Switzerland, located directly on the river bank: its view over the Rhine, the island of Werd with its little monastery, and the lower part of Lake Constance is so idyllic that only an extremely naive artist would dare to paint it. I was preceded by two children, Anne and Hans, and after me two more, Georg and Dorothee, followed, all at rather short intervals. In 1932 we moved to Arlesheim, because my father wanted to live near a city so as to enable his children to

* Pastor Heinrich Albertz (SPD) who, as mayor of Berlin, was ultimately responsible for the brutalities committed by the police and the shah's agents against students protesting against the visit of the Persian shah and Farah Diba on June 2, 1967.

attend gymnasium.* That, of course, meant Basel and its Humanistisches** Gymnasium. In Arlesheim, two more brothers were born—Christoph in 1933, and Markus in 1945. When that latter year I visited my mother in the maternity ward of the hospital in Basel, I heard the battle thunder of German and French artillery across the border. A relatively small bridgehead was won by the French not far below the city of Basel; and lots of Baslers had climbed to the tops of the harbor silos to watch the fighting with their field glasses. German troops who fled into Switzerland for safety and internment were abused and spat upon in the streets by the Swiss population.

We were thus seven children in all; my oldest sister, Anne, was twenty-two years older than my youngest brother, Markus. No pill was available in those days, and my parents observed the rhythm method—the wrong way around. What foolish and brutal hypothesis: that this or that child might perhaps, or even normally, not have been born. For it is pointless to count backwards when it comes to children.

To be part of a large family enlarges the network of human relations dramatically, especially after you reach school age: you meet your brothers' and sisters' friends, and they get to know you. For the parents, the large number of children is above all a great burden, a house full of duties and unmanageable individuals and children's noise. We all met our obligations and grew up to become good citizens. All five brothers went to the Humanistisches Gymnasium in Basel, on the Münsterplatz, the square across from the cathedral—a school that still regards itself as the most important in Switzerland.*** There I had good

* Special public high schools for academically talented children. Graduation from such a school is a prerequisite for admission to a European university.
** One oriented toward the humanities—i.e., the curriculum is dominated by classical languages.
*** Founded in 1589 as the first Latin school, it has long been part of the public school system of the canton Basel-Stadt.

academic grades but always bad conduct marks. It was at the hands of certain teachers that I came to know injustice for the first time. Conduct was rated only when unsatisfactory: the appropriate box in the grade book was filled in with either of two formulas, "gives occasion for censure" or the severe "very reprehensible." In my final year, the teachers at last gave up. I never understood for what kind of behavior I was actually taken to task. I often had a feeling of defenseless rage, especially when I saw that my father took my conduct marks so seriously, as if they were proof of inferior morals.

Unfortunately, nearly all my teachers were boring; but that couldn't have been the reason for my bad conduct, because I never let my boredom show and was rather attentive and strove to learn just enough to earn the grades my father admired so much. On the other hand, our particular school had the advantage of not requiring any effort during the last four years* while at the same time introducing us almost automatically into what was considered to be the educated world of the day; hence, I had time to read Nietzsche, Dostoyevsky, and Büchner for my own pleasure. On the school bench I sat out the solemn texts of Horace and Virgil; I probably developed my dislike for Plato during this period, because the teacher was only interested in grammar. We also had to translate texts by Ovid and Catullus, at least the nonerotic sections, carefully selected for being safe. In retrospect, my explanation for bad conduct marks is that I probably attracted more attention than the other pupils. But why?

Graduation was an enormous relief. I went on to law school because I thought that pursuit would allow me the most free time for writing. I was initially encouraged to write by Kutter and then through my contacts with Fritz Dürrenmatt, who at

* Corresponding to the senior high school years, or the ninth through twelfth grades.

that time was writing his first plays in Basel and whom I went to see frequently. But then the study of law gave me fascinating insights, especially in retrospect to my school days and my poor conduct marks. As a pupil I thought I was completely defenseless, at the teachers' mercy. Then I realized that all power is tied to law: I could at least have requested a justification for my bad conduct charges, perhaps filed a motion of appeal and the like. That everyone had rights, that he can find these rights spelled out in the constitution and the codes of law, that the powerful must respect them—all this came to me as a great enlightenment. Responsibilities exist as well; they too must have legal foundations and limits. Order is not a matter simply of the subordination of the less powerful but of written law. Already in the first semesters I began to ponder the question why the courses at law school are concerned exclusively with applying existing statutes to specific cases and why, at the same time, the much more interesting question is not asked—namely, whether the laws are right, and how they must be fashioned in order to be just, practicable, and comprehensible to the average citizen. That was for the jurists of the day a totally nonjuridical question—in fact, a purely political matter. Hence, it is again the power that determines the law. I've never been able to accept that. As a result of more than twenty years of reflection, my monograph *Doctrine of Legislation* finally took shape. Today, I would write it in a completely different way, but the time is too short. As a preliminary study, a doctrine of justice would be needed that is well versed in the ways of power and thus capable of controlling and managing it. How can we make the law effective in dealing with power? That's the core of the entire problem, especially in regard to practice. Why do nearly all reforms invariably fizzle out? Why does Mitterrand, for example, have to retract his whole program piece by piece because the rich and the mighty arrange a giant flight of French capital to other countries, Switzerland not last among them, and otherwise sabotage his measures? Power must be reckoned with, from the beginning, when programs are designed. The only alternatives are probably radical revolutions or gradual reforms that just manage to be acceptable to the rich. Perhaps both can be realized only in a world state: Pax Americana or, if necessary, Pax Sovietica. But this idea, too, is a horror. A single giant machine would control everyone. Today at least the rich and mighty can trek from one country to another with their money.

The second part of the *Doctrine of Legislation* ought to be practice-oriented to a much greater extent. It should contain all the information in the form of concrete instructions how to make laws that are simple and that truly fulfill their purpose. How does one prevent the rich French from transferring their money to Switzerland? How can one create incentives that will induce them to cooperate and keep the French economy from falling apart? Must it always be that the rich get richer and the poor get poorer and that things get a little better for the poor only when the rich are doing excessively well? From a worldwide perspective, this question has become meaningless anyhow: the poor people of the third and fourth worlds are producing such a tremendous overpopulation that they are forced to use up quickly whatever is left—the little wood that grows in Nepal, for example, or in the African plains. To be sure, the great ravishers and destroyers are once again the rich peoples of the Northern Hemisphere, who are selling arms to the poor nations and in return are taking the wood from the tropical forests, which will be wiped out in twenty years.

After my law studies, I did my practical training at the district court in Arlesheim and at the superior court in Liestal. These were in part very fun-filled times, often spent drinking in the company of friends—no sophisticated jurisprudence but, in retrospect, plenty of human warmth. The best judge I ever saw was the superior court's chief justice, Paul Gysin. He was friendly and patient—exasperatingly patient. The right to a judicial hearing was overfulfilled in his court. When I think of those sharp judges, some of them in Zurich—I won't name them because everyone knows them—those sharp judges who think that fast and tough actions administered without a shred of self-doubt and with pompous, authoritative mannerisms have anything to do with law and justice, then I recall Paul Gysin, his circumspect approach, his scrupulous and hesitant deliberation; his judgments, even when they had to be severe, were always manifestly just and accepted by almost everyone affected by them. Later, when I became superior court clerk, some of the old guard retired, and among the younger judges some would take the stance of the tough judge. By that time, however, I was able to prevent many bad decisions with the aid of Paul Gysin and the effective application of my juridical craftsmanship.

In 1955 I became assistant professor at the University of Basel; Professor Germann, who held the criminal law chair, was my sponsor. This was probably my most productive period: teaching and research in addition to my clerkship at the superior court. In spite of all this, I had, so it appears to me in retrospect, an enormous amount of leisure time. Lots of conversations with friends and girlfriends, the latter sometimes spending the night with me. I was living again in a house on the bank of the Rhine at the time, in the St. Alban Vorstadt in Basel.

In 1961 I became an associate professor in Mainz and again lived right on the river, where it is twenty times as wide as in Stein am Rhein and three times as wide as in Basel. Almuth and I married. We lived on Taunusstrasse on the sixth floor, without an elevator, and with a coal stove in the living room, yet rewarded by a view, grand and wide, out over the Rhine and extending as far as the Taunus, which to German eyes is already a mountain. After only six months I was offered a chair at the University of Göttingen, which happened only because the faculty in Mainz had made the mistake of appointing me to a mere associate professorship. In Germany, this means that you are not "locked in" like an ordinarius [full professor], who, as a result of collusion among the country-wide ministers of education, cannot accept a new position for a period of three years. I turned down the offer from Göttingen and became a full professor in Mainz.*

My first appointment in Mainz had less to do with achievement than with chance and luck. Since the faculty at Mainz knew me only from my publications, which nobody wanted to read anyhow, they sent the associate dean of the faculty to Basel to look me over. He didn't want to hear any of my lectures, mind you, but rather to meet me at the Hotel Jura. The dean, Werner Niese, was not only a brilliant legal scholar but also a talented musician—he played the viola—and very interested in art. When he first met me at the hotel, I took the opportunity of showing him the original paintings of Roualt and Klee, as well as some German expressionists that were hanging on the walls there, as the hotel's owner collected art and was a friend of some of the artists. Niese was delighted. We talked only of art and music, then went to have tea with Germann and afterwards to my apartment in St. Alban. Niese never had tasted any Veltliner wine, so we made up for this. I put his musical knowledge to the test by putting on a record of Mozart's "Dissonance" Quartet. Of course, I played only the beginning, which sounds like a twentieth-century composition. Niese was unable to identify the composer. When I let the record play on, he was completely in awe of the supposed breadth of my knowledge. After several days, the offer arrived—that is, the written invi-

* Had the original appointment in Mainz been at the full professor level, the University of Göttingen would not have been permitted to make an offer within three years after the appointment in Mainz.

tation from the Cultural Ministry in Mainz to contact its director in order to negotiate the details of the position.

In 1969 I received simultaneous offers from the universities of Frankfurt and Zurich. I hesitated a long time, since I had friends in Mainz and Frankfurt. Almuth was the decisive factor; she loved Switzerland very much, knowing it only from vacations. So we came to Zurich and built a house in Gossau, on a hillside with a view of the Alps around Glarus and Central Switzerland. Lots of comfort: two bathrooms, a shower, a heated outdoor swimming pool, and later a sauna as well. Upstairs, I had an enormous study with a cathedral ceiling. Our house was one of the highest on the hillside in that zone, only five minutes from the forest; beyond was a marsh and the entire landscape of Zurich Oberland, hills of moraines left by the last and next-to-last Ice Ages. On the Zurich faculty, I was soon considered an outsider, partly because of my "leftist" outlook, which actually was only the most extreme aspect of my individualism. I often thought that the faculty would not have offered me the job if they had known me beforehand. But I could be wrong.

My daughters, Rebekka and Sibylle, were very different from each other ever since they were very small. Rebekka spoke perfect German sentences when she was only one and a half, always had fancy ideas, and nearly always obtained what she wanted from me. Sibylle was even-tempered, quiet, steady, very witty and sociable, always surrounded by friends, less of a loner than Rebekka. Especially when I think of Rebekka and Sibylle, I feel pain that I must leave.

In 1977 I went through a crisis: the thought that nothing in my life would change anymore, the thought of being a prisoner of possessions and social ties depressed me. I found it difficult to concentrate or work. After long conversations with Almuth, I sold the house and we took separate apartments in Zurich.

Later, we divorced. This new chapter of my life was followed shortly by the last. This chapter is now truly totally new.

In regard to my life, I made too many mistakes. I should and could have overcome the crisis. I should have tried to change my life, not the external circumstances. Nevertheless, I have done much that was beneficial, more than my share.

The curriculum vitae is complete. What shall I call this last period? Curriculum mortis?

I have to urinate more frequently and use Spasmo-Cibalgin more often, to the point that it constipates me. I'm again tired, and it's only four in the afternoon.

Laax, May 31

On Friday a phone call from Gerda Rosenbusch. First: I should sit down. Then: Ernst [her husband] is dead. As he was returning by car from Tuscany to Zurich, near Rhäzüns, at seven in the evening, a chunk of rock from the cliffside fell through the windshield and smashed his skull. Would I give the funeral oration? Yes, of course.

I've already dictated it. It went as usual. For two days I thought about nothing else, especially the strangeness of his death, which, in a way, was the best thing for Ernst Rosenbusch, better than the alternative of a slow brain death; then I jotted down notes, accumulating ideas; and finally I dictated the whole, in one stretch, without making use of the notes yet still retaining in the resulting text the entire long thought process that preceded it. At the same time, I realized afterward, the notes would have been of no use. They all were outside the main train of thought, dead ends.

He who is going to die shall talk about the dead. Gerda

185

arranged that perfectly—probably without giving it a thought. But didn't Ernst have better friends than me? Certainly many who knew him much longer than I did.

Christoph and Eva were here for two days. That's always very nice, but in the end Eva gets on my nerves, and I naturally get on hers as well.

Again one of these beautiful evenings; I am able to tell which birds are the first and which the last to stop singing. On the pond are two coots and a family of mallards.

Birdsong time table: until 9:15 (daylight saving) chaffinches, which then suddenly fall silent. The cuckoo can be heard until 9:30. At around that time a song thrush further down the valley begins to sing; and a little later, at very close range, an ouzel, but only for a short while. Until 9:15 the swallows fly across the evening sky, and I was wrong in maintaining that they were immediately followed by the bats—it takes longer. I am waiting. The birds that are audible longest are the ouzels, with their warning call. Now, at 9:35, the cuckoo starts in again. Twilight is giving way to darkness; the fieldfares are rasping now and then. I also heard an isolated robin when I went out onto the balcony, but the bats are still not here, only the chirp of the crickets. From afar the voice of a bird I can't identify, probably a song thrush. Tinkling cowbells. Still no bats (10:00); hardly any light.

Zurich, June 10

Yesterday I dictated the end of the manuscript of the second volume of *Criminal Law*, and now I feel as always in such a situation: I fall into a void, everything bores me. As soon as I pick up something to read, I put it away again. I don't feel like doing anything, feel tired, despite the fact that I'm physically rather fit, except for periods of increasing pressure and pain in my bladder.

The world is full of wars again—senseless wars, as everyone says, as if there could be sensible wars. What else could be expected from people like Galtieri, Begin, and Thatcher? Two of the nations at war are atomic powers: Great Britain and Israel. If the British lose in the Falkland Islands, who knows what will come to Thatcher's mind? And who knows what Begin will do with his atom bombs when the two superpowers threaten to throw him back into his former boundaries? At the same time, the Iranians are marching into Iraq, which originally attacked them. Naturally they are all fighting for their rights. If the apocalypse should come from Israel, it would be an evil confirmation of the prophecies that originated from that land. This world has a beginning and an end. Jews and Christians have always known that. Is the Messiah to appear over Jerusalem in an atomic flash?

June 13

I keep having problems with the type of unfairness to which I feel entitled as a dying man. But, then, everyone is dying too. Since the word went around that I have cancer, many acquaintances write or call me on the phone, want to see me while I'm still alive. Apparently, it doesn't occur to them that I might not want to see them, and that they act according to the conventional view that those who are going to die soon wish to see as many of their old friends as possible. I react unfairly to those to whom this gesture really means something.

June 14

The invitations are piling up; I keep postponing, making promises, sometimes refusing. For a time now, I've been sleeping ten hours a night (always with three interruptions), and sometimes half an hour during the day as well. Sleep is only semideath; consciousness is somehow still present—one is aware of one's body, of the bedcover, of the pillow that has moved out of place.

A sermon by Bossuet (1627–1704) on the unity of the Church extends over fifty-five closely printed pages in my French edition of 1869. The man must have preached for three hours. The whole thing is nothing but a paean to the Catholic Church: "She is beautiful, great and terrible." At the very end, the Protestants get their turn but not by name, in keeping with the rest of the sermon, which never contains any concrete details: "Think of the misfortune of the peoples who have broken the unity and have thereby cut themselves into so many pieces that in their religion they see nothing but the confusion of hell and the horror of death." "These free thinkers are already appearing among us . . . Let us defend against them and their treacherous charm of novelty the rock upon which we are built, the authority of our traditions in which all previous centuries come together and the antiquity which joins us to the origin of all things. Let us march the roads of our fathers, but let us stay with the old morals as well, as we march on in the old faith." In between, always great praise for the French kings.

Thus did the Church engender atheism.

Bible quotations are used like any other citations from classical antiquity wherever they are thought to apply.

Bossuet was a star preacher for an audience of the rich and the mighty. He gave them just the dose of bad conscience they could bear without pain.

The dilemma is this: The spirit needs actualization and continuity; to maintain continuity through tradition requires organization; organization invariably produces power and propels the same breed of people into the seats of power. The sole spiritual tradition that functioned passably without losing its soul was that of the prophets of ancient Judaism, an epoch of a good five hundred years, admirable because it represented a sort of institutionalized conscience that nevertheless remained free and continued to exert a restraining influence on power.

The enemy one is fighting must remain abstract, anonymous, and collective; otherwise the aggressive spirit flags. Ultimately, good battles are fought only in the name of principles. Often the opponent is transposed into a past he has long left behind him. Christianity, socialism, etc. are always best refuted by attacking them for ideas they stood for at least a hundred years ago. One fights yesterday's enemy. That also saves the effort of seeking information about the latest state of affairs.

The Nordheim crematorium and its entire surroundings appear much more old-fashioned than the Grossmünster or the Predigerkirche.* The fiery faith in burial by fire has long been dead. What remains are the buildings, which exude an atmosphere of death, if only because they are being used exclusively for funeral services; their attempt to imitate the gloom of an old church is only depressing. Funeral services ought to be held in multipurpose buildings, such as churches, where people are baptized and married, where they sing, preach, and sleep. Death ought not to be separated from life. Nor should it be displaced into hospitals and old people's homes. But modern society has come to accept

* Another landmark church of the Old Town.

these separations, has even welcomed them, is perhaps happier for it, but without hope. What has been achieved ultimately are mere conveniences, as with dishwashers and washing machines.

People don't say "He has cancer"; they say "He is seriously ill."
Cancer is not called by its name. All other diseases are called by their names: "He had a stroke," "He had a heart attack," and so forth.

June 15

That faith in health has become a substitute religion (Thou shalt not smoke; Thou shalt not abuse alcohol; Thou shalt keep physically fit) and the fact that quacks of all kinds are so popular may in some way be related to the miraculous healing activity of Jesus, which in his time had meaning but today can only be taken as metaphor. The miracle as a form of religious proof is extremely vulnerable, especially to explanations resulting from scientific progress, but even more so when confronted with a faith that has no need for miracles, because it rightly holds that God doesn't need such trickery, either. Certain mental activities surely can influence biological processes, which, however, is of no significance to God's truth. Jesus would adduce very different proofs today. Neither have the prophets, with few exceptions, performed any miracles. Miracles always provoke suspicion. The thought of God does not.

Open the Bible to whatever page you wish, it always puts you in a reflective mood and provokes thought processes that go deeper than the purely operational. Bible study as a basic course for freshmen, in association with a plausible theological-historical analysis?
If my cancer were now to disappear suddenly, I don't think

190

I would become more Christian or "religious." I just would be amazed. Perhaps I would begin thinking anew.

June 22

Reading Trotsky's *My Life*. I recalled the 1950s, when I followed, probably at Fritz Lieb's suggestion, the beginnings of the Stalinist era in literature, especially the Moscow show trials which resulted in the liquidation of Stalin's last opponents. Trotsky had been wiped out a long time before that. He was doubtless the greatest mind of the Russian Revolution, more brilliant, cleverer, and more courageous than Lenin, who in 1917 remained in hiding until the dice were cast.

The Russian Revolution was probably morally justified in view of the mindless and brutal tsarist regime. In cases of too great injustice and suppression by too much power exercised by too few people, even a violent revolution may be justifiable, though unjust by itself as an instrument of change. The problem is that one never knows what the revolution will bring forth: a Napoleon, a Stalin, a Khmer Rouge. Revolutions thrive on extremely short-range goals. Trotsky writes:

> Our humanitarian friends of the neither-hot-nor-cold species have explained to us more than once they could see the necessity of reprisals in general, but that to shoot a *captured* enemy means to overstep the limits of necessary self-defense. They demanded that we show "magnanimity." Klara Zetkin and other European communists who at that time still dared speaking their minds to me and Lenin—insisted that we spare the lives of the men on trial. They suggested that we limit their punishment to imprisonment. This seemed the simplest solution. But the question of personal vengeance in times of revolution takes on a rather special significance that defies all humanitarian clichés. The struggle is for nothing but power,

a struggle for life or death—the very essence of revolution. What sense does it make, under such conditions, to imprison people who hope to seize power in a few weeks and imprison or destroy those who today are in command? From the point of view of what we consider the absolute value of the human personality, revolution is to be condemned no less than war, including, by the way, the entire history of mankind. Yet the very concept of personality itself has been shaped only as a result of revolutions, a process that is still far from complete. In order that the concept of personality be infused with real meaning and the semi-contemptuous concept of "masses" may cease to be the antithesis of the philosophical-privileged idea of "personality," the masses must lift themselves by the lever of revolution, or, more exactly, by a series of revolutions, to a higher historical plane. Whether this path is good or bad from the point of view of normative philosophy, I do not know nor am I interested in knowing, to be truthful. But I also know definitely that this is the only way that humanity has found so far.

Revolution is the most primitive form of political change, also the most painful: Trotsky has come to this conclusion from personal experience. The revolutionaries' idealism (not to be confused with that of the putschists) justifies in their eyes the sacrifice of others, just as they themselves are prepared to be sacrificed. Add to this a sense of being at the center of action, especially obvious in the case of Trotsky when, from his legendary railroad car, he built and commanded the Red Army, leading it to its final victory. The sense of participating actively in history, the primitive joy of combat and victory leave no room for thoughts straying into the more distant future. For this more than any other reason, all revolutions tend to reach goals that are quite different from their original vision.

Trotsky was always second to Lenin. Lenin was his authority

and the justification of his actions. This, much more than the intrigues of those around Stalin, caused his fall from power. Unlike Lenin and Stalin, Trotsky was not power hungry. When Lenin was mortally ill and then died, Trotsky lost all support in the revolutionary power structure. As Lenin's second-in-command, he could freely fight out differences of opinion with Lenin. But later these were used against him as sins against Leninist dogma.

The Russian Revolution was, after all, not much more than a putsch, even though the basis for a revolution certainly existed: the majority of the population was dissatisfied, hated to go on with the war; the country was dissolving into chaos. Thereupon a small clique, the Bolsheviks, seized power, undercutting democrats like Kerensky by methods essentially no different from those of South American putschist generals.

Trotsky also saw the blindness of revolutionary developments:

I am not engaging here in the philosophy of history, rather I'm recounting my life against the background of the events to which it was linked. But I cannot help noting in passing how zealously chance serves necessity. Generally speaking, the laws shaping the historical process are reflected in chance events. In the language of biology, one might say that what appears as historical necessity is in fact the result of the natural selection of chance events. On this foundation arises the conscious human activity which imposes artificial selection on chance events.

I must add that Fritz Lieb, my mother's cousin, was one of the truly great spiritual leaders of Switzerland's social democrats of the left, a deeply religious evangelical Christian as well, professor of theology at the University of Basel and friend of Karl Barth. In the Russian Revolution he saw the great Christian soul of the Russian people; only after Stalin's seizure of power did he become unsure. He was naive about power, unable to perceive how it takes hold in and through political machines. Lieb was an anti-Stalinist, certainly not a Trotskyist, though he greatly admired Trotsky, which I find not difficult to understand in view of Trotsky's outstanding intelligence. Compared with Trotsky, Stalin represented mediocrity itself, a weakness pointed out again and again in Trotsky's later writings. Power figures who reach the top through or within organizations are mediocre almost without exception as a result of the very process that produces them. This applies to political machines as well as to business and science. That Stalin later was victorious in World War II he owes only to Hitler's megalomania. Fritz Lieb was highly intelligent, extremely well read, and inimitably absent-minded. While he was known internationally, his local fame derived mainly from an incident when, as a member of the Basel City Council, he shouted "Sauhund!" (something like "Bastard!") at a conservative member who was vilifying the social democrats. His distraught mind produced some linguistic confusions as well: I remember the wonderfully mixed metaphor when he said in a lecture that "Potemkin villages were stamped out of the ground like mushrooms." (*"Potemkinsche Dörfer wurden wie Pilze aus dem Boden gestampft"*).

Trotsky describes his fall from power as follows:

> If I refused to take part in the pleasures that were becoming increasingly the norm of the new governing class, so not for moral principles but rather because I wished to be spared the torture of the most dreadful boredom. Social evenings, frequent ballet attendance, drinking parties with their inevitable gossip about those not present, had for me no attraction whatsoever. The new ruling elite became aware that I did not fit in with their lifestyle. Neither was there an attempt of drawing

me into it. Hence conversations stopped when I appeared and the participants went their way with signs of embarrassment vis à vis each other and hostility toward me. If you like, one might say: this means that I was beginning to lose power.

All of this occurred, of course, only after Lenin's death, including the following:

Gossiping over a bottle of wine or returning from the ballet, one smug bureaucrat said to another: "He can think of nothing but the permanent revolution." Closely linked are accusations because of my behavior as an unsociable outsider, because of my individualism, aristocratism and so on. "But why should the revolution be the beginning and end of everything, after all, one has to think of oneself as well"—that sentiment was translated to "Down with the permanent revolution!" The resistance against the theoretical demands of Marxism and the political exigencies of the revolution gradually assumed for these people some form of struggle against "Trotskyism." Under this banner the petit bourgeois in the Bolshevik was unleashed. These developments constituted my loss of power and determined the form which this loss took.

In a much more harmless context, but by precisely the same mechanism, individuals may be cut off from power—for example, as directors on the boards of corporations, members of management teams or scientific institutions.

Trotsky unmasks another mechanism of the manipulation of power: "If people originally regarded Lenin as a revolutionary leader, he soon became the high priest of a religious hierarchy. Over my protests, a mausoleum was erected on Red Square which to a revolutionary is disgraceful, even offensive. The official books about Lenin evolved into similar mausoleums. His ideas were cut up into quotations for false sermons. With his embalmed corpse they fought against the living Lenin and—against Trotsky."

Revolutions, the French Revolution not excepted, are by their very nature nearly always seizures of power by relatively small groups in the revolutionary situation of general rebellion and widespread chaos. They are preceded by infighting among these small groups, between the Jacobins and Girondists, between the Mensheviks, the social revolutionaries, and the Bolsheviks, etc. Victory by one of these groups over the others, which is almost inevitable because otherwise chaos and civil strife would continue, has two possible outcomes. Either the victorious group will be dominated by one man (Lenin), or it will split into factions who fight each other until again one man emerges as the dominant figure (Stalin after Lenin's death). Once the revolution is over, the single ruler toppled or dead, it is quite possible that they are again succeeded by a ruling clique, but one whose members don't fight each other—a situation exemplified by the present power system of Soviet Russia. Often somebody will grab the position of sole ruler only out of fear that somebody else would do it first and then liquidate him. The group might also agree on a single ruler (Brezhnev) in order to avoid just this kind of infighting and liquidations.

I mention the story of Trotsky's elimination from power only because it is typical of what can be observed everywhere on a large as well as on a small scale: the outsider is pushed out as soon as he has lost his protector. It could be the case of an unpopular assistant professor whose faculty mentor has retired.

Trotsky's elimination from power reflects a very simple principle: nobody can be powerful alone. Each ruler needs subordinates who help him subordinate others. Stalin, for example, had long before Lenin's death built up the GPU, or, rather, brought it under his or his confidants' control. Had Trotsky had such an organization at his command, he would have been able to send the others packing.

Makers of history see themselves as such and are regarded as such by others because they believe history can be made. In reality, history is made almost exclusively by chance events. The whole thing is nothing but a great maelstrom about which we know only that it has a beginning and an end. Moreover, the recorded history of mankind is so short as to be not worth going into.

Much larger is the view of the transitory nature of all existence, evoked with such power in the poem "Vergänglichkeit" by Johann Peter Hebel* in which he describes Basel the way it would look after an atomic war—a poem everybody ought to know.

Examples in literature that have a much greater visionary power than their authors ever knew, intended, or were able to conceive: in most cases they are to be found in little stories, fairy tales, fables, or poems. Goethe's "Sorcerer's Apprentice" is one: he describes our time, which he had no way of foreseeing—the uncontrollable nature of modern technology.

Some of the Grimm brothers' fairy tales. "Hans in Luck" can be understood at one level as a parable of the state of contentment produced by the simple life (Diogenes), while from an opposite point of view, the tale could exemplify the exploitation of the working man by dealers and traders.

June 24

Many of the fairy tales collected by the Grimm brothers contain more wisdom than all of philosophy. They are parables, which

* Johann Peter Hebel, 1760–1826.

197

reflect forever recurring events, eternal human truths, sometimes in such concentrated form that one could derive from them socio-psychological laws. Most of the fairy tales, however, especially the best known, are nothing but imaginative entertainment, unless one virtually forces a metaphysical meaning on them. For example, "Cinderella": the poor and humble shall be raised on high.

A prime example of the injustice of historiography is the tale of Mr. Korbes. "Four little mice, a little hen and a little rooster, a cat, a duck, an egg, a pin, a needle, and a millstone met on a trip whose destination was to be Mr. Korbes's house. Korbes was not at home, so they all hid in his place. Then Mr. Korbes came home, went to the fireplace and as he wanted to light a fire, the cat threw his face full of ashes. He ran quickly to the kitchen to wash himself when the duck squirted water into his face. He wanted to dry himself with the towel, but the egg rolled toward him and broke and glued up his eyes. He wanted to rest and sat down on the chair and then the pin stuck him. He became enraged and threw himself onto the bed, but as he laid down his head on the pillow, the needle stuck him, so that he cried out and wanted to run out into the wide world. But when he came to the house door, the millstone jumped down and killed him. *Mr. Korbes must have been a quite evil man.*" Which means: fate is always just (a maxim maintained in nearly all fairy tales); from the punishment one deduces the crime. Absurd; to be taken ironically, perhaps, but this is the way it is.

The best analysis of visions of eternity is unfortunately not represented in my collection, but I remember the tale from my childhood. A rich man and a poor man arrive simultaneously at the gates of heaven. St. Peter admits them and explains to them that all their wishes will now be granted but that they will have to describe them to him precisely. The rich man's wish is to have a large castle with an enormous park and a lake in front, a large staff of servants, good food daily, and so forth; the poor man's wish is to sit forever before God's countenance. Both wishes are granted. The rich man tires of his "eternal" life after only a few years: no changes ever, and beyond the border of his large estate, the void. He is in torment, tries to divert himself, feels imprisoned; he climbs one day to the attic of his house, opens a little hatch, and sees a small shimmer of light radiating from God's countenance. From now on, he spends his eternity standing day and night on a high chair straining to gaze through the little opening, weary of everything else. In the end, God tells him that he, the rich man, has suffered enough and likewise may take his place before God's countenance. And thus the rich man is finally redeemed. The tale, being a sort of allegory for purgatory, must have been invented by a Catholic mind; yet it contains the metaphysical answer to the quest for the concrete eternity. Every eternity becomes hell if it consists of concrete details. Nor are ideas of eternal youth and such of any help, unless we assume that man could, as a physical creature and without succumbing to habituation, experience eternity as something constantly changing and full of new surprises. That, however, would be the real fairy tale.

An old love and great flame of mine wrote me a wonderful letter a few weeks ago. Now comes the mailing of two books about consciousness expansion, on esoterics, reincarnation, karma, experiences of afterlife, etc. I'm embarrassed. The lady who sent the books would like me to read them with an open mind, and I can do this only by taking random samples, which immediately convince me that they are all absurd speculations— a kind of rhetoric that poses as thought and knowledge but, of course, regards itself much superior to science, while in reality it is nothing more than an excuse for unrestrained muddling and the inability to think. In the end these are but contributions to the promotion of ignorance that is culminating in a colossal idiocy. In addition, of course, the monetary greed: certain words in one of these books are marked with an encircled R, indicating that they are protected under the trademark convention, which from a legal point of view is completely ludicrous.

My apartment, facing exactly north without an exposure to the south, in winter a tomb, is now very pleasant in this beautiful weather. The long days are less of a strain, because the shade comes rather quickly. Only the terrace is in direct sunlight, too hot and bright during the day but enveloped in a transparent and mild luminosity in the evening. The swifts dart through the air, these pure creatures of the air that are never on the ground or able to take off from it, capable only of clinging to and nesting on walls. No other form of life is so wedded to the air.

June 26

The desire to immoralize oneself in world literature, to go down in the history of art or music or even in the history of world events, probably means that one has an ambivalent relationship to eternity. Eternity is regarded as part of life. After I'm dead, I no longer have any benefit from people talking about me for some time, whether for a few hundred or a thousand years.

If, on the other hand, I were to live on in some form as the same personality after death, I would care even less. Thus, the desire for one's own immortality assumes that one doesn't believe in an existence after death. To be exempted from this conclusion are magical views such as those of the Egyptians, who believed the afterlife to be an extension of this life and in need of tangible means from it. Ramses II has broken all records in this regard. His colossal statues have been left all over the Egyptian landscape. If what he (possibly) believed were true, he would now be the most important man in heaven. Already in times of ancient Greece and Rome (Horace declaring his poems to be *aere perennius,* more enduring than iron ore) and again since the Renaissance, self-immortalization has been indeed part of life and an enhancement of life's pleasures, provided that human history will continue for millennia—a questionable assumption today. The medieval builders of cathedrals, whose names have remained largely unknown, had an intact relationship to eternity. They worked for God's glory or simply in order to make a living, with no thoughts whatsoever of immortalizing themselves in their works; for immortality was, in any case, taken for granted, be it in heaven or in hell.

These recordings, to make it clear, are not guided by any such ideas of eternity. I merely want to present my situation as average and, at the same time, exemplary, in order to convince the reader that it makes sense to examine the issues of dying, death, and notions of the beyond while we are still alive. If this attempt fails, I shall destroy these notes before my death.

The pain in the bladder comes and goes, regardless of the drugs I take.

Peter Schneider, my former colleague at the University of Mainz, called me on the phone yesterday, as he always does when passing through, and told me that he had been thinking a lot about my theory of the inevitable and predictable self-destruction of planets inhabited by living creatures. Schneider thought it had much in common with Manichaeism, which believed that the world was the work of the devil and that it would end in redemption through God, a belief St. Augustine once shared. I don't like the scheme. I explained to Peter my ideas of oases of meaning, which, viewed within the basic Manichaean model, would mean that the divine Beyond forever penetrates the here and now, even if we can grasp the whole only as meaningless desert. But what little are we able to comprehend?

I have to alter my will. I don't want money from my estate to be spent for the publication of these notes (at my daughters' expense). Either the stuff gets printed or it doesn't. This decision, too, makes me feel relieved (like the decision not to have the surgery). I leave it, so to speak, up to nature how I will fare now and after my death.

"Death by choice" [*Freitod*] is a verbal protest against "suicide" [*Selbstmord*]. The term has never gained a foothold. It is a polite euphemism. It also conveys the idea of acting by free choice when killing oneself. Reality is different. Without despair or being trapped by external circumstances, nobody kills himself.

Recently an association called Exit has been founded which engages in very sensible educational efforts, including the problem of "death by choice." Their main concern is to enable the individual to escape the automated machinery of medical technology—which is very good. But their program should also teach people that dying and death are always imminent and that one should prepare oneself in good time.

Karl Reber comes to my mind all of a sudden. I don't know why: we haven't seen each other for at least fifteen years, I'm sure. With admirable determination and abruptness he decided one day to seek a divorce and to live exclusively as poet and homosexual. When I was a student, he admired everything literary I put out, even in conversation, and later he kept borrowing money and never paid me back, although I didn't have any money either. Now he is a poet for the cognoscenti, a kind of poet of literary delicacies [*Literaturleckerbissendichter*], reasonably well known. A pity we don't see each other anymore.

June 29

Strong pains since noon, almost to the limit of what is tolerable. The medicines are without effect, even the new ones that Christoph sent me. Only very slowly, toward evening, have the pains been subsiding.

Joy has its own meaning; pain must derive meaning from a purpose. Pain as warning symptom: that is the simplest, medical explanation—suffering for a cause. Maybe pain still has some intrinsic value; I don't know, have difficulty believing it, even though pain is more a part of everyday living, of human existence, than joy.

Zingg told me that for him death was always the enemy, nothing else. Everyone has to talk that way when somebody else's death is at stake, especially the physician. To one's own death it is possible to gain a more neutral relationship.

It is not right, however, to see merely a simple contrast between joy, pleasure, well-being on the one hand and pain, grief, and despair on the other. The longest periods in the lives of most people lie in the realm of the masked pain, the masked grief, and the masked despair. It seems impossible to take joy in one's work on an assembly line, as a little clerk in an office. Perhaps only through pain—and that would be its totally different, unbiological meaning—do we become aware that life is mostly toil, interrupted now and then by little oases of meaning. Thus pain would have a metaphysical meaning, especially as masked pain, as destruction of meaning, by revealing that this world, at least since the existence of man, is dominated by evil and that the transcendent good succeeds only occasionally in bringing joy to the individual. Developed logically, this thought means that joy and good deeds are signs from a better world beyond.

Of course, the trivial explanation is more plausible. The totality of world events follows a physical-biological course, indifferent to anything else, neither recognizing its own need of redemption nor striving for it, either.

When I am dead, I shall know all this, at worst only at the very last moment, when I realize that now, now nothing exists anymore.

June 30

After ten drops of morphine solution—that's how far I've come—the pain subsides slowly and finally disappears altogether. Instead I get tired; of euphoria not a trace.

The philosophers of law have again been rather busy in recent years. I have read several of their books, in particular the monumental *A Theory of Justice* by John Rawls, which by now has become well known in Europe as well and is considered one of the books of the century. On the basic idea of "fairness" he erects a complicated and what appears to me incoherent edifice. The problem of power arises only marginally.

If I had at least two years left, I would devote it to a comprehensive presentation and substantiation of the following proposition: what we see and experience everywhere as tangible reality is injustice. To suspend above it an ideal free-floating structure of justice is meaningless—the good king, the noble parliament, the good and sensible people, etc. We should begin instead with injustice—and already I hear the objection of how to define it, not knowing first what justice is. Let us not be deceived by words: injustice is the original human condition, justice the result of critical analysis and reflection. Hence, justice ought to be called un-injustice. Justice is observable only in the destruction of injustice. If, however, we take injustice as our point of departure, we are immediately confronted with power. If we wish to establish justice, which means abolishing injustice, we must acquaint ourselves with the mechanisms of power that produced injustice and either dismantle them or oppose them with countermechanisms that in turn require power. Not a single book of legal philosophy has so far been able to change the fact that the extent of injustice has remained the same. Nor will Rawls change anything apart from bringing new fodder into the libraries, which is then rehashed and thrown to the young, piecemeal. Thinking that engages in mental masturbation is perfectly permissible as long as it doesn't pretend otherwise. But if it claims to improve conditions, then it must document its assertions. Now it is true that most philosophers and legal theoreticians don't even make this claim but merely ruminate over what would be good and just, without any further pretensions. It seems inevitable that at some point the patience that makes such occupations possible by providing space, money, and labor will come to an end. For injustice is spreading at an ever-increasing rate. I would never in my wildest dreams have thought it possible that Zurich's criminal justice since the riots, and in its riot cases, hardly differed from Turkey's military justice, which seven years ago I was able to observe when the International Jurists Commission sent me as its representative to attend military trials in Ankara.

Subject: antiinjustice philosophy. Much effort has been devoted to this very subject by a number of historically effective philosophers and legal theoreticians, from Montesquieu to Marx. They proceeded from mechanisms of injustice and conditions of injustice to show how these may be replaced by something better. Separation of powers (still one of the greatest ideas), abolition of monopolistic capitalism; the Puritans earlier: abolition of slavery, etc. Only by this process did the world become partly more just—"partly" because injustice grows by itself and continues to do so; justice must be made to prevail by attacking ceaselessly at their weakest points the mechanisms of injustice and the power on which they rest.

Scholarship, too, keeps succumbing to its own inner logic. The areas of research and its tools are already given. But the analysis of power structures lies beyond the field of legal philosophy, which tends its flower garden without worrying about a flood or the collapse of a mountain in the near future. To practice legal philosophy means to become a good legal philosopher, to author a few publications, and finally to write a big book. The field is always exactly predetermined and circumscribed.

Reflections on how to prevent atomic war would already be beyond the pale of legal philosophy even though this ought to be one of its most important subjects. The writers and thinkers remain forever subordinate; the real action is the work of Stalin and his ilk.

Last Thursday I saw B. at a party, and he told me my theory of the destruction of planets populated with intelligent creatures as if it were the result of his own thinking.

July 4

Twenty-nine percent of the people in our country die of cancer; 33 percent, of heart and circulatory diseases. Hence, I belong to the first third. Mere numbers cannot be the reason that cancer appears so sensational and existentially disturbing to the others and engenders so much compassion. According to its percentage of the total, cancer ought to be a rather ordinary, mostly lethal disease. Most likely the trouble comes from the word "cancer," which the physicians, too, are avoiding. They call it "carcinoma" or, better yet, "CA," similar to "GO" for gonorrhea. A disease named for an animal: a custom normally reserved for innocuous conditions like the kind of chafing soreness between the buttocks resulting from long hikes and called "wolf" in German.

I am also concerned with demythologizing cancer—especially since I keep coming across books written by people with cancer. Does cancer spur the urge to communicate? Why don't people suffering from heart disease write about their impending death?

July 5

Rebekka proved to me yesterday in a cut-and-dried—or at least cut—way that a dwarf-giant must always be larger than a giant-dwarf. In German compound words, she pointed out, the second denotes the basic category: a dwarf-giant, therefore, would still remain in the basic category of giants, the giant-dwarf in that of the dwarfs. Hence, a giant-dwarf could never attain the stature of a dwarf-giant.

Have read Arnold Hottinger's book *Islam Today*, which is mostly a compilation of quotations from Islam's "church fathers" as well as from its contemporary theologians. This alone is revealing enough. Islam is not original, if this can be said about a religion; rather, it is a copy of the Judeo-Christian religion, stricter in its monotheism than Christianity with its Trinity. Muhammad was only a prophet, not the Son of God. Instead, he was a great victor and conqueror, perhaps the kind of figure the Jews have in mind as the promised Messiah. There are sharp divisions between believers and unbelievers, the redeemed and the damned. Islam is a success-oriented religion, without an understanding of the awesome symbol of the crucified Jesus in which the Almighty demonstrates his solidarity with the failures, the defeated, the powerless. This criticism of power, whose beginnings reach back to the Jewish prophets, is completely lacking in Islam. It feeds on its own success, as at present in Iran; it will become weaker with its failures. That failure in itself might be a form of success is beyond Muslim imagination. The prescriptions of Islam's later theologians are all alike: if only we convert again totally to the teachings of the Koran, then we will again have the power to conquer the entire world and convert it to Islam. The longer this success fails to materialize, the weaker the faith that should make it possible. Islam certainly offers no alternative to Western nihilism, although modern Muslim theologians keep touting their religion as such a solution.

Laax, July 6

Pain is easy to localize (headache, stomach ache, etc.), but very difficult to describe in terms of quantity and almost impossible with regard to quality. The physicians speak of "tearing," "shooting," "stabbing," "searing," "spasmic," "diffuse," etc., pain. But how, for example, should one describe the terrible pain resulting from being hit in the testicles? No single direct word exists for the quality of a particular pain, such as those used for colors (red, green, etc.) and shapes (round, square, etc.). Pain, according to the physicians, is something purely subjective. Moreover, its lack of language makes it difficult to deal with. The pain I am now experiencing is dull and heavy, but I can't say anything about it because I can't relate it to some outside experience of a similar nature. Pain may be dampened by medicine, sometimes driven away entirely for prolonged periods. At other times some sort of schizophrenia develops: euphoria, yet at the same time the presence of pain as a silent, stern observer.

Everyone has an infinite variety of pain, yet he is not able to communicate a single kind if the listener has not experienced exactly the same external event that triggered the pain. And even then the communication is uncertain. Is a knife stab in the arm perceived in the same way by everybody?

Laax, July 9

The landscape has again changed completely since I was here last. Alpine midsummer: the summer pastures, still under deep layers of snow only a little more than a month ago, are now all green, as if no snow ever existed there. The reeds are again standing high, their growth advancing steadily into the pond. The shadows are sharp in the glaring sunlight, and still it seems as though the light were dampened by its own brilliance.

Today, toward noon, I went skiing on the glacier of Vorab. I was anxious to find out how I would manage; but it went as usual, except that the snow was much too heavy. Does that mean that it took more effort than before? Apart from tiring quickly, I feel a certain lack of enthusiasm. One ought to start at eight in the morning, when the snow on the glacier hasn't yet turned soft; but that's too early for me.

From the slopes toward Falera the noise of haying machines can be heard, fortunately from far away. Work is going on in the countryside.

At the edge of the pond two herons have settled in; I heard for the first time their shrill, hideous screams. These disturb me, because until now I have seen the heron only as a beautiful statue, motionless and silent.

I have better control of the pain; at least it seems so at the moment. Since I've started taking several drops of morphine solution with my sleeping tablets, I'm rid of the pain during the day as well, to the extent that I can think of other matters, which is almost impossible when the pain is strong. Even Jesus no longer preached when he was tortured and later hung on the cross.

In these recordings I've said too much and too little. I wanted to give meaning to my dying and death, a meaning also for others in the same situation. I have not succeeded. Nevertheless, I could at least recommend this place in Laax to someone doomed to death. The last rays of the sun just barely stroke the tips of the firs across the pond; this and the dark slope to Falera conjure something almost impossible to express in words, an image that one would like to view again and again, even for the last time and knowing that it was for the last time. Here, on such an evening, it would be easy to die.

Yet the questions posed before remain. I want to examine them again tomorrow in a rigorous, entirely existential fashion: God, Meaning, Death.

Meaning would really include everything: it is the all-encompassing question.

At the moment, as I look outside, I have a very clear feeling that the earth is rolling, away from the sun toward the stars. In the morning this impression doesn't arise; it is a feeling of evening.

Laax, July 10

Too many wrong associations: God and the organized, very secular Church; God and eternal life after death, in the beyond; God and the legal statutes, etc. The only association that matters is: God and meaning. Life is not meaningless without God, but death is. There are, of course, substitute gods who give subjective meaning to death, such as fatherland, the future of the revolution, steady progress, and so on. But the substitute gods are all short-term, shortsighted, subject to the ephemeral nature of historical forces.

Trotsky writes at the end of his testament: "Whatever the circumstances of my death: I shall die in the unshakable faith in the Communist future. This faith in humanity and its future gives me the strength now that no religion could ever impart." In this view the future is taking on the role of the promised kingdom of God. Trotsky keeps silent about the temporal dimension: two hundred years or two hundred billion? Evidently, his God is not eternal but bound to time.

On the other hand, Trotsky developed prophetic visions of conditions that to him meant future happiness but which we today, as a result of their partial realization, perceive as apocalyptic. Trotsky foresaw atomic energy already in 1926 and genetic engineering in 1932.

> The atom contains in itself an immense hidden energy, and the greatest task of physics is to set this energy free, pulling the cork to allow this energy to burst forth. This will open the way to replace coal and oil with atomic energy which also would become the most important motive power. . . . Limitless technical possibilities will open up to a liberated mankind.
>
> Once he has managed to control the anarchic forces of his own society, man will begin to work on himself, put himself into the mortar, into the chemist's retort. For the first time, mankind will regard itself as raw material, at best as a physically and psychically half-finished product. Socialism will mean a leap from the realm of necessity into the realm of freedom also in the sense that present man with his contradictions and inharmonious nature will prepare the way for a new and happier race.

211

Comparing these visions with our reality cannot fail to bring home the truth that what we figure out in our heads invariably looks quite different once realized in practice. For this reason alone, the road to an earthly paradise doesn't exist. Thus, we are happy enough today for all of this century's architectural and urban construction projects that have not been realized and sad about those that have.

July 11

On the lower part of the mountainside rising toward Falera a shooting range is being used for target practice nearly every Saturday and Sunday afternoon. Most unpleasant is waiting for the next shot.

And what will the sharpshooters do in the next war?

Since the last world war, hundreds of local wars have raged all over the globe to this day; and this will continue until all local warring parties have acquired the atom bomb. Thirty-five million killed—more than the blood toll of World War II. The dying, past and ongoing, is brutal, crueler than dying from cancer. Nor did any of the victims have the time or the strength to describe their dying. Nothing unusual: for dying as a victim of war or genocide is, according to man's nature and history, the most natural death.

The cancer patients who have the privilege of writing the history of their illness and dying ought to be less interested in their own biographies and thanatographies than in articulating dying for all those others who are less privileged. Otherwise these cancer books are nothing but a particular literary genre characteristic of our affluent society. The authors are concerned only with life, how to hold on to it, how to enjoy it even in its last few weeks. Why, then, talk about dying and death at all? All complaints by the victims against their dying of cancer seem unjust and narcissistic and filled with self-pity when we think of the millions who have been killed unjustly.

Still, dying can be experienced and described only as a highly individual act. In this regard there is no collective death. In this view, too, the awesome significance of Christ's dying on the cross becomes apparent. He was alone and died, inevitably, as an individual; yet at the same time His dying was the dying of each individual, including the hundreds of millions who have since died violently at the hands of other men.

In my little book *Jesus and the Law* I argued years ago that Jesus's postulate of loving one's enemy not only was something radically new in all of Jewish and ancient thought but also highly realistic for today because of the possible self-annihilation of mankind. Today this insight is gaining ground in the face of the unending stockpiling of atomic warheads. Yet Jesus too was aware that while love of one's fellow man is natural and hence not meritorious, loving one's enemy simply overtaxes the human psyche. The Falklands war, in particular, made it clear that the peoples are the ones who want war, sometimes more than the governments. Only when the dreams of victory are giving way to the reality of the victims are the peoples' eyes slowly beginning to open.

Jesus's thesis can be shown to be realistic by a very simple consideration. What would happen if, for example, the Americans or the Russians were to disarm unilaterally and totally? For the people, nothing at all—only peace. But the ruling machines would not survive such an event. The Kremlin could occupy Europe but not digest it; instead, it could blackmail America—but to what end? And what would America do with a Russia it had forced to its knees? At most, provide what would be good for the Russian people: peace, freedom, democracy; but also, on the other side of the coin, capitalism.

The vision is realistic, but reality is not. In a confrontation

between America and Russia, the peoples will demand toughness, strength, and war, just as the British and Argentinians did
in the Falklands conflict. Hence, it would take an atomic war
to bring mankind to its senses, because only then would it realize
what its dreams of victory were actually worth. Yet only few
would be left to share this insight.

Laax, July 24

For one week I was in Sent visiting with Anne, Hans,* and
Mother. While hiking in the nearly intact landscape of the Lower
Engadine, I was surprised that I could keep up with the others
quite well; they hardly had to pay any attention to my condition,
or else they did it so I wouldn't notice. Hans, a geologist, is
interested in every detail of the earth's history, especially in the
formation of the Alps, a very complex affair. We are in a region
called the Lower Engadine Window; here the uppermost layers
are the oldest, because the newer layers were pushed under the
older ones, as was the case in nearly all foldings. But almost
everywhere the oldest layers were eroded away, except in the
Lower Engadine, if I got it right.

The sign "God" obviously cannot substitute for explanations—
that is, it cannot be used to complement scientific knowledge,
contrary to what some pious people still believe. God as origin,
creator, and source of order is a sterile concept, unable to cope
with the question of morality and the question of origins. A
decent order would never have admitted man, who tears everything down again. And the question of origin leads to infinite
regression: who created God; and who created whoever created

* The author's oldest sister and her husband.

214

God, and so on? The Jews of the Old Testament knew better: God is a totally different dimension; eternity abolishes time, space, and causality. We catch a glimpse of God in the oases of meaning of our existence. More cannot be said, except, at best, in the form of musical expression, which is so abstract as to approach the metaphysical.

The pond is now completely overgrown with green reeds— beautiful, too, now in the rain, which is drawing a fine veil in front of the forest.

Natural or practical atheists I call those who justify their atheism neither by claiming to fight the power and the mistakes of the Church nor by a carefully reasoned agnosticism. They merely say: the earth is round and was not created in seven days, and arguments invoking God have long been used, especially by the Church, to justify all kinds of crimes. Such ideas may at one time have been a necessary stage of human thought and its liberation. What has been consistently overlooked, however, is that neither the existence of so many variations in the ideas of God nor the failed proofs of His existence can in any way prove His nonexistence. They want a miracle, something inexplicable; only then will they believe. What remains inexplicable, however, is nearly everything that cannot be bottled into the narrow vessels of causal thinking. Hence, only the position of the agnostic is consistent and honest: we know almost nothing, certainly not the answers to the questions that truly move us. Only this position opens again the way to faith and hope. The practical, natural atheist stops thinking at this point. He questions no further, because to him these are idle speculations. And that is false, of course; for reason can distinguish between the absurd and the meaningful even in the metaphysical realm.

———

Everywhere people suspect that I am trying to find consolation for myself and others in the thought of individual life after death. Yet I'm searching only for meaning. And that is much, much more.

How enviable are people like Heinrich Albertz who breathe, live, and act in an unquestioning and admirably naive Jesus-the-Savior faith. No matter what leaps they take, they'll always land in God's safety net.

The past three days I spent with Peter Schneider at his house in Serneus. Our friendship has not aged. Everything he reads, and he reads a lot, he brings to life so well that afterward the book itself is a disappointment. But his greatest talent lies in interpretation and argumentation. Out of a completely banal novel by Walter Jens he can extract a quite profound philosophy that would have never occurred to the author. His debating skill matches at least that of the West German Supreme Court, which is why his briefs have won and lost so many cases there. As I had always feared, the court has now become a superparliament, although I tried to suppress these apprehensions in my textbook on legislative doctrine. The West German Supreme Court says: every word that I utter is valid law. That is supposed to apply even to a casual or gratuitous remark in the written opinion. Purely political questions are treated as matters of constitutional law in a definitive way. In the end, this is bound to result in a complete immobilization of society in a net of unalterable legal norms. That the West Germans give more credence to a court consisting of nine men per chamber than to the parliament they themselves have elected is in keeping not only with their particular weakness but with that of every parliamentary system lacking elements of direct democracy. The people should really have to eat only those soups that they cook for themselves. The Germans, though, seem to prefer fewer and outside cooks.

Schneider is reading a French book about Manichaeism. The world is the devil, but in the end God will overcome the world and the devil. There is only good and evil, black and white. Christianity struggled for a long time with this doctrine. Immediately, the political joined the religious: the history of the Balkans can be explained only by this process. The Cathars, one of the Manichaean movements, it should be recalled, in the West gave their name to all heretics ["Ketzer" from "Kathar"]. Manichaeism does not solve the question of meaning. Like all religions, it presumes that it is impossible for a good God to create a bad world. In the Judeo-Christian religion, this dilemma is solved with the fall of man: man corrupted a world originally created perfect by God. The Manichaeans explain this question of much-exaggerated importance by saying that God is still struggling with the devil; only in the end will He be victorious. But what is the point of this sham battle resulting, nevertheless, in so many real deaths?

Not having to face these doubts about the metaphysical mechanics of salvation, how much easier is it for the practical atheist: the world is good for those who are doing well, bad for those who are doing badly.

When I discuss things with Schneider, and he paces the room back and forth with long strides and wide-reaching movements of his arms, it is exactly as it was twenty years ago in Mainz.

He says that when he thinks about death, he always returns to his childhood faith.

Laax, July 25

Everything requires an effort: breathing, too, has once again become difficult. My indecisiveness has reached a high point. I don't leave the house, even though it isn't raining. Nothing appeals to me, nothing tempts me. These dictations, the disease, the pain, the thought of death—they've all become habit.

To imagine eternity as eternity, even if unimaginable, is perhaps the final achievement on our planet, brought forth by means of its ultimate product, the human brain: spirit which might yet be a particle of Him through whom everything has been made and is being perceived. But the realm of meaninglessness is extended tremendously by the question of eternity.

Tomorrow I'm driving to see Max Frisch in Berzona. From an absolute low point, any movement can only lead upward. This last period is more demanding than any before: not knowing how things will continue with my work, with my disease, with my dying; not knowing what will happen to those who will no longer have me, Rebekka and Sibylle above all. Incessantly, I'm thinking of both of them. Somehow I would like to leave them a wholesome world, which is of course impossible. New pet names for them occur to me all the time, in addition to the old ones.

Zurich, August 3

Four beautiful days in Berzona, two of them in the rain. But the rain didn't reach the fullness and endless duration of the true Ticino-style rains that Frisch describes so drastically in *Man in the Holocene*.

The house is located below the cemetery, which was put about a hundred and fifty yards away from the village, so that the village didn't lose any tillable acreage. I had hardly arrived when Alice found out the freezer had quit—apparently some time ago from the way it smelled; and we threw all the meat into a pit, about 400 francs' worth, as Frisch observed. So we endured the four days as vegetarians without any harm. Frisch is a master cook, though he will probably go down in history under a different title. The loss of the meat inspired him to invent all kinds of vegetable, egg, and flour combinations, all of them superb. He is a master of soufflés and au gratins, of omelets stuffed with vegetables, of baked vegetable tarts. With mushrooms, of course. Meat is brought to Berzona only once a week by a butcher with a truck.

All the greenery, on the other hand, grows by itself. The boccie court is completely overgrown, not only with grass and weeds but with saplings as well. The steep slope below the house is getting more and more overgrown with shrubs, and the trees that were already big are growing larger. It had all been intended for his former wife; but when they separated, vegetation took her place. Frisch worked for days with two Italian laborers, felling trees and clearing brush in order to free at least the immediate area around the house from the green strangulation. To no avail: the plants react instantly when man moves away. The longer Frisch remains in New York, the more clearing he has to do afterwards. The clearing process has even taken hold of his writing: he is hacking away at his typewriter all morning and then strikes everything out, reformulates, rewrites, redeletes, changes until he achieves the very terse form, with many gaps the reader has to fill in for himself, this severely compressed expression that distinguishes his latest works.

I wouldn't recognize Alice anymore from reading *Montauk*. She moves in a livelier, lovelier way; perhaps the dreams of the old man have made her into what he really dreamed of. There was only one brief disagreement, which dissolved quickly. Of course it was about washing the dishes. The way a third party sees it: he showers her with compliments and she responds with displays of tenderness and cheerful spirits. Suddenly she throws her arms over his shoulders from behind and snuggles up against him. To my questions, she replied that she did indeed feel a little like Alice in Wonderland.

Zurich, August 5

It is possible to keep the pain within tolerable limits by the use of conventional medicines, like Cibalgin and Zomax. The morphine drops are only rarely necessary, fortunately. But I have to take the pills more frequently now. Maybe it has to do with the enormous fatigue that sometimes overtakes me and refuses to be resolved even in sleep.

Zurich, August 10

Last week I had breathing difficulties again. On Saturday, Christoph, who had to come to Zurich anyway, listened to my chest and noticed a wet sound: again water in the lungs. Now I take six different kinds of pills, can breathe normally again, but my heart is banged up. Heart muscle damage, left side—all from the viral infection I had in April, if it really was one.

I'm annoyed about my cautious, slow movements.

My brother Hans thought it was not conclusive that intelligence and evil have evolved together from common causes. According to his reasoning, selection, on which evolution is founded, actually operates only to a limited extent by means of competition but on a much larger scale by means of environmental changes— heat, cold, droughts, and so on. This is indeed correct; but at the same time, every species must assert itself against other species, and the winner in this competition is always the more intelligent or the one with the fastest rate of reproduction. Human intelligence, which alone is my concern here, developed, as Hans finally had to concede, in the struggle against other species as well as against its own species. The shrewder, more cunning Odysseus finally triumphed over other species and over other groups of his own species.

This process leads inevitably to the destruction of every inhabited planet. My theory is as exact as Darwin's, but of course even more unpopular than his. Neither is it correct to look at the whole matter from the other side, arguing that our moral demands have nothing to do with reality and hence are irrelevant. Nevertheless, the destruction of all life can only be termed evil. That man is highly developed intellectually and underdeveloped morally is certainly true but explains nothing. The explanation lies in the selection mechanism, which favors evil to the point where it destroys itself and nearly all other life. What finally survives need not interest us: bacteria, insects, certain deep-sea fish. The sole final selection test: resistance to atomic radiation.

The large majority of Israelis still support the merciless, criminal, senseless campaign against Lebanon. If the attack on Beirut fails definitively, the same people who now support it will hold their government responsible. Still, there are many critics and opponents today, even soldiers who refuse to obey commands and get away with it: at most they are transferred or discharged. A remnant of prophetic consciousness may have survived here; the cry to turn away from the path of injustice, even if it means civil disobedience in wartime, must be tolerated—this alone justifies Israel's claim to her tradition. As long as this is the case, it makes no sense to call Israel a fascist state.

They share with the Arabs the most beautiful salutation I know: "Shalom [or Salam] aleichem"—Peace! Nowadays this phrase strikes me as purely hypocritical, but one has to recognize that it is meant only for one's fellow man, not for the enemy. Jesus's original invention of loving one's enemy has never taken hold in the international marketplace.

The substructure of our aggressive biomass will always remain stronger than the very thin moral superstructure.

Haddad, archbishop of Tyre, will go down in history as long as there is a history, probably even in legend. When Israeli tanks were moving toward Tyre, he ran up to them at the edge of the city, asking to speak with the columns' commander. The commander of the very first tank raced his engine and screamed: "Get out of the way!" The archbishop, accompanied by a helpless Swiss Red Cross delegate and one of his priests, stood firm, legs apart, in front of the tank and repeated his request. The entire column remained at a standstill. Amidst the laughter of the Israeli soldiers, he was taken to the commanding colonel: "You should be glad I am even talking to you." The discussion led nowhere. The officer climbed back aboard his tank. Haddad, thinking that his mission had failed, provoked the colonel with: "Won't you show some human magnanimity for once in your life? When do you actually plan to attack Tyre?" "At twelve-thirty." "But it's already twelve-fifteen." "Right! In a quarter of an hour. And that's it. Good-bye." The archbishop: "I promise you'll find no armed resistance in Tyre; we don't have any heavy arms. The PLO doesn't have any positions in the city." He told the truth: the PLO had evacuated the densely populated city some time earlier. The Israeli colonel thought it over. "My goal is to keep the loss of my troops to a minimum. I'll give you two hours." The archbishop ran back to the city with his companions.

Within several minutes, all the church bells of Tyre started to ring as Christian and Muslim clergy urged the population to leave the endangered city immediately and to proceed to the beach. Hardly had the people withdrawn from the city when the Israeli tanks moved in. When a few youthful Palestinians shot at them with light weapons, they responded with heavy fire and reduced seven hundred houses to rubble. Nevertheless, the Israeli storming of Tyre cost not a single life. Thus, in part verbatim, the report in *Der Spiegel* of August 2, 1982.

Everybody should have witnessed this situation: the archbishop, planting himself in front of the tanks, stops a military operation for two hours by arousing the conscience of the enemy, which is then rationally translated into the military consideration that it would be important to lose as few of one's own soldiers as possible. Such images should enter history, not victories, conquests, and triumphal parades.

Zurich, August 14

Several days ago German television reported that the swifts had already flown south and the swallows were gathering for migration. Somehow I was saddened, because the swifts belong to the sky, especially in the milder evening light. Today I was almost happy when I saw a whole swarm of Alpine swifts circling above the Predigerkirche, with their trilling call, which besides their imposing size distinguishes them from the city swifts. Both are so totally one thing: birds of heaven.

Conversations with Dolf Vogt are analytical, essaylike. Why are there architects? Shouldn't the profession be abolished? Individual architecture in cities is always destructive: a glass-and-steel structure next to a medieval half-timbered house. The architects are commissioned to do a particular work, and insofar

223

as they aren't restrained by ordinances, they indulge their whims and fancies without inhibitions. On the site of the neoclassical physics building, next to the university, they want to erect a futuristic superbuilding shaped like an ocean liner. They regard themselves as being creative but are in fact destructive. And what they are building out of steel and concrete will remain as a skeleton even after an atomic war. No such thing as self-decay in such buildings—at best mere desolation through neglect.

Our era is the first in which buildings are torn down with the full awareness that something worse will take their place. Until the 1930s architects at least believed they were building better and more beautifully than their predecessors; and this was even more true during the building boom at the turn of the century. Only now do we know that in order to erect bleak and ugly structures, we are destroying more beautiful buildings. This is nihilism. We live in a nihilistic age, nihilistic also in the sense that profit has become the measure of all things. Naturally there are many fig leaves—for example, productivity, high standards of living, and, when they run out of ideas, prevention of unemployment. Work at any price that others pay for. Work in the arms industry, manufacturing serial death in the name of defense, work that is literally nonproductive in every respect, especially since the war machinery—the combat planes, tanks, etc.—must be replaced every five to ten years because of obsolescence. For as soon as the new arms go into production, the finished plans for the next batch are at hand. The obsolete junk is sold to the developing countries: there it doesn't matter one way or another how many human beings and peoples kill each other off.

We recognize nihilism by the fact that means have been declared as ends in themselves: money, work, profit.

That nihilism in the form of usurious exploitation, as the product of land speculation, is at the same time showing a

hideous face, that at least we owe to the architects who yielded
to nihilism. Here, surely, the aesthetic judgment is subject (in
every sense of the word) to the moral one.

Laax, August 25

Ernst Jünger, the aesthete of World Wars I and II, is to receive,
at eighty-seven, the Goethe Prize of the city of Frankfurt. That's
how long they've let him wait. He, too, if I've correctly understood the interview I've read, is searching for morality—above
all, for ways to justify (not apologize for) his attitude and development. Of course, no regrets, only complaints about having
been misunderstood. His courage and bravery in World War I
are admirable, less so his intellectual and moral faculties. Somehow, he reminds me of a *Stehaufmännchen,* the weighted pop-
up dolls that always bounce back right side up. Thus, he continues to live, at his old age, healthy as a horse. When I visited
him in 1947 in Kirchenhorst near Hannover, because his the-
atrical herosim fascinated me, he still smoked cigarettes, one
after the other, including all of mine that I had brought with
me from Switzerland. (Apparently, he has since given up smoking.) He was sitting, a small man with a stern, shrill voice,
forever looking like a lieutenant, behind his antique table, and
taught me his (then current) political theory: that the Russians
would now have to be taken very seriously and any European
order would have to be shaped according to their conceptions.
When I kept interrupting, as I had been taught as a student,
with liberal ideas of constitutionality and democracy, even em-
phasizing the American model, he countered less with arguments than with rigidity and became increasingly irritable.
When he had smoked my last cigarette, I took my leave and
began the two-hour walk back to Hannover. Later I was told
by Armin Mohler, who was for several years Jünger's secretary

until he too fell out with him, that Jünger complained bitterly about me. What a naive Swiss Mohler had sent him! Actually, Armin Mohler hadn't sent me at all but merely had given me the master's address.

One ought never visit authors whose books one enjoys reading. Or at least one should have known them before they became famous, rather than trying to get acquainted afterwards. If you get acquainted by chance, take it as a matter of course and enjoy it as you would enjoy the friendship of a nonfamous person. Quite often, however, this will not be possible.

Christoph called, and I described to him the development of the old and the appearance of the new symptoms. He said that in January he would have given me less time; so I am at least surviving his prognosis—although not by much, as I realize more and more. Everybody is asking him about my health. Thus, I have to keep reporting being alive, just like the locomotive engineer with the foot on the "dead man's pedal."*

My test, to have somebody who appears in them read my dictations, came out negative: the testee found my presentation biased and struck off her name at the few places where she was mentioned with such force that the cover of the paperback book she used for support was completely scratched.

My sister Anne wrote to me and sent me the English original together with the German translation of J. D. Salinger's best- (or, better, perennial-) seller *Catcher in the Rye*. The book seems to be known to everyone except me. I'm reading it now. Unfortunately, I'm mostly interested why such a small book, his-

* A pedal that is released should the engineer suddenly die (e.g., from a heart attack), which then stops the train.

torically unique, becomes such a hit that the author, who appears to have written barely anything since, is still able to make a living from it after more than thirty years.

A call from Rebekka: she is flying to Poland on Saturday, into the midst of the prospective political turmoil. After her return I'm supposed to give her private lessons in criminal law. She insists on making an effort to study hard so as to pass the college entrance exam. She wants to enter law school and study criminal law with me before time runs out. All this *in amore et memoria patris.*

Laax, August 27

On the phone again with Zingg about the reduced intervals between trips to the bathroom, about the reduction of the bladder volume, about the pain. Above all, I wanted to know what the immediate prospects were and how things will look at the end. Zingg is so factual and at the same time so compassionate that talking to him is in itself a form of therapy. After our first talk, in January, I believe, he had thought that I would break down mentally within six weeks at the latest and overturn all my decisions. He was amazed and impressed that this didn't happen and wanted to know how I was able to stand up to the stress. As to the end, it became clear to me from his explanations that any surgery would not make sense now, as it would only shift the medical problem from one place to another. Moreover, I would again be at the mercy of the hospital. The pain can be eliminated or at least greatly reduced, first with drops and later with injections. The situation in the hospital would be less desirable in this regard too, because one would be dependent on personnel: pleading and begging for a pain-relieving injection. With my disease I can die at home as well, the only requirement being that somebody be present at the end who is competent and authorized to give injections. My question: how long can the pain be eliminated without seriously impairing consciousness? Probably until shortly before the end. The morphine, Zingg explained, produces a strong euphoria associated at high doses with hallucinations, but once these high doses were required, one was going to die anyway because the body no longer had any strength left.

It has become cold. The rain is falling with a monotonous lulling sound into the foggy dusk. The pond has been completely grown over. The reeds are still green.

When the sun comes out, it gets quite hot again. Bulky flies are bumping with full speed against the windowpanes, buzzing back and forth until they finally find the open window. They never learn. If the collisions with the windowpanes were lethal, there would in time only be flies that recognize windowpanes. The genetic material learns only by the penalty of death. The human genome is incapable of learning because man as an individual always finds a means of averting death—and hence, he won't survive in the end.

Dying also announces its approach by the conversion of eros into agape, not only in him who is to die but also in his lovers. Should anyone think that eros is more intense than agape, he is mistaken.

Laax, August 29

At exactly 7:04:05 p.m. the sun went down today behind the mountain that rises above the village of Falera, which itself cannot be seen. The sunsets are now again taking place in front of the house, although still much farther to the west than in September, when I was here for the first time.

I'm reading Salinger's book with great pleasure; everyone will read it with great pleasure, and that, I believe, is the main reason for its success. It is never boring; at no time has the author felt compelled to continue when he was not inspired—no artifice, etc. That is probably why the book is so good rather than because of the fact that the author has an eighteen-year-old portray himself and is able to sustain the gimmick to the end. *Surtout pas trop de* profundity. That is left to the reader and is easily accomplished by generalization. The story: a youth flunks out of school, doesn't know how to break the news to his parents, and embarks on a wild goose chase through New York. The generalizations: odyssey of youth in search for self, problems of failure, the much greater sensibility of youth to injustice, routine, boredom, and, especially, deception. The life of a normal, robust, and successful adult can only be a sham.

Zurich, August 31

Yesterday evening Peter G. came by, and we went out for dinner, to the Zimmerleuten, of course. He told me the story of how I had brought him a whole basketful of bunnies when I came to see him in the hospital when he was recuperating from an appendectomy at the age of fifteen, and how they ran all over the room and kept slipping on the polished floor. His roommate, a grown man with a fractured arm or something, was thrilled, and so was Peter, of course—we were both enthusiastic rabbit breeders. When the nurse, who was both strict and tolerant, came in, she said only that in half an hour—the end of visiting hours, anyway—the animals had to be gone. The incident made Peter insanely happy, and he just can't believe that I have no recollection of it at all. I may have repressed the memory of such events because of their possible similarity to those other, also repressed, experiences that had led to my bad conduct grades.

The past is reaching for me: yesterday a phone call from Elisabeth Cabasse, born Brunet, with whom I fell insanely in love some thirty-five years ago, hence also unhappily. Shortly after, she married a man whom she had met accidentally because of me. The two ran into each other at the Italian consulate in Paris while applying for visas, which she was doing at my behest, because I had suggested a trip to Italy. We then took it together as planned, though we hardly touched each other. A little later, she fell in love with Cabasse, became pregnant, married him, and together with him built from scratch on his inventions a business that must be very substantial, for they own factories, a private plane, a yacht, and a mansion in Brest—probably because at that time government subsidies were available to those who wanted to start an enterprise in the provinces. She is coming to Zurich to exhibit their audio speakers at the FERA trade show, and I'm supposed to come to her booth tomorrow, and then we'll have lunch together. The only problem is that starting at noon tomorrow I'm not allowed to eat anything, because Dr. Spiegel, Haemmerli's physician in charge, wants to X-ray my gastrointestinal tract.

At the office visit this morning, I described to him the symptoms that have so far developed. He examined everything and said that the nodule that is palpable on the lower abdomen near the surface is almost certainly a metastasis. The nodule on the left clavicle could be a lymph-node metastasis but for its location (too far distal). So it seems that I must be satisfied with one metastasis for the moment. I wouldn't be unhappy if the metastases should overtake the primary tumor, because it would mean a gentler death. Nevertheless, the likelihood remains that the bladder will close up first—which implies that I will have to use very strong painkillers. Unfortunately, I'm rather pleased that the physicians, who in the beginning tried to make me opt for surgery, all were betting on the wrong horse, and that my decision, which I made only for myself because I felt clearly that I would not want to live differently, was right. If the metastases are already palpable, they must have been present long before last December, when the tumor was first diagnosed.

Elisabeth has not the slightest inkling. I'll have to explain it to her tomorrow. She will survive it, I'm sure.

Still, it's interesting that things long past are turning up on all sides. It might reflect the history of the cancer in my own body: it probably was dormant for a long time or working away unsuccessfully until it finally found a spot from which it was able to destroy my body.

Zurich, September 2

The strict form of a true dramatic stage play, which requires a "gathering knot," a construction in which a central event holds the key for all the action (Sophocles, Shakespeare, Schiller, Kleist, Dürrenmatt in the early plays), demands of its author more concentration than any other literary genre does. The form keeps him from digressing, from writing on even when he runs out of ideas. If he does anyway, the play will immediately be recognized as a failure. For this reason, only very few writers have in the course of time dared to involve themselves in genuine drama.

The novel, by contrast, allows for much more flexibility, and nearly everything is permitted in the diary. I'm reading Andre Gide's *Diary, 1942–1949*. The author himself admits that he frequently lacks inspiration, and it depresses him. Yet he feels compelled to write at least half a page nearly every day. The great writer knows that everything he writes will be printed. Therein lies a great temptation: because others think he is important, he finally believes it himself, so as to think that every thought that crosses his mind, and every little experience, is worth communicating. Only the diary, not really meant for the public, is the appropriate form for this. Apart from a few *historical* exceptions—for example, Pepys, whose diaries are of historical interest as the perspective of an individual observer of his time—diaries are also unsuitable as a vehicle for the type of literary fame that assures more or less automatic publishing. Another counterexample: the diary of Anne Frank.

If somebody writes a diary of literary ambitions, which need not be the case, then he must at least heed the law of exemplary significance. His experiences, his way of describing them, his view of contemporary events, and his evaluation of what he is reading must make visible the general through the medium of the individual. Often it is precisely the diaries not written for publication that have succeeded in this. (See the above examples.)

September 3

In the West German weekly *Der Spiegel,* Helm Stierlin, professor of basic research in psychoanalysis and family therapy, inks a violent article against Jesus. Not only Christianity but Jesus Himself, he contends, conspired to make peaceful coexistence impossible. While, according to Stierlin, Jesus was loving, humble, and so forth, he was also "merciless, unyielding, intolerant, and prone to violence." To document his claims, he uses statements in which Jesus pronounced judgments of damnation, threatened people with hell, etc. He is particularly disturbed that Jesus tore apart families by saying that He had come to separate the son from the father, the daughter from the mother, and so on. The author writes that he has read anew the Gospels and especially the Sermon on the Mount. However, what he cites, "Thou shalt love thy neighbor as thyself," is already found in the Old Testament as well. By contrast, in the Sermon on the Mount, it says:

Ye have heard that it hath been said, Thou shalt love thy neighbor, and hate thine enemy. But I say unto you, Love your enemies, bless them that curse you, do good to them that hate you, and pray for them which despitefully use you, and persecute you; That ye may be the children of your Father which is in heaven: for he maketh his sun to rise on the evil and on the good, and sendeth rain on the just and on the unjust. For if ye love them which love you, what reward have ye? do not even the publicans the same? And if ye salute your brethren only, what do ye more than others? do not even the publicans so? Be ye therefore perfect, even as your Father which is in heaven is perfect. [Matthew 5:43–48]

Jesus was certainly no family therapist; but He saw the conflict between love of one's fellow man and love of one's enemy. Stierlin missed this contradiction completely. All wars are essentially fought for the protection of one's own family, for the defense of one's own people—thus, for love of one's fellow man. With love for one's enemy they could not have been justified. Hence, when Jesus demands the dissolution of the family for the kingdom of God, it necessarily includes the call for peace and tolerance, just as God lets the rain fall on both the good and the evil.

There remain those undeniable utterances in which Jesus damns those who have no mercy—the judges, the powerful. No doubt this is how Jesus thought; no man can think otherwise. Can we cure a Hitler, a Himmler, a Stalin with a therapy of love? God may see this all very differently; His grace can have no blind spot, and we shall receive new eyes to see likewise.

The metastases are clearly progressing. We don't need to deceive ourselves, remarked Dr. Spiegel; and he's quite right. Meanwhile, several other suspicious spots have become noticeable. Now, it can't take too long anymore.

September 8

In my present condition, I can't possibly keep myself going till the end of the winter semester. The pain relievers make me tired, sometimes nauseous.

A few days ago, I saw on television a film about J. Robert Oppenheimer. Oppenheimer was spirit and soul of the giant team of top scientists who built the first atomic bomb in Los Alamos. With so many prominent scientists participating, it was an honor to be part of the team. Most interesting were the interviews with the participants, most of whom are still alive. The Jewish scientists expelled by Hitler were particularly afraid that Hitler was going to build the atom bomb. Einstein warned Roosevelt, who then ordered the Defense Department to put at Oppenheimer's disposal all financial means necessary to carry out the project as quickly as possible. Hitler's death should in fact have made the atom bomb superfluous, but it was completed anyway. One of those interviewed said: "Nobody has built the atom bomb, nobody really." Another: "I can't explain why we continued working on the project after Hitler's downfall. Apparently, we were simply too fascinated with the work." A third: "After Hiroshima I quit nuclear physics and turned to completely different fields. Never would I work on such a thing today." Nobody quit after Hitler's destruction, not even one.

The apparatus was simply too strong. The compulsive power of external circumstances: billions of dollars had already been sunk into the project—how could one just abandon it, unfinished as it was? At a time when all other Japanese cities had already been destroyed by conventional bombs, the American general staff had intentionally spared Hiroshima and Nagasaki for the big bomb. Frank Oppenheimer, Robert's brother, said with complete honesty: "When the bomb was dropped, my first thought was, let's hope it's not a dud. Only then did I think of the victims, of the endless suffering, the gigantic destruction, and I was ashamed."

Zurich, September 13

A day-long session of the court of cassation, which has never happened before. I managed it well, while noticing at the same time how my colleagues showed great consideration, asking if I didn't want a break, which I declined, as things really went very well. We were in session from 9:00 to 11:30 and again from 2:00 p.m. It doesn't bother me at all that everybody knows about my condition; I've already dictated the letter in which I explain my resignation.

Drive to Basel. Klärli drove me in the impossible Mini [Morris] that lacks any decent shock-absorbing suspension.

Megge—who just had his seventieth birthday—is sitting at a table in his studio, slumped in his chair, the gray hair hanging down onto his face. His girlfriend has brought him a bowl of gruel, and now he is spooning it in slowly and with long pauses.

When I had called, nobody had answered the phone. I knew the neighbor in the house; his wife told me: "Yes, he's very ill." "What's wrong with him?" "You'll have to see for yourself."

Megge, mentally still absolutely alert, is telling me about his illness and his repeated surgeries. Since he suffers from exactly the same type of cancer, I am able to fill in everything the doctors apparently didn't tell him. The tumor closed up both ureters, blocking the kidneys and the excretion of potassium. In the hospital his bladder was freed from the cancerous tissue by surgery—without anesthesia, because he would not have survived it in a comatose condition. During surgery Megge lost consciousness because of the pain. With stimulants they brought him back to the world of pain. Subsequently, he recovered enough that his bladder could be removed entirely, this time under anesthesia. Since then, he has been relatively free of pain but is growing visibly weaker. He is telling all this with a detached serenity and a tinge of irony. The only thing that bothers him are the frequent coughing attacks, which sometimes seem as if the world were coming to an end. He now is getting codeine and is doing better.

My diagnosis of Megge's condition is arrived at rather quickly: terminal cancer, metastases throughout the whole body.

In the hospital Megge didn't eat and lost more than forty pounds within a short time. Now he is eating gruel, raw eggs for protein; fruit he likes too. Meat, cheese, and that sort of thing he is no longer able to handle.

He can no longer paint, because he can't remain standing for more than ten minutes; nor can he draw, because he can no longer control his hands. He sits at the table in the middle of his studio, smoking cigarettes, reading the newspaper, often taking naps.

And so I see, surprisingly and for the last time, an old friend. He doesn't complain; he is just letting it happen—probably doesn't want to know too much, either, or at least doesn't want to have it verbalized. His thoughts are entirely clear; but his medium is not language, it is drawing and painting.

Afterward I went to see Gschwind on the Steinerhof. Gschwind was his same old self, going full blast, in a good mood, one idea chasing the next. He even managed to get serious, which is not so difficult in my case. Death as a hypothetical thought he rejects; dying he considers very important, dying as an art. The patient must learn it unaided, since the physicians dodge it.

September 14

The law is flexible—or should one say "bendable"? You can always override formal arguments with arguments of substance, and vice versa. Thus, about a year ago, in a social-democratic flyer quickly gone with the wind, I criticized the city council's decision directing the state's attorney's office to conduct the case against the Zurich riots on an "accelerated" basis. My argument that this would be an invitation to the prosecutors for summary justice and sweeping judgments, always a typical sign of political justice, was dismissed by invoking the supervisory authority of the city council over the state's attorney's office. This, according to my opponents, was simply the law. Since subordinates usually are overzealous in their obedience, it was not surprising that it resulted in that grotesque scene when forty-six accused were herded with their defense attorneys into a courtroom to watch and listen over closed-circuit video as the five witnesses, all policemen, testified against them: all of this was apparently no violation of their civil rights as guaranteed in paragraph 14StPO, a conclusion confirmed by the majority opinion of the court of cassation as well who found that the mere anticipation of trouble would have created the necessity to curtail the rights of the accused. It is obvious, however, that it could have been easily arranged for the accused to confront the witnesses singly or in small groups.

Injustice for Peace and Order, a book by my former doctoral student Peter Robert Schneider, keeps provoking a lot of excitement. The State Council of Zurich, supported by an overwhelming majority of the population, has refused a request by a few social democrats to have a parliamentary commission investigate the riot justice, which has now lasted for nearly two and a half years, in terms of both the individual decisions and the overall trend and bias. Here again the *formal* argument was most welcome: we do have, after all, a separation of powers, and nobody ought to lecture the judiciary, even post factum. That may well be; but why wasn't the same formal argument used earlier against the city council?

For a while I thought that the only way to force the practice of law onto the path of justice was to have a rule according to which formal arguments can be used only against formal arguments and substantive arguments only against substantive arguments. I admit that this is a naive idea, exactly as naive as the hope that justice one day may no longer be political—that is, no longer adapting itself to power.

In the present situation, even the members of the judiciary are able to cover their shortcomings with clichés: heeding the voice of the people provokes criticism just as much as not heeding it.

Tonight I'm expecting Heidi A.* I've given her the transcript of my dictations to read, and she is very enthusiastic about her new editorial assignment. I, too, am anxious to hear her always perceptive reactions, even though I've already decided not to change anything.

The last war fought by Switzerland ended in the battle of Marignano (1515), on foreign soil. Since that time, the Swiss can imagine a war only as a Morgarten, a Sempach,** or a Mari-

---

* Heidi Abel, well-known personality of Swiss TV and friend of Peter's who died of cancer not long after him.
** Morgarten and Sempach were famous battles in which the Swiss peasants wiped out the Austrian equestrian armies coming to the support of the local ruling classes.

gnano, never as a Vietnam or a Lebanon. The Swiss go to military shows as if they were going to a museum. A jet fighter squadron roaring over their heads at three hundred feet makes them shudder with holy awe. When a tank unit near Frauenfeld takes a hill defended by an imaginary enemy—with live ammunition, mind you—this has the appearance of a solemn act rather than a preparation for mass killing. The danger of the militia system: the whole people identifies with the military. A military mentality is part of being a good citizen. It is always a tacit assumption that Switzerland will never attack another country but will only have to defend itself. Whether these assumptions are still valid today, when an offensive advantage accrues automatically to the party capable of better protecting its civilian population from atomic attacks, is highly questionable.

Schneider's book is almost universally criticized as a cheap piece, a biased, distorted presentation. Personally, I am able to evaluate only the matter concerning the few cases cited in the book that came before me as a judge of the court of cassation, and hence all I can say is this: everything Schneider writes about these cases is true. Precisely this may be the reason why government executives, superior court judges, and district attorneys are so upset about it. Equally correct are Schneider's findings about the predisposition of the Zurich courts, submissive to authority and obsessed with order—attitudes that are even supported by the Supreme Court in adopting a literal interpretation of the statute on the breach of the public peace: anyone who knowingly participates in a "riotous assembly" inciting violent action is committing a crime. Were the purpose of this type of justice to restore quiet in Zurich, the task has undoubtedly been accomplished. The only ones left are the secret artists who with their spray cans decorate the outside of every other house with some kind of graffiti, a slogan or a clumsy drawing. Spraying as liberation: that is what we have come to.

Zurich, September 20

Telephoned Zingg to let him know that I have quite a few metastases. He thought that these might now actually overtake the primary tumor. I feel like someone to be broken on the wheel whose sentence has been commuted to death by beheading. The metastases result in a complete disintegration of the entire organism and its individual organs.

Today my colleague Robert Hauser came for a friendly visit. I had called him last week and asked him to take over as thesis adviser to one of my students, as I was unable to continue supervising the student's work. Before Hauser's visit, I learned that in a recent edition of the *Neue Zürcher Zeitung* he had reviewed Volume 1 of my textbook *Criminal Law* together with the general part by Schultz and the one by Stratenwerth. Moreover, I had an opportunity yesterday to take a quick glance at the review; I felt slightly irritated without being able to say why. We talked a little about my discussions of art and criminal law on page 114 of the book. I thought that he had generalized my ideas in a way that could mislead the reader into believing I would give absolute precedence to fundamental constitutional rights over the criminal statutes. But I was quickly mollified when he shared my view that criminal norms had to be interpreted in conformity with the constitution and assured me that his criticism was not to be understood as indicated above. We then quickly concluded that we still disagreed about the relationship between works of art and religious feelings.

He brought me fresh apples from his garden. I ate one right away. I never had liked apples, but this too has changed recently, for reasons related to my condition, I believe. Zingg asked me, "Do you still like meat?" Only then did it occur to me that I'm not so keen on it any longer.

Later, when I handed over the thesis that I can no longer supervise, Hauser asked: "Is this my punishment for the displeasure my review caused you?" The ex–prosecuting attorney required a compelling excuse, which I furnished by pointing out that I had requested the thesis transfer *before* his review had appeared.

Since the day before yesterday I've been running a fever ranging between 100 and 102; today at 5:00 p.m. it was 102. Christoph said that it must be an infection of some sort (no need to be very specific any longer in my case); and it would certainly be a more pleasant death if I were to die of pneumonia instead of metastases.

Ballweg,* too, showed up yesterday. He is such a loyal friend that one could take, within the entire spectrum of possible opinions and political viewpoints, a position diametrically opposed to his without losing his friendship. This, too, is perfectly consistent with his fundamental position in legal theory: in the realm of the philosophy of law, there is only rhetorical discourse, never truth. A cool agnostic. And suddenly he said to me, "You must fight the cancer—eat nothing but brussels sprouts and cauliflower, and drink red beet juice along with it." Where might the irrational find refuge if it is banned even from the philosophy of law? In medicine, of course.

If only I knew how to store energy! I would solve not only the problem of this planet but also my own very personal one. In

---

* A colleague of Peter's from Mainz.

the evening, when the mood is good for dictation, I'm drained of all energy.

Thursday, September 30

From last Sunday to last Monday, I took too much morphine. Total loss of sense of time. Three days in a row I asked Frisch if we were to meet tonight or tomorrow night. The third time, he gently pointed out to me: "Today is not Friday, as you seem to think, but only Thursday." We then drove in his old Jaguar over the Forch and Pfannenstiel hills to the Restaurant Buech. The writer Albin Zollinger often went there, the last time three weeks before he died; he used to sit at the same table at which we were eating. Max urged me to have fresh, spiced chanterelles as an appetizer, with a white burgundy. Always trying to eat as lightly and as little as possible, I then chose as entrée a filet of lake perch with lemon slices.

When we drove back, it was raining, and we sensed that along with the mild weather the summer had passed, definitively.

The Final Days

BY REBEKKA NOLL

I had flown to Poland on August 28, 1982, to observe the demonstrations in Warsaw. At the beginning of September I received
a telephone call from my father. To my question how he was,
he replied: "Not so good—please come back." I was alarmed,
because it was not his usual way of telling anybody, not even
his friends, in such a direct fashion that he needed them. Hence
I flew back on September 9. In Zurich, however, things were
as usual. A few visits to the emergency room were necessary for
flushing kidneys and bladder, but he was always able to return
home in the evening. I had a key to his apartment, brought him
the mail, took care of the grocery shopping, and got him the
morphine from the pharmacy. My father was weaker, yet he
did not in any way change his everyday life. Sometimes he
seemed somewhat distant; apparently, being in pain, he had
taken morphine. He complained only once or twice, softly and
casually.

It must have been toward the end of September when I woke
up with a start at two in the morning. I recognized my father's
voice calling my name from the street below. When I went to

the window, he said he could not get into his apartment; somebody had tampered with the lock. I tried with my key and
returned to tell him that it worked. He took my key and went
home.* He refused my offer to go with him. I watched him
secretly from my second-floor bay window. In the middle of the
street, he turned and, despite the darkness, looked straight into
my eyes, as if he knew I was standing there and watching him
walk away. Then he walked on, slowly, like an old man.

From then on, I no longer had a key for his apartment.

One day in the beginning of October, my morning phone call
went unanswered. Nor was there any sign when I rang his bell
and knocked on the door of the house. None of his friends and
acquaintances knew where he was. For two days he could not
be found, until a political friend came to tell me that he had
found my father in the little park around the corner, and that
he appeared to be not quite sober. Immediately rushing to my
father's place, I found him on the stairs, with large, shining eyes
and disheveled hair, a bottle of orange juice in his hands, a
sweater pulled halfway over his head; he was apparently on the
verge of leaving the house again. "What are you doing here?"
I said. "I'm going to get undressed," he replied with great
significance, waiting intently for my reaction. "No—let's go to
your apartment instead," I said, and he followed without resisting, quietly submitting to my authority, which I was not used
to. He lay down on his bed, and only then did I see how
exhausted he was. He was so thin; he was trembling and sweating and his pulse was very rapid. Clearly, he was hallucinating.
Asked where he had been for the past two days, he replied:
"Looking for young, talented painters." I was not able to get
more out of him. To this day, nobody knows what happened

---

* Rebekka and Peter lived in the center of the Old Town, about a three-
minute walk from each other.

during this time; walking through the streets in his confused state, he must have lost his way, until he managed to get close to where he lived. It was sheer luck that nothing happened to him, for he had a lot of money on him and apparently had taken too much morphine, as I concluded from the fact that several suppositories were missing from the apartment and nearly his entire supply of morphine drops was used up. I decided to stay with him in his apartment from now on.

He remained delirious the entire day, and the following day as well. Later, he wanted to know, in minute detail, what he had told me under the morphine. He was ashamed to have lost control and decided then and there to stop using morphine entirely. From that moment until his death he didn't take any pain-relieving drugs at all. His appetite was completely gone, and he was frequently nauseous.

Friends kept seeing him, and although his conversational activity was clearly diminished, he remained fully alert. One evening, when I had stayed out longer than required for buying some tea, he got very restless, making worried phone calls. According to Frisch, he developed some sort of antennae that allowed him to distinguish my steps on the stairs from those of the others. It seemed as if our relationship had intensified and clarified, and that we were closer to each other than ever before.

One morning I called from the kitchen: "Shall I fix you your yogurt with cottage cheese?" (It was easy to digest, and I had gotten him to eat it.) No answer. I went to his room, where I found him bent over trying to put on a sock. He looked at me with large, clear eyes and said, "Lobster." I was astonished: "What?" He: "Lobster." It dawned on me: "Should I buy you a lobster?" "Yes." He also wanted a small bottle of champagne and a Bürli [a kind of roll]. I did the shopping and set the table. He sat down, and for the first time he again ate with a good appetite. It was a gray October morning; the swallows were circling the tower of the Predigerkirche, and I felt very solemn. I therefore played a record, the one already on the turntable. I didn't know at the time that it was the B-minor Mass and that my father had selected it for his funeral service. Suddenly he put down his silverware and ceased moving. With raised forefinger he looked into my eyes for a long time, in silence. I merely noticed a change in the music and gave it no further thought. Only at his burial service did I understand the meaning of this gesture: at this point in the Mass, the "Crucifixus," Christ's crucifixion and entombment are expressed in a somber, chromatically descending motif ("sepultus est"). Then, all of a sudden, with an overpowering burst of trumpets and timpani, the chorus rings out the triumphant "Et resurrexit"—He is risen. This is what my father was signaling me.

The physician couldn't tell when my father would die. My father knew that it would be soon. Once he asked the doctor: "People die at four in the morning, don't they?" "Oh, no," the doctor replied. "There's no rule—it varies a lot." My father looked at him with a mixture of amusement and pity, as if he were sorry for the doctor's ignorance.

Thursday, October 7, was a strenuous day. My father was lying exhausted on his bed, and I was sitting on the edge of the bed, holding his hand. As I watched his face, he opened his clear blue eyes and asked softly: "Bekkesli, how are you?" Tears welled up in my eyes, and I had to look away. When the lump in my throat would not go away, I got up and went to the bathroom. There I wept. When I returned to prepare my bed on the sofa, I was still sobbing silently. He asked: "Bekkesli, are you crying?" I didn't know what to say. Had I said yes, it would have meant an additional strain for him; had I said no, it would have been a lie. So I answered: "A little." Then he began to cry. I was in despair. "And if this is hell?" he asked. I couldn't stand it any longer and lay down next to him. Moments of panic seized him; he tried reading a court document, then my article on Poland, and finally the automotive page of the newspaper. When nothing seemed to help, he shouted despairingly: "Why does nobody take me out of here?" A clay bird on the bookshelf threw a shadow on the wall that looked like a Buddha. He said something about a big monkey and made repeated references to hell. I tried to comfort him as best I could. It occurred to me that somebody else had endured this agony, and I talked to him about Jesus on the cross. Even the Son of God despaired in the face of death. He sat up and ran his hand through his disheveled hair. When he rubbed his waist, I asked him if he was in pain. He answered: "No—these are the pangs of death." Toward morning we finally fell asleep.

Friday was peaceful. My father was quiet and withdrawn. Max Frisch came and said good-bye, and they embraced. My father thanked him for their time together.

He went to bed early, and a few friends came for a last visit. I had fetched my mother and sister, feeling the time had come. Heidi Abel, a good old friend of his, showed up too. My sister slept in my father's room on the sofa; I lay down next to my father on his bed, while my mother and Heidi Abel were conversing in the living room. Soon there was silence. All were asleep except for my father and me. I was supporting his heavy head with mine, was dabbing the sweat from his face, feeling now and then whether his heart was still beating. Suddenly something startled me, despite total silence and darkness. I called my sister, but she was fast asleep. I threw myself over my father and held him in my arms. Then he began to heave deeply and painfully. I thought to myself, My God, how can you let anybody suffer like this! and, almost at the same time, Yes, God does let people suffer. At that moment my father ceased breathing. Only then did my sister stagger into the living room and wake the others.

My father died on October 9 at four in the morning.

Funeral
Oration

BY MAX FRISCH

Our circle of friends among the dead is growing.

In December of last year, after Peter Noll had replied to my routine question on the phone "How are you?," first, half-laughingly, "Fine, thanks," then, dryly, "I have cancer"—we met in the Zimmerleuten not far from here. He has known the bad news for three days, and I find him fully composed and in good form, a man who still enjoys life. But the medical results are clear and without hope: half a year, a quarter, at most a year. He knows exactly the score, and rejects surgery—that too is clear. It's his decision. He refuses to die as a disabled object of medicine. How, then, does one die? Among other things, we talk about death by choice (in technical terms) and about medically assisted death (in legal terms) and move on, during the meal, to subjects we would have discussed anyway, and we both don't feel this to be a form of escape. There is no escape. Why not laugh? His Socratic calm would indulge anything except consolation. Then, while waiting for the check, a pause, and he returns to his request; "You have some time yet" is how he explains his request for a funeral speech at the Grossmünster nearby. When the bill is finally paid and the time for a decision has come, he gets my pledge.

That is why I stand before you today.

As a person without official function.

What does an agnostic have to say in a church?

When he was ninety, Ernst Bloch, at an outdoor breakfast, said the only thing he was still curious about was dying (he wasn't ill at the time)—dying as the one experience he hadn't had and couldn't learn from books. It was not a symposium but a breakfast with friends; probably not everyone at the table heard it when he added: he could not imagine that after death there was simply nothing.

Others say it differently: I simply cannot imagine nothingness.

Peter Noll, a pastor's son and schooled in Protestant thought, independent in his thinking and delighting in the play of ideas, often bold in his visions in a way that made him appear cynical to those who knew him only superficially, never preached to me—and we were together often during his last nine months, be it at home or in taverns. The wish that one who had learned to think as Peter did would write down for the rest of us what he is thinking and how he is experiencing the world in the certain knowledge of his approaching death, even while still skiing in Laax, so that we may discover what he believes to the very depth of his suffering, or what he doesn't believe as he attains his ultimate lucidity, before the morphine impairs not his sensibility but the language to express it—this wish of mine, expressed not without hesitation, causes him a moment of embarrassment, for he had already begun to write such a log book. And this log book grew; it is now complete.

———

Three evenings on the Nile—

(That was at Easter time.)

Its banks are green wherever they are flat and thus can be flooded by the Nile's fertilizing silt; as soon as the land rises, the desert begins. A complete desert. Across the river the barren mountains, bleak as bones during the day, lilac in the dusk; the sky above, violet, after the huge sun has set; two or three sails on the river, which now appears brighter than the sky, its waters now flowing silently, without glittering.

We viewed:

The Valley of the Kings:

their tombs all ransacked—

Ramses as Man-God:

his mummy duty-taxed as dried fish—

What did the ancient Egyptians believe?

They believed inexactly, thinks Peter.

Why the mummies?

We are sitting on the balcony, bare feet on the railing, drinking whisky and talking about the fashionable best-seller tales: light effects at the moment of dying, and so forth, as guaranty for a life after death—

He prefers speaking to Socrates.

And again to Jesus . . .

The drive to Edfu was too much: his physical breakdown on the fourth day, the long night behind venetian blinds; outside, the heat and the Nile, black; the mountains across the river like light ash and farther away than they are in reality. And a day behind the blinds; sometimes Peter wants to know what I am doing. And I don't know it, either. Outside, the sun and the glittering river, palms at the desert's edge, hoofs clattering, mixed with the honking of horns, and an Arab gardener again watering the lawn in front of the hotel. And then the second night: again the braying of that donkey. As he sits at the edge of the bed, naked, what is Peter thinking? His eyes very small: what does he see? Returning from the toilet: not much, he says, mostly blood. And the following day, as we drive to the Luxor airport, ahead of us, on the bumpy road, an Arabic funeral procession, which Peter (as I learn later) didn't notice; finally the Swiss Rettungsflugdienst [rescue flight service] in the scorching desert. We fly (Peter with an infusion needle attached to his arm) over the Valley of the Kings, later over Crete, then Mycenae, presumably, but it is night. I force myself not to look away; the result, a bag full of urine-blood, has disappeared; the color persists for another half-hour on the Western horizon.

What he remembered:
He had been ready to die and really quite reconciled, so he says later, wholly and fully reconciled.

His preoccupation with Jesus, whom he always saw differently than he is viewed traditionally by church-state-society: *Jesus and the Law, Jesus and Disobedience.* I quote:

Today Jesus would be charged not only with the illegal but also with the un-Christian character of His behavior. For in the meantime (that is, since Christianity has been recognized by the state), it has become a Christian virtue to obey the authorities under nearly all conditions.

Further:

The opposing view, that Jesus stated with the exemplary force of His life, can only be sustained in the legitimate rebellion for freedom and the very daring appeal to God's commandment to be free. He who accepts this commandment will have no peace; he will always be an outsider, but he will attain a serenity and detachment that enable him to be forever immune to all other powers, to their threats and temptations.

252

Thus it is written in the lay sermon that Peter Noll, professor of criminal law, preached on December 1, 1978, in the Predigerkirche in Zurich.

Our friendship was also political, to a large measure.

To watch us walking uphill along the Spiegelgasse: slowly, like two old men. But he is no old man. That changes the relationship to death—though we do have something in common: we both are no longer controlled by an engagement calendar stretching years into the future. No food in my house, he says; no, not even cheese or such—hence, we go out. Gradually he is using morphine (that's what I hear), but we talk about other things— Israel, for example. What he has to say is logically sharp and clear, but he speaks more slowly. His eyes are set deeper in his face, that is my impression; and even though his mind is present, his gaze suddenly seems to be coming from far away. And again shortness of breath; then he smokes a cigarette anyway, even if only briefly. Death is not merely the end (which would be a kind of solace), nor has it anything to do with old age, which he will be spared: aging as the experience of a protracted decline. Rather, death is from the beginning and without end.

Peter Noll . . .

The natural and naive yearning to speak once more to a dead man—which, alas, is not possible. Friday morning at ten, before I drive to the airport, the brief embrace, during which he remains seated, and we both know: perhaps we will see each other again; probably not. "You know," I say, "that I am fond of you"; he says, "I thank you for this time."* When I leave the house, he

* The Swiss German "Ich dangg Dir für die Zyt" is difficult to render in English: "die Zyt"—"this time"—refers to the time of his illness, when Frisch's supportive friendship meant so much to Peter.

is not alone. He dies hours after midnight; and there, where the news catches up with me, it is not midnight yet. . . .

Peter is buried.
We are gathered in his memory.
His body is buried.
Once in Ticino, as we were sitting on the little porch with wine and summer lightning . . . it is sultry but not raining . . . suddenly a smell of decay—my property borders on the cemetery, but the smell comes from the woods below. No wonder, since the previous day I had thrown the spoiled meat from the freezer, which sometimes goes on strike when a thunderstorm hits, down into the woods. And suddenly he laughs; for both of us, silently, think at this moment exactly the same thought, and as I meet his very bright blue eyes, I know that they belong to someone who is free, not afraid of knowing what he knows, and expecting the same from us.

We are gathered in mourning.
To praise a dead man publicly and to proclaim in public that he will be missed is the customary expression of our honest grief in our ignorance of death. No face in a coffin has ever shown me that the just-deceased misses us. The contrary is more than obvious. How, then, can I say that the circle of my friends among the dead is growing larger all the time? The deceased leaves me the memory of my experiences with him: three evenings on the Nile, yes; or that last lunch on top of the autumnal Pfannenstiel. . . . He, however, the deceased, already has an experience that still awaits me and that cannot be transmitted—unless it should come to pass through a revelation in faith.